# Futuristic Romance

*Love in another time, another place.*

## PARADISE IN HIS KISS

Before he could stop himself, Devyn leaned down and captured Alix's moist, sweet lips.

Alix gasped at the contact of his mouth against hers. All thoughts fled her mind and left her sitting there like a fool. She knew she should push him away. Instead, she opened her lips, welcoming him into her lonely, isolated world.

Inhaling the warm spicy scent of him, she wrapped her arms around his strong shoulders, drawing him nearer. She felt like the mythological tyrilian girlbeast who allowed itself to be lured by a lover, knowing that at the end of the act its mate would only incinerate it, its life forever sacrificed for a moment's pleasure.

But she didn't care. Instead, she wished she could melt with Devyn, become part of his beautiful world where the slave girl could be forgotten. A place where she could be free.

# Paradise City

## Sherrilyn Kenyon

LOVE SPELL  NEW YORK CITY

*For Rickey Mallory, Diana Porter Hillock,
and Kim Henson Jones,
thanks for your encouragement and support.
And for my husband, Ken, for eating lots of pizza.*

LOVE SPELL®

August 1994

Published by

Dorchester Publishing Co., Inc.
276 Fifth Avenue
New York, NY 10001

Printed in the United States of America.

# Paradise City

# *Chapter One*

Devyn knew a lot about women, gambling, and medicine, but what he knew about a ship's maintenance system wouldn't fill the empty space of a miser's wallet. He was hot and tired, and more than ready to fly off this miserable, backward space station, but he couldn't get clearance until his ship stopped flashing warning lights at the landing bay's controller.

As he pulled open the panel for the rear leading hook, his anger boiled. "What's wrong with this stupid thing? Twenty minutes looking for a—"

"Excuse me. Your rear stabilizer is down."

Devyn froze at the sound of the husky female voice that reminded him of a soft, cool caress sliding down his naked spine. Without conscious

Sherrilyn Kenyon

effort, his mind flashed on an image of what the woman who possessed such a voice must look like. His body burned with desire.

Suddenly, the idea of staying on this stifling station for a little longer seemed appealing.

A sly smile curved his lips as he closed the panel and stepped around the back of his ship to face the woman of his dreams.

His smile faded in slow disappointment. The woman standing before him was nothing like he'd imagined. Instead of a gorgeous seductress, she looked more like a lost puppy.

A faded red cap covered her head, shielding her eyes from him. Her nondescript brown hair fell over one shoulder in a thick braid hanging to her hips. She wore a baggy, brown battlesuit that had seen far better days. Even her boots were scuffed and worn out.

From what he could see of her face, her features leaned toward plain. The only interesting part of her was her chin, which she lifted with pride. Stepping closer, he noticed the small cleft.

"What did you say?" he asked.

An intriguing blush spread across her cheeks. She pointed to the rear of his ship. "Your back stabilizer is down. I think that might be what you're looking for."

"Hmm," Devyn mumbled, grateful someone knew what was wrong with the damned thing. He moved to check on it.

"Are you Captain Kell?" she asked, following a step behind.

Devyn slammed the stabilizer plate back into its original position. Wondering what she could want with him, he turned back to face her. He'd learned a long time ago to be suspicious of people who came looking for him. "Maybe. Who are you?"

She extended a small hand out to him, her features stern and determined. "Alix Garran. I heard you were looking for a new crewmate, and I'd like to apply for the job."

Accepting her answer, he took her hand and noted the calluses there as he shook it. She might not appear much older than an adolescent, but her hands told him she was used to hard work.

Normally he wouldn't consider someone so young for a member of his crew, but right now he'd take on the devil himself as long as he could operate the flight checks and get the *Mariah* back into space. "I need an engineer and a gunner. You got any experience?"

"Well, I was born on a freighter and have worked on one since I was old enough to hold a wrench." She shifted the backpack on her shoulder and lifted her head with an arrogance he found admirable for her age. "I know how to run preliminary flight checks, keep logs, and I can fix any engine malfunction with a piece of string and a drop of sealant."

Devyn laughed. For some reason, he didn't

doubt that last boast in the least.

He leaned against his ship with one hand and narrowed his eyes on her. "My last gunner was killed in a run-in with the HAWC. The *Mariah*'s a runner; do you have a problem with that?"

She met his gaze unflinchingly, and he noticed the strange dark blue shade of her eyes. "I won't run drugs or slaves."

"Good, neither do I."

"Then I don't have a problem with it."

Devyn pushed himself away from his ship, pulled a cloth out of his back pocket, and wiped the grease from his hands. "How old are you?" he asked, not wanting to assist a young runaway.

"Twenty-four," she answered without hesitation.

Devyn lifted a disbelieving brow. He wouldn't place her at more than sixteen. "You got any ID?"

She reached into her back pocket, pulled out a small wallet, and handed it to him.

Devyn studied the picture and the birth date. He had a good eye for forgeries, and this ID was either the best he'd ever seen or authentic. Deciding on the latter, he handed it back to her. "You're a long way from Praenomia."

She shrugged her thin shoulders. "My birth was registered there, but I've never spent more than two weeks on a planet in my life."

He smiled. "Then you're used to recycled water and air."

"And bad food, boredom, and stuffy noses," she added with a wistful sigh.

"Then why do you want to sign back on to a ship?"

She put her hands in her pockets and looked up at him with probing eyes that struck a long forgotten chord inside him, a chord he had hoped was forever severed.

"It's home to me," she said dispassionately, "and I have to make a living. I don't know how to do anything else."

That was one reason Devyn understood. Something about the dark tranquility of space seemed to comfort even the most troubled of souls, including his own.

He scanned her competent stance. She seemed honest and capable enough. At worst, she had to be better at maintenance than either he or Sway.

Their next destination was only three days' travel time. If she didn't prove to be as good as she claimed, he could always fire her once they reached Nera. "The job's yours if you want it."

A puzzled look crossed her face. "Don't you want some credentials?"

He shrugged. "Most people don't have any for this kind of work. You spotted the stabilizer with hardly any effort. Hell, I've wasted almost half an hour looking for it." He smiled at her. "You obviously know something about ships."

She returned his smile, and he became entranced with a dimple in her left cheek.

Devyn ran his hand through his hair and took a deep breath. What was wrong with him that such a waif could affect him so easily? Maybe Sway was right and he did need to break his celibate nature. "We're getting ready to launch, so if you have any gear or good-byes jus—"

"Just this gear," she said, shrugging her backpack off her shoulder. "And no good-byes."

Devyn frowned at the catch in her voice. "None?"

She clenched her teeth, and he had the strange sensation she fought against tears, but her eyes betrayed nothing. "My father died a few weeks ago. I don't have anyone else."

He nodded in sympathy. He'd never lost anyone close to him, but he could imagine how hard it would be to lose one of his parents. "I'm sorry."

She looked around the bay as if his words embarrassed her. "Don't worry; it won't interfere with my work."

"Well then, uh . . ." Devyn paused in an effort to remember her name.

"Alix," she supplied with an odd half-smile. "My dad wanted a son." She looked down at her body and pulled at the loose material over her breasts. "I guess he didn't miss by much."

Devyn noted the bitterness in her voice, and a strange surge of protectiveness ran through him. "You don't look like a boy to me."

Her smile returned and sent a wave of heat through his body.

"Yo, Dev! Your *mom*'s calling." Devyn cringed at Sway's gruff, mocking voice. He knew the next word before Sway shouted it out. "Again."

Devyn loved his mother dearly, but her constant, friendly calls were a source of extreme aggravation. But for once, his mother couldn't have had better timing.

"C'mon," he said to Alix, moving to the ship's ramp.

Sway met him at the top of the ramp with a snide smile that made Devyn want to slug the arrogant *prato*. But what the hell, they'd been friends for too long for him to take offense at the dorjani's normal taunting ways. Besides, he actually enjoyed Sway's caustic comments.

"Are we ever going to get off this rubbish heap? Between your mom and the locals, I'm growing moss."

Devyn handed him the grease rag. "You're green all right, but I always thought it was from the mold growing on your brain."

Sway rumbled his version of a laugh. He caught sight of Alix standing in Devyn's shadow and sobered. "Who's the *frelin?*"

"Our new mate." Devyn stepped aside to give Sway a full view of her. "This is Alix. Alix, meet our navigator, Sway Porrish."

He looked back at Sway and warned him with his eyes to keep most of his usual snappish comments to himself. "Why don't you show her where to bunk while I take care of my call."

From Sway's face, he knew the dorjani had to stifle a smart-ass response. But at least his friend was wise enough to hold his taunts.

"Follow me," Sway said.

Alix walked down the narrow corridor of the ship, her heart hammering against her ribs. She hated being on a new ship, surrounded by strangers. For the first time in her life, she didn't know every crevice of machinery, every chink in the cold, steel walls.

She wanted to go home. But the only home she'd ever known now belonged to whoever had bought it in the auction. Her throat tightened. She clenched her teeth, refusing to cry any more tears over her lost ship. She'd done what she had to, and there was no going back.

If she were careful with her pay, she ought to have enough money to put a down payment on her own ship within four or five years. Then she'd be free—the one thing in life she truly craved.

Her thoughts turned to the captain, and an unexpected tingle filled her. He was something she hadn't counted on. Most runners were a lousy lot with rotting teeth and smelly bodies.

Her first instinct had told her to ignore the posting for a new crewmate, but after checking with the crewmembers of other ships, she'd learned the *Mariah*'s captain had a solid reputation for fairness and ran a clean ship. Alix had figured as long as the ship stayed clean, it didn't matter about the crew's hygiene. And heck, after putting up with Irn's disgusting habits and repulsive advances over the last year, almost anything else had to be better.

But Captain Kell was more than just clean; he was marvelous. From his shoulder-length dark brown hair to the toes of his expensive black boots, nothing about him reminded her of the runners she'd come across in her travels.

And his ship! Well, that surprised her most of all. The *Mariah* couldn't be more than a year or two old—something miraculous given how little money most runners earned. Obviously, the crew made a lot from their less than legal efforts. Maybe it wouldn't take very long to get her down payment after all.

"You can bunk in here," Sway said, pushing the controls to open a door.

Alix's eyes widened at the large sleeping compartment. The bed in the room occupied as much room as her entire private chambers on her father's freighter. Rich, blue carpet lined the floor. She'd thought only aristocrats had ships with carpet in them.

Without a word, she stepped inside and ogled the rest of the furnishings.

"I'm sure Devyn will want to run over the ship with you, but he'll probably wait until after we launch."

Alix frowned. "Who's Devyn?"

"The captain."

"Oh," she said, feeling somewhat stupid. No one had bothered to tell her his given name. "So how many other people make up the crew?"

Sway leaned his back against the open door frame and folded his arms over his chest. "Just the three of us. You got a problem with it?"

Alix pursed her lips as she scanned Sway's body. He reminded her a lot of Captain Kell— both of them had attitude disorders.

They were also about the same height, and had the same lean, muscular build, but Sway wasn't quite as handsome to her. Of course, she'd never been partial to humanoid dorjani life-forms, and Sway's yellow eyes with slit pupils unnerved her.

"I've never had much of a problem with men chasing me around decks, if that's what you mean. As long as neither of you gets desperate, I think I can manage."

Sway laughed, a deep rumbling sound that reminded her of thunder. "I think you'll fit in pretty well with us." He tucked one of his multitude of blond braids behind his left ear. "This isn't sexist or anything, but can you cook?"

Alix wondered at the strange question. "Nothing fancy, but I do all right."

A smile curved his lips. "Thank God. I'm sick of eating processed food."

"And I'm sick of listening to you complain about it."

Alix's heart sped up at the sound of Devyn's deep voice. She told herself not to feel this way; her heart and body had done this to her before and she'd been crushed. Men weren't interested in small-boned, small-chested women who looked more like their brothers. Besides, she didn't need anyone. She was here to work for the captain, not make sweetie eyes at him like a lovesick moron.

"If you two don't mind, I think it's time we get out of here," Devyn said.

Sway nodded and left.

Alone with the captain, awkwardness consumed her. Alix studied her feet, wishing she could think of something to say. But as usual when she was around a handsome man, her brain couldn't focus on anything except the way his shirt clung to his muscular chest.

She knew if she looked up, she'd meet his beautiful dark brown eyes that were tinged with a hint of sadness and forget everything she knew about men.

"Your cooling unit isn't stocked, but we'll take care of that at our next stop. There's plenty of water and other liquids in the galley if you start dehydrating." He cleared his throat. "Take your time unpacking and whenever you're ready, the control room is at the bow of the ship."

Alix nodded, still not willing to look up. She heard the door slide shut.

Swallowing the sudden lump in her throat,

she finally glanced at the door and sighed.

She'd seen the look of disbelief in Devyn's eyes when she'd told him her age. His reaction was normal, but for some reason it bothered her more that he had done it.

"What's wrong with you?" she said with a groan, dumping her backpack onto the bed. "You ought to be happy you get to spend time with two handsome men. Probably be the only time in your life that you can."

Her father's laughing voice echoed in her mind. He'd often told her men would never look twice at her, and she knew he was right.

But what did she care anyway? Love was a give and take—the more you gave, the more people took. She didn't have any use for it. Life was hard enough without the added misery of a broken heart. Besides, if Devyn ever found out who and what she was, a broken heart would be the least of her problems.

It didn't take long to unpack her two pairs of pants, three shirts, and two pantsuits from her backpack and place them in her storage closet. Alix folded her backpack up, stored it in the closet next to her clothes, then decided to join the men for the launch.

Slowly, she made her way down the ship's corridor, dragging her finger along the sleek, cool steel wall. A soft tilt told her they were leaving the station, but the smoothness of the ride astounded her. On her old ship no one could stand, let alone walk, during a launching.

As she neared the control room, she heard Sway and Devyn singing. Loud music filtered into the corridor at a pitch she knew must be deafening from the interior, but even so their voices managed to drown it out.

Frowning, she pushed the control to open the door and stood back to watch the two of them serenade each other from their chairs. A laugh bubbled up through her.

The music stopped. "*Frelin* at six o'clock," Sway said in an embarrassed voice as he straightened himself up in his chair.

Devyn swung his chair around to face her. It was obvious her presence didn't bother him in the least. A smile curled his handsome lips. "Hope you don't mind our taste in music. We get a bit strange every time we launch."

"Strange?" Sway scoffed. "We act like bloody idiots."

Alix smiled and pulled her cap from her head. She brushed her hand through her damp bangs and tucked the cap into her back pocket. "Don't let me stop your normal routine. I can go back to my room if you want."

Devyn shook his head. "You might as well get used to us. Better to find out on a short trip if we're going to get on each other's nerves. I hate taking long trips with people who annoy me."

Sway made an odd noise that Alix couldn't quite identify. Devyn ignored it.

Taking the engineer's seat, Alix ran over the ship's settings, amazed at the updated equipment. "You've got a great ship."

Sway snorted. "Only the best for little Devy."

Devyn gave him a lethal glare.

Alix frowned at Sway's snide comment, wondering what had prompted it.

"My parents bought the ship for me," Devyn explained. "You'll get real used to them hailing us. Check over the frequency and make sure you know it. If I fail to take a call, my mom thinks the worst and starts calling out Rescue Probers to find me."

Alix lifted a brow in disbelief.

"He's not kidding. I'm actually amazed his mother ever let him out of her sight."

Alix stared at Devyn. "Does she know what you do?"

He nodded. "That's why she bought the ship. She wanted to make sure I"—he cast a warning glare to Sway—"didn't get hurt."

She told herself not to laugh, but even so, she couldn't quite stop the smile breaking across her face.

Devyn returned her smile. "Go ahead and laugh. God knows, I do. At least I've never had to doubt how much my parents love me. I'd much rather have my mom calling twice a day than not caring whether I'm dead or alive."

Alix's chest tightened from familiar pain. She wished she could have said the same about her father, but in truth he had cared more about his bottle and freighter than he'd ever cared for her.

Devyn stood. "C'mon. I'll show you around the ship."

Alix rose to her feet, her mind still on her dad. Even though he'd been a callous man where she was concerned, she missed him terribly. In fact, she missed a lot of things she never thought she would.

She followed Devyn around the ship, listening to him explain various engine specifics, and the location of gauges she'd be responsible for checking and maintaining.

As he ran over the logs, she frowned. "We're flying into Paradise City?" she asked, a tremor of nervousness running through her.

"Yeah, we'll stop on Nera Seven in three days, then head out to PC. Something wrong with that?"

"I've heard it's a rough place since the rebellion broke out. Not even runners or assassins are safe there."

Devyn shrugged. "I'm not worried."

Alix cocked a brow at him, doubting his mental abilities. He'd seemed sane enough at first, but now she had to wonder about him. "All right, but if I end up smeared against a wall, I'll never forgive you."

Devyn leaned across the panel in front of her, his head less than three inches from her own, and pressed a couple of switches. The crisp, fresh scent of his after-shave filled her senses. She stared at the smooth planes of his face, wondering how it would feel to touch the sun-darkened skin with her fingertips. How his lips would taste. . . .

He glanced up at her and she looked away, embarrassed by her thoughts.

"I don't let my people get hurt," he said in a sincere tone.

"What about your last gunner?"

A blush spread across his cheeks, and he dropped his gaze back to the panel. "I lied. He ran off with his lover at our last stop."

She raised her brows, shocked by his confession. "Why'd you lie about it?"

He shrugged again and continued to program coordinates into the computer log. "I thought you were a kid trying to leave the station because you were mad at your parents. I figured my words would make you think twice about signing on to a ship."

Alix smiled at his kindness, but before she could say anything, a whistle rent the air.

"Devyn!" Sway's anxious voice broke them apart. "I've got six Probers up here asking for the captain. You'd better get up here, quick."

Devyn pushed himself away from the panel. "Better get strapped in. Looks like we're going to have a bit of trouble."

Alix went rigid, knowing all too well the type

of trouble he meant. "You want me to take the guns?"

He shook his head. "Only as a last resort. I'm a runner, not a smuggler."

"Is there a difference?"

He gave her a strange look that she couldn't define. "Runners are motivated by a lot more than money," he said before dashing down the corridor.

Alix thought over his enigmatic response as she followed him. Just what kind of man had she signed on with?

Finally, she decided she liked his convictions about the guns. She'd never enjoyed firing at others, and she was grateful he obviously felt the same way.

As she entered the control room, the hailing channel buzzed in her ears. The captain of the lead ship demanded their call letters and codes. Devyn disregarded the strident tone and strapped himself in.

Sway turned around in his chair and tossed her a bag. "Keep that handy."

"Why?"

Before he could answer, Devyn took the controls, and the ship lurched to the right at an angle she hadn't thought possible for a ship the size of theirs. Grateful she hadn't eaten a large lunch, she gripped the arms of her seat.

For close to ten minutes, the ship bucked and dipped like some crazed beast trying to sling off a rider. Sweat covered her face as she struggled not to undignify herself with her heaving stomach.

All of a sudden, Devyn fired the retrorockets and the ship jerked to a crawl. Alix looked up with a frown, only to wish she hadn't.

Before them, three Probers waited with a tractor net spread out in two directions. The other probers were closing in behind them.

A trickle of sweat ran down her cheek. She swallowed the lump in her throat and tightened her grip on the armrests.

They were about to be caught and jailed.

# *Chapter Two*

"Surrender your ship, crew, and cargo," a gruff voice demanded over the hailing channel.

Sway pulled his legs up to his chest, laid his head on his knees, and covered it with his arms. "Dev, I really hate it when you do this," he mumbled.

Alix swallowed in fear. By now she'd learned enough about the captain to realize he wasn't going to surrender. In fact, he stared at the surrounding ships with a smile on his face that told her how much he delighted in toying with the authorities.

"Alix," Devyn said. "Put your head down and take a deep breath."

He didn't look at her, but from the tone of his

voice she could just imagine the gleam in his eyes. Quickly, she duplicated Sway's position.

Through a miracle of his piloting abilities, the ship dropped straight down. Alix's stomach lurched straight up. The ship's gravity field switched off automatically, and the unexpected weightlessness hit her like an asteroid.

Alix gripped her legs, her body rigid in expectation.

Then, just as she thought she'd definitely be sick, they stopped descending. They drifted for half a heartbeat before Devyn fired the engines. The sudden force lurched her back against the seat with an impact she was certain would leave a long bruise down her spine.

Within a minute, they hit hyperspace and flew out of the sector.

"Everyone all right?" Devyn asked as he flipped the gravity back on.

"I think I just gave birth," Sway growled.

"Me, too," Alix mumbled, her stomach still pitching.

Devyn shook his head. "This is the thanks I get for saving us from jail? No 'Gee Captain, great flying,' or 'Wow, how'd you do that?'" He gave a heavy sigh as he ran over the settings. "Leave it to me to get a crew of old women."

His words amused her, but she couldn't quite bring a smile to her shaking lips. He was right, though. That was some of the best flying she'd ever seen.

Sway wiped an arm across his sweat-covered brow. "One day, someone is going to make the markings on this ship, and then we will be in trouble."

Devyn shrugged off the warning. "They might, but there's never been a HAWC prober born who could outmaneuver a Laing."

Alix looked up at the mention of the Laing surname. Everyone in the business of freighting knew of the infamous family of smugglers.

"Your aunt and uncle would be proud of you, no doubt," Sway said. "But your mother would have your ass if she ever saw you do what you do."

Devyn swung his chair around to face Alix. "Any complaints you want to add to his?"

Startled by his sudden attention to her, Alix focused her gaze on his playful brown eyes. She wasn't used to men who joked about life and death, and the things in between.

A strange surge of emotion filled her, but she couldn't quite name the sensation. She shook her head. "No complaints, Captain, but as soon as my legs can walk again, I think I need to lie down."

"C'mon, I'll help you to your room," Devyn said, unstrapping himself.

Alix started to protest, but her words stumbled on her tongue as she looked up at him.

Maybe it was the lighting, or her shaky nerves, or maybe her leftover fear. Alix wasn't sure what caused her sudden muteness, but as she watched him, she knew she'd never seen a man so handsome, nor one so desirable.

He unstrapped her and his warm, strong hands helped her up from her chair. A half-smile played across his lips with a devastating effect on her. No longer sure if her shaky legs were a result of the flight or the man, Alix slumped against his long, lean body.

Devyn draped her right arm over his shoulders and held her wrist with his right hand. He wrapped his other arm around her waist. Alix trembled at the intimate contact, wishing she were the type of woman who knew how to play coy games. "I think I can manage to make my way."

His gaze burned into hers, and for a moment she feared he might be able to see past her defenses and detect the way he unnerved her. "It's not often I get to play the gallant. Don't interfere with my good deed for the day."

Alix smiled, her heart hammering. What she wouldn't give to be free from her past, to be a beautiful, blonde socializer who could seduce Devyn with a smile. Her smile faded in disappointment.

Who was she fooling?

He was just being thoughtful, as he'd said. He'd do the same for Sway, or any other crewmember.

Still, the heat of his body warmed hers as he

led her out of the control room and down the corridor.

"That was some really good flying," she said. "How'd you know a hyperspace opening was there?"

That gorgeous smile appeared. "I have my uncle's star charts that detail every opening in the trigalaxies."

Alix frowned. "Your uncle?"

"Calix Laing."

Shocked by his words, she stumbled against him.

He tightened his grip around her, preventing her from falling. Alix's heart beat even faster. "Are you really a Laing?"

Devyn nodded, his features serious. "Son of a Laing bounder and a Kell clinch. Somehow fitting I ended up on the dark side of justice."

Alix came to a complete stop. Bounders hunted down criminals and turned them over to the government authorities who paid the most for them. Clinches made their living by stealing secret government documents, and selling them to enemy governments. How two such opposite creatures could come together and breed the man beside her, she couldn't imagine.

Devyn released her and stared at her with an odd, almost hurt expression. "Does my parentage repulse you?"

She shook her head in honesty. "No, but I'm curious about how they met."

29

He shrugged and the humor returned to his eyes. "My mom was hired to track my dad down and arrest him."

"And I thought my parents had a rough relationship," Alix mumbled before she could stop herself.

Devyn cocked an eyebrow. "I know your father ran a freighter. What about your mom?"

Her heart hammered against her ribs. She squelched the sudden burst of panic before she gave herself away. He must never know about her mother. No one must ever know. She couldn't even think about it without her head becoming light and her sight dimming in mortal terror.

"She . . ." Alix paused while trying to think up a believable lie.

She shifted her gaze to the floor, hoping he couldn't detect her deceit. "She disappeared when I was just a kid. I don't really remember her."

Skittish about the turn in their conversation, Alix sprinted the rest of the way to her room.

"Alix?" Devyn called, but she didn't even hesitate.

He frowned at the frightened look he'd seen on her face when he'd asked about her mother. Tempted to go after her, Devyn decided it would be best to give her time to get used to him and sway slowly.

Trusting strangers wasn't easy for most people. In all honesty, he envied her suspicious nature.

Trust had gotten him into one predicament too many in his life.

Alix sat on the bed holding her pillow to her stomach. She wasn't sure how many hours had passed, but her parched throat begged for something to drink.

Well, she didn't have much choice. She had to go find either Sway or Devyn and get something to drink before she dehydrated to the point of illness.

With a reluctant sigh, she swung the pillow aside and rose. She decided to try the control room first. If her luck held, Sway would be there, and Devyn would have already gone to bed.

Reaching the control room door, she pushed the touch-activated lock. The portal opened and she sighed in disgust. Since when had luck ever been on her side? Devyn stood to her right, leaning over a panel.

He glanced up at her. "I'm glad you're here. I thought I was going to have to wake you."

Alix frowned at his tone, which landed somewhere between frustration and relief. "What's wrong?"

"I've got a fluctuation in the radiation shielding and I think gamma rays are leaking in."

Alix's eyes widened. She didn't like the sound of that at all. Stepping up to the panel, she ran over the gauges. They had pulled out of hyperspace and were traveling at fifty percent light speed.

She glanced over the diagnostic test Devyn was running and saw the leak.

"Where's the shield's power source?"

"I'll show you," Devyn said, leading her back to the corridor.

Halfway down the hall, he stopped and pushed the controls for a lift to the lower deck. "The air gets a bit thin. If you start getting sick, let me know."

She cocked her brow. "Believe me, if I start getting sick, you will know."

Without responding to her sarcasm, he stepped into the lift. Alix followed, but quickly wished she hadn't. The small compartment forced them together in an intimate proximity she found horribly unsettling. She bit her lip and tried not to brush up against his hard, muscular body. All too well, she remembered how it felt to be in his arms.

"When did you notice the leak?" she asked, trying to distract herself from her thoughts.

"A few minutes ago. I was about to go to your room." He looked down at her and smiled. "What brought you out?"

She licked her dry lips. "Dehydration."

A deep frown creased his brow. "Why didn't you say something before I brought you down here?"

The anger in his voice startled her. "Why are you growling at me?"

"I don't know. I'm frustrated, and you should

32

have told me you were dying of thirst!" For such a reasonable response, the tone of his voice wavered on violence.

"Well I'd rather die of thirst than radiation poisoning. I daresay it's less painful."

Devyn laughed, his breath falling against her cheek. "I guess you're right."

Alix stared up at him, her body trembling. Never in her life had she been so attracted to a man. Maybe the knowledge that she couldn't have him caused the strong attraction. Whatever the source, all she wanted was to taste his lips and feel his arms around her once again.

With a soft whir, the door opened. Relieved and despondent, Alix stepped out. She reminded herself why she must never open herself up to Devyn or anyone else, but still her heart hammered a denial.

Devyn led her to the engineering room and punched in a sequence of keys to open the door. "The code to enter the room is Claria."

A wave of disappointment ran through her at the mention of a woman's name and the note of obvious affection in his voice when he spoke of her. "Claria?"

"Sway's wife."

Alix lifted a brow in surprise. "Sway's married?"

"Yeah. Claria's a political assassin for the dorjani government. Since she travels so much, and they don't have any children for him to watch, Sway stays with me."

Alix frowned at him. "That sounds odd."

A quirky smile curved his lips. "Only by most humans' standards. The dorjanie are matriarchal. The males can't do anything without female consent. The men even take their wife's name."

She found his good humor infectious as he stared at her with those playful eyes. She could just imagine having that kind of control over Devyn. The thought appealed to her greatly.

He entered the room and started checking over the system's gauges. "I'm Sway's legal chaperon, which is why he gives me such agony about my mom's calls. He considers it justice over the way I taunt him about Claria."

Alix wondered at his words. "How did you get responsibility for him?"

"His mother is an old friend of my father's. Since we grew up like brothers, Claria knew I wouldn't let Sway get into trouble." He glanced up from the panel. "What about you? Do you have any siblings?"

A cold, twisting lump coiled in her stomach, and she feared for a moment she might be sick. *Don't think about it,* she warned herself. Alix dropped her gaze and looked over the control panel for the shield's leak. "No. I told you I don't have any family ties."

"Sorry, I forgot."

Alix hadn't meant for her reply to be so curt. She tried to ignore her guilt—and his presence—as she concentrated on her task, but it wasn't easy.

It didn't take long to isolate the leak and correct it. "There," she said, stepping back. "It's all fixed."

Devyn checked the gauges.

She studied his frown of consternation and smiled. "How is it a pilot of your abilities doesn't know anything about ship's maintenance?"

Devyn laughed and looked up at her. "I'm a pilot, not a mechanic. All I know is how to check things and fly them, not fix them. What about you? Can you pilot?"

She shook her head. "I can do a launch sequence, but that's about all. I couldn't get near the directional controls unless my father passed out."

Alix bit her lip in shock at the slip she'd made, but she couldn't seem to help herself. There was something about Devyn that stripped away all the careful barriers she'd built for herself. The thought terrified her.

A flicker of anger touched Devyn's eyes but quickly vanished. Could he possibly have any feelings for her? She disregarded the possibility. Men like Devyn Kell had no use for women like her.

"Is that why you became an engineer?" he asked in a low voice.

Alix brushed her hand across her cheek, skimming the tiny scar just below her right eye where

35

her father had slung her against a control panel a few years ago after she had made a simple mistake. "No. My father didn't like paying the extra money to hire an engineer, so one day he handed me a wrench and a manual and told me to fix the side stabilizer or get off the ship."

Devyn stared at her in disbelief. The blasé tone of her voice told him more about Alix than the words themselves. Her father had been a real bastard. Even so, she hadn't let him hold her back. A surge of admiration ran through him. "I bet you fixed it like new."

Alix snorted. "No. It went out before we could even complete the launch. Ended up busting one of the cargo bays and losing half our shipment."

Devyn studied her halfhearted smile. "I'll keep that in mind if one of ours ever goes out."

She gave him a guarded look that made him regret his words. He'd meant them as humor, but obviously she didn't appreciate it.

He stared at her eyes. They were such an unusual shade, probing, intelligent, and pain-filled. For some reason, he wanted to soothe away the agony that blazed in defiance of him and the whole universe.

Before he could stop himself, Devyn cupped her cheek. The softness of her skin surprised and delighted him. Despite her rough, prickly defenses, she was an attractive woman with a quiet assuredness he found refreshing. He hadn't been this attracted to a woman in a long time.

He knew he should walk away from her. She was a member of his crew, and business and pleasure shouldn't mix. But he couldn't seem to stop himself from touching her soft cheek, or brushing her lips with his thumb.

Alix opened her mouth to speak, but no sound came out. Her cheek burned under the weight of his fingers. She wanted this kiss, and a small voice inside told her it was more than mere want. She needed it.

His hands tightened on her face. He closed his eyes and dipped his head toward hers.

"Devyn? Where are you?"

Silently, Alix cursed Sway's dorjani hide for the interruption. Just a few more seconds and he could've called without her wanting to strangle him.

Was one kiss too much to ask?

Devyn blinked in confusion, as if he were waking from a dream, then dropped his hands from her face and took a step back.

Her skin still tingling, Alix wanted desperately to return to the mood, but it was too late. She sighed in disgust. Luck would never be her friend.

Devyn moved to the wall intercom. "What do you need?"

"I need you to get your ass up here and assure Claria Alix is human and that you're not going to leave me alone with her."

Devyn rolled his eyes in obvious frustration.

Alix laughed.

"I'm on my way," he said with a sigh.

She stepped away from him. "Ever wish subspace transmissions were impossible?"

"Only every time my mom or Claria calls," he grumbled.

Alix's smile widened.

They remained silent the whole way back to the main deck. Devyn stepped out of the lift first. "The galley is all the way down the corridor on the left. Search through the cooling unit until you find something you like."

Alix stared after him as he walked toward the control room, amazed he had remembered her thirst.

Her throat tightened as longing raced through her. If only she could trust him with her secret. But she knew better. She'd lived most of her life under dire, soul-wrenching threats, and she wasn't about to put such a weapon in Devyn's hands.

With a sigh, she crossed her arms over her chest and headed to the galley.

What she wouldn't give for the type of friendship he and Sway shared. Someone she could talk things over with, release the darkest secret of her soul.

*Don't think about it,* she told herself. *As long as you don't open your mouth, no one will ever know; you'll be free.* She must always keep her secret, no matter what.

The next two days passed quickly. Alix did her best to avoid being around Devyn and Sway. For the most part, she succeeded, and they only passed briefly in the corridors or galley.

She sat on her bed, listening to the whir of the engines as Devyn and Sway brought the *Mariah* into the docks on Nera VII. The two of them had invited her to dinner at one of the local pubs.

Alix pulled the tie from her ponytail and let the long, thick, heavy hair hang down her back.

With a deep sigh, she ran her hand over the rough material of her beige pantsuit, wishing she had more suitable clothes. Just once, she'd like to look at least halfway attractive.

A knock sounded on her door.

"Come in."

The door slid up to reveal Devyn. "We're getting ready to go eat. Are you joining us?"

She nodded her head. "How long will we be here?"

Devyn rubbed his left hand over his right arm. "We're supposed to be meeting a supplier for dinner. As soon as we eat and exchange partial cargos, we'll leave."

Alix gave him a suspicious look. She'd never known a runner to be open about cargo exchanges. "So where are we eating?"

His eyes glowed with mischief. "The Runner's Den."

Alix laughed; now she understood his lack of secrecy. "Why doesn't that surprise me?"

Devyn didn't comment. Instead, he extended his arm to her. "Shall we? I'm hungry enough to eat Sway's cooking."

Alix's heart pounded in response to his gesture. Before she could stop herself, she wrapped her arm around his. She swallowed at the contact, her body throbbing from the close proximity.

Apparently oblivious, Devyn led her out of the ship and into the landing bay, where Sway stood at one end talking to a group of men. He looked up and caught sight of them.

Devyn headed toward him. The fact that he didn't release her arm surprised Alix. No one had ever publicly claimed her before.

"Is Taryn here?" he asked as they joined the group.

Sway nodded and scratched his chin. "He beat us here by about half an hour."

Devyn gave him a satisfied grin. "Then let's find him."

Sway excused himself from the group, and they made their way out of the bay and into the long main corridor that ran in a circle around the space station.

Like most stations, shops lined both sides of the corridor. They passed a number of people and aliens, their arms filled with a variety of goods.

Devyn stopped outside a door painted with an encircled freighter—the universal sign of a runner's or smuggler's haven. Alix pulled away from him, no longer quite comfortable in his embrace.

Sway opened the door and led the way into the dark room. Voices and music mingled in the air, making her ears throb. She'd never cared for these types of places. Too many years of pulling her father out of them left her with bitter memories Alix wished she could erase.

Banishing the thought, she followed behind Sway and Devyn as they made their way through the pub to one of the tables in the back.

A handsome, dark-haired man sat at a corner table with an extremely attractive redhead in his lap. Laughing with each other, the couple were locked in an intimate embrace that brought heat to Alix's cheeks.

Devyn glanced at Sway with a disgusted frown, then shook his head. "Don't you ever get tired of playing the traveling rogue?"

The man looked up with a smile. His gaze swept over Devyn, Sway, and her, and Alix had the strangest feeling he took in more than just their presence. "C'mon, Dev, be nice. Prenna and I have known each other for years."

Alix stifled her laugh at the skeptical look on Devyn's face.

The redhead pushed herself out of the man's lap. "I'll see you tonight?"

He nodded. "I'll be there."

The woman gave him a hungry smile, then turned a hostile glare to Alix and her companions before making her way through the crowd.

Devyn held a seat out for her. Amazed at the gesture, Alix sat down across from the stranger, who eyed her curiously.

"Who's *your* friend?"

Devyn took a seat at her right and Sway on her left. "She's my new engineer," Devyn said. "Alix, meet another of my childhood friends, Taryn Kyrelle."

Taryn dipped his head to her. "Nice to meet you."

Alix nodded.

Devyn sat forward in his chair and caught Taryn's attention. "Did you get all the medical supplies I asked for?"

Taryn sat back and crossed his arms over his chest. "I got them, but you should know the HAWC Keepers at Paradise City have been scanning cargoes for perillian and antibiotics for the last two weeks. Someone told them a large shipment would be coming in, and that its destination was for the rebel Outposters in the mines."

Alix's heart skipped a beat. The last thing she wanted was a run-in with the HAWC. An elite military organization, the HAWC had charters from all the major governments granting it the right to act as judge, jury and executioner against anyone it deemed a threat to intergalactic peace. More than one rumor claimed the HAWC served only itself, and she knew crossing the HAWC would be the last mistake she or Devyn ever made.

Devyn narrowed his eyes at Taryn and clenched his teeth. For the first time, Alix sensed what a dangerous man he was. "Any idea who leaked?"

Taryn shook his head. "No, but I'd be real careful."

"I'll guard my back."

"And I'll guard the rest of you!"

Alix looked up at the sound of a sultry female voice. Her mouth opened in stunned surprise. The most beautiful woman she'd ever seen leaned over Devyn and kissed his cheek.

Hair as black as space cascaded from the top of an assassin's skullcap down to the woman's tiny waist. Unbelievably tall and dressed in a skimpy black suit that barely covered the necessary parts of her body, the woman had a figure Alix would kill for. She wore one blaster strapped to her left hip, and the silver handle of a dagger peeped out of the top of her shiny black thigh-high boots.

Meeting the woman's friendly gaze, she realized the stranger was Deucalion. Not even the oddity of Deucalion eyes—white pupils surrounded by red irises—detracted from the beauty of her face.

43

"Someone ought to tie a bell to you," Devyn said, hugging her tightly. "I hate the way you sneak up behind me."

The woman laughed before making her way around the table to hug Sway. "Oh, I've missed you guys!" she said, emphasizing her words with a tight squeeze. "So where's Golan?"

Devyn sighed. "He ran off at our last stop. Alix here is our new engineer."

"Hi," the woman said as she took a seat between Sway and Taryn. "I'm Zarina, but you can call me Rina."

Alix smiled at the sincere friendship in Zarina's eyes but noticed the uneasiness of the men.

Zarina looked around at them and caught their sudden rigidness as well. "Don't tell me," she said with a tired sigh. "We've got business to discuss. Would you mind giving us a few minutes?"

Taryn tipped his glass to her in a mock salute. "Since you already knew our thoughts, why did you disturb us?"

She pierced him with a malevolent glare. "Suck an asteroid berry, you pirate snot." Zarina glanced to Devyn and lastly to Sway, both of whom were trying to stifle their laughter at her words.

Realizing they weren't going to interfere on her behalf, she sniffed in mock hurt. "Fine," she said, lifting her chin defiantly. "Rather than ruin your fun, I'll find someone who'll help me waste some time." Her gaze followed a handsome man passing their table.

When she stood up to go after the man, Taryn grabbed her wrist. "Alix, would you mind taking Zarina to the restaurant four doors down? You can put the food on my bill."

Zarina snatched her arm from his grasp. The look on her face could have melted steel.

Stunned, Alix didn't know what to do.

With an imperious toss of her head, Zarina rounded the table. "C'mon, Alix. Let's leave the boys to their games."

Still somewhat confused, Alix followed Zarina out of the pub. Zarina stopped in the hallway, turned around, and glared at the door. Her eyes glittered with malice as she leaned against the outside wall, crossed her arms over her chest, and tapped her fingers against her upper arms. "They make me furious!"

Before Alix could say anything, the door opened to reveal Devyn. He gave her a sheepish look and turned toward Zarina. "I'm sorry, *shanna*. You know how Taryn is."

Zarina narrowed her eyes. "Six weeks. I've been with him for the last six weeks, and I'm about to kill him!" She faced Devyn and her expression changed to pleading. "Will you take me with you when you leave?"

Alix and Devyn exchanged shocked glances. "You know I can't. I'm heading to Paradise City. Your brothers would tear me apart if they found out I took you to a war zone."

Zarina dipped her head in a coy pose and smoothed the collar of his shirt like an old lover after a long separation. "Please," she purred.

Clenching her fists at her sides, Alix wanted to snatch the thick mass of black hair from the woman's head.

Devyn shook his head, a smile hovering at the corners of his mouth. "You know better."

Zarina's gaze hardened. She dropped her hands and gave him a feral snarl. "Fine. When I kill him, remember you could have prevented it."

Devyn laughed and handed Alix his debit card. "Don't worry about the price. Just keep her eating and out of trouble."

Their hands brushed as she took the card from him. A chill spread up her arm at the unexpected contact.

His gaze dipped to her lips, and Alix could almost swear a hungry look darkened his eyes, but he quickly looked away. He cleared his throat, then turned to face Zarina. "Behave," he warned her before reentering the pub.

Zarina pursed her lips into a becoming pout until the door closed behind him. She looked down at Alix and smiled. "You've got a crush on Devyn."

The words startled her. "What?"

Zarina nodded, a knowing smile on her face. "I saw the look the two of you exchanged when you touched. The heat from it almost scorched me."

Alix opened her mouth to deny it, but wasn't sure what to say.

"Don't worry. I know just the thing you need to get his attention. Listen to me, and we'll have his gorgeous body in your bed before another week elapses!"

# Chapter Three

Heat stung Alix's cheeks as she stared at Zarina in disbelief. "How do you know what it takes to get Captain Kell in—"

"Relax," Zarina interrupted her. Shaking her head, she said quietly, "You could give Taryn lessons in hostile tones."

She took Alix by the arm and started walking slowly down the corridor. "I have no physical interest in Devyn. He's like a brother to me. He, Sway, and my brothers used to terrorize me when I was growing up. Not that they've changed much now, but at least I can get away from them on brief occasions."

Alix frowned at her words. "Why do your brothers leave you alone to travel with Taryn?"

Zarina laughed and squeezed her arm. "Taryn *is* one of my many overbearing, overprotective, overly obnoxious brothers."

Alix scanned her suspiciously.

"I know we don't look anything alike," Zarina said with a sigh. "Taryn looks like our mother, who's human, and I look like our Deucalion grandmother. Leave it to me to get all my father's recessive genes. You can't imagine what it's like looking Deucalion while your mother and siblings look human."

Alix bit her lip, a wave of empathy washing over her. She understood only too well the isolation and bitterness that came from being different. "I'm sorry. I didn't mean to insult you."

Zarina shrugged. "Don't worry. I'm used to it. Anyway, back to you and Devyn."

"There's nothing between us," Alix hastened to assure both herself and Zarina. "I work for him and that's it."

Zarina pulled her to a stop and probed her with a stare that seemed to see all the way to her soul. "But you want more?"

"No," Alix said calmly, knowing she denied the truth. "All I want is enough money to buy my own freighter and have my own life."

Zarina cocked a suspicious eyebrow. "Alone?"

"Alone." Alix had the distinct feeling Zarina didn't believe her, but Zarina said nothing else as she led the way into the restaurant.

They ate their meal in a chatty camaraderie.

Alix found Zarina a good listener, with more insight than a sage, and a sense of humor that kept her laughing throughout all six courses.

As they finished their rich triata cream dessert, Zarina locked gazes with her. "You know, Devyn's not the pacifist you think he is."

Alix looked up with a smile. "I can't imagine him hurting anyone. He's just too nice."

Zarina shook her head. "Stay on his nice side. Believe me, you don't ever want to see him angry."

Licking the back of her spoon, Alix thought over Zarina's words. "He doesn't even have weapons on his ship. Systems disrupters are the only protection we have. For a dangerous man, he certainly has mild toys."

Zarina's face turned serious. "Never underestimate anyone. Devyn knows he can outfly anything a HAWC Prober or enemy might have, and the disrupters are just a safeguard in case he has a malfunction while being chased." She scooped up a large spoonful of cream. "Trust me, Devyn isn't the type of man you want to cross."

"Okay," Alix said with a smile. "I'll do my best not to try his patience."

Zarina returned her smile and set her spoon on the table. "I don't know about you, but I can't eat any more."

Mischievously, she glanced around the room. "Why don't we take my brother's card and buy ourselves something expensive and useless!"

"Excuse me?" Alix asked.

"Don't look so shocked. He deserves it after sending me off like an errant child. The least I can do is erode some of his balance."

Zarina's words and obvious dislike for her brother confused her. "If Taryn bothers you so much, why don't you buy a shuttle ticket to go wherever you want to?"

Zarina pursed her lips and declined using Devyn's debit card for their meal. Instead, she ran Taryn's debit card through the table payment slot and punched in an enormous tip. "Taryn is the lesser of my banes. If I abandon him without a proper escort, my parents will sic ten bodyguards on me for the rest of my natural life."

"What?"

Zarina rose to her feet and led Alix out of the restaurant. "Our father is the Kirovion Emperor," she said, her voice full of disdain. "If not for my brothers and their extremely overprotective natures, I'd be stagnating in the summer palace, and not out here annoying Taryn."

With a speculative frown, Zarina paused in front of a clothing shop and eyed several pricey dresses. "In fact, my staying with Taryn is punishment for disappearing from my brother Tiernan's side while he was visiting a friend in Quiyarda Square."

Zarina sighed and scanned the other shops around them. A slow smile curved her lips.

Alix shook her head in amusement. By the look

51

on Zarina's face as she headed into the jewelry shop across the corridor, she knew Zarina had found her revenge.

Zarina paused in the doorway to allow her to catch up. "My parents figured Taryn would keep a tighter leash on me." She walked up to a long glass case in the center of the store and pointed to a huge, expensive taria necklace. "Now, if I have to wear a leash, that looks like a most attractive one. What do you think?"

Alix widened her eyes in appreciation. The clear, perfectly formed necklace would dazzle anyone. "I think your brother will kill you for spending that much money."

Zarina smiled like a hunting virago after its prey. "Won't he, though?"

Despite herself, Alix had to laugh. Zarina's carefree good humor wouldn't allow anyone to fault the princess for her shortcomings. "So how is it Taryn doesn't have a body-guard?"

"He does. Didn't you see the two Deucalions sitting at the table next to his in the Runner's Den?"

Alix shook her head.

With a half-smile, Zarina took her hand and led her to the glass window at the front of the shop.

"There's one of them now," she said, waving at a tall Deucalion male who stood outside the shop with a stern frown on his face as he watched them. "He joined us in the restaurant not long after we sat down, and he won't let me out of his sight until I get back to Taryn."

Alix stared at the Deucalion, wondering how he had escaped her attention. "I didn't even notice him."

"You're not supposed to. They hang back until someone unfamiliar approaches; then they make their presence known rather rudely."

Zarina turned around and headed back to the case. She stopped a passing saleswoman and pointed to the necklace. "I'll take that, please."

Though Zarina was about as spoiled as any person Alix had ever met, she possessed a strange charisma. It wasn't that she demanded anything; she just assumed no one would ever deny her requests.

Alix watched the clerk take the necklace out of the case and hand it to Zarina. Without a care for the price, Zarina gave the clerk her brother's card. Alix shook her head in amusement. She couldn't even imagine having enough money to afford one small taria ring, let alone the necklace Zarina was securing around her neck.

Moving to stand next to Zarina, she frowned. "I think I'm confused. Sway, Devyn, Taryn, and you come from such different backgrounds. How did all of you meet?"

Zarina smiled and patted her shiny new leash. "Devyn's father and Sway's mother worked for my father. They ended up good friends, and by the time all of us were born, they were inseparable, which made us inseparable."

"Hey," Zarina said, going to the next case. "That's perfect!"

Alix frowned and looked down at the dark blue vizier choker. Her mouth opened at the intricate workmanship that had interlaced white and clear tarias with the vivid blue stones.

"I'll take this, too," Zarina said to the clerk.

After the saleswoman handed it to Zarina, she turned and placed it around Alix's throat.

"What are you doing?" Alix asked breathlessly, a chill rising on her neck from the coldness of the choker.

"It's a perfect match for your eyes," she said, turning Alix to face a mirror. "See how it makes them darker? That'll get Devyn's attention."

Shocked, Alix just stared at the sparkling choker around her throat. Her mind couldn't comprehend Zarina's generosity. "You're buying this for yourself, right?"

"Don't be silly," Zarina scoffed. "What would I want with a blue choker? It'd look queer with my eyes."

Afraid to touch anything so costly, Alix unfastened the catch and handed it quickly back to Zarina. "I can't take this."

Before Zarina could protest, Devyn and Taryn entered the shop.

Taryn had a fierce look on his face as he pierced

his sister with his gaze. "How much did you bleed my account?"

Zarina ignored the question, placed the blue choker in a box the saleswoman had provided, and handed it to Alix, her hands lingering on Alix's. "I want you to have this," she said with a sincerity that brought a lump to Alix's throat, "so don't say no, or you'll hurt my feelings."

She looked back at Taryn and tossed her hair off her shoulder with a careless shrug. "I'll reimburse you for Alix's gift. But you owe me my necklace for what you did last night."

A blush spread across Taryn's cheeks, and Alix wanted to know what had happened so badly she almost asked. But from Taryn's face as he walked to the clerk to retrieve his debit card, she didn't think it wise.

Devyn cleared his throat and diplomatically changed the subject. "We need to get back and swap freight. I'd like to dock in Paradise City by the end of the week."

Taryn returned and handed Zarina another box. "You might as well have the earrings, too," he mumbled gruffly before leading the way out of the store.

A slight smile played on Zarina's lips as she stared after her brother. "I really hate it when he's nice. He knows just what to do to make me feel guilty."

Alix smiled at her dire tone.

Pursing her lips, Zarina linked arms with Alix

and Devyn, and the three of them followed Taryn back to the bay.

"Where's Sway?" Alix asked.

"Claria came in not long after you two left," Devyn said. "He should be on board the ship."

Zarina's arm tightened around Alix, and she gave Devyn a calculating smile. "So, Dev, when are *you* going to calm down and get married?"

Anxious in spite of herself, Alix looked over at him. An angry tick beat in his jaw that surprised her.

"You know the answer to that," he said, his voice hard, his gaze brittle.

Alix swallowed at his strange reaction. Normally, he appeared so even-tempered that she couldn't believe just a question could elicit such an emotional response.

His eyes filled with pain, Devyn left them and went to open the cargo hatch of the *Mariah*. Biting her lip, Alix looked to Zarina for an explanation.

Zarina sighed and shook her head. "It's a long story. I keep hoping he'll get over it, but I guess it just epitomizes his career in the HAWC."

"Devyn was in the HAWC?" Alix asked in disbelief.

"Yes," Zarina answered, her voice shaking. "But don't ask him about his training. He gets in a nasty mood at the mere mention of it."

Alix watched Devyn program the cargo robots

to exchange crates with Taryn's ship.

She just couldn't quite believe everything Zarina had told her about Devyn. In the last three days, he hadn't even raised his voice to anyone. Everything he did, from evading probers to dealing with irate controllers, he did with a calm, good-natured gentleness.

"I'd better go see if I can help him," Alix said. "I'd hate to be fired so soon."

"All right, but just remember what I told you about men and how to attract them."

"I'll remember," Alix said with a smile, thinking about all the outrageous things Zarina had suggested she try, things she knew she could never do. "Thanks for the choker. I've never had anything so nice, or beautiful."

Zarina returned her smile. "You deserve it, and more. Take care of yourself, and watch Devyn's and Sway's backs."

"I will."

Zarina nodded her head before walking toward Taryn's ship.

As she placed her hand over the box in her pocket, a warm rush flooded Alix. She'd never met so many kind, generous people in her life.

Her heart light, she made her way to Devyn's side.

"Alix," Devyn said when he saw her nearing him, "could you please check the front quarter panel and see if we can squeeze in another crate up there?"

"Sure, Captain," she said, moving to the front of the ship.

She pulled open the compartment. With a grunt, she tried to move one crate over, but slipped and cut her hand. Hissing at the pain, she pulled her handkerchief out of her pocket and wrapped it around the cut.

"I thought it was you."

Alix tensed at the sound of the all too familiar voice. The one voice she'd hoped never to hear again.

Slowly, she turned around to face her father's old navigator. "Hi, Irn," she said with a politeness she didn't feel, knowing rudeness would only bring out one of his temper bursts.

No doubt he just wanted his wages. She had tried to pay him, but he'd disappeared after her father's murder. She stepped down. Might as well pay him now and get rid of him.

He stood to her left with four men she didn't recognize. Her throat tightened. Irn always lost what little sense he possessed when he was with a group of men to impress. She hadn't seen him in six months, but even sixty years wouldn't be long enough to forget his long, stringy hair and the unholy stench that clung to his body.

He leered at her and there was no mistaking the lust that burned in his eyes. "I've been hoping to come across you."

Alix clenched her fists at her side, debating what to do. She wished she had her blaster with her. The last time they'd been together, he'd ended up ripping her shirt before she managed to dissuade him from rape.

*Pay him off before he asks,* her mind warned. She reached for her wallet. "Look, why don't you—"

"You don't order me around no more," he said, looking at his friends to see their reactions. "I'm claiming freeman's rights. From now on, I own you."

*No!* her mind screamed. Her vision dimmed in panic. How could he possibly know her secret? She gripped her makeshift bandage, trying to think of something to do, but her mind was numb.

Irn grabbed her wrist.

Instinctively, Alix snatched her hand away. "No one owns me!" she snarled.

He backhanded her.

She stumbled backward, her sight dimming, and she fell against the ship.

Enraged to the point of murder, Alix pushed herself away from the ship and struck out at him with her good fist, catching him on the chin. He fell to the ground.

Irn's hate-filled gaze bore into hers as he wiped the blood from his split lip. "You'll pay for that, bitch," he said, pushing himself up.

Her heart pounding in her ears, Alix tensed for his attack.

He reached for her, but his hand froze inches from contact.

Devyn wrapped his arm around Irn's throat and held him in a headlock. "What's going on?" he asked in the calmest voice Alix had ever heard.

Before anyone could answer, Irn's cronies attacked. Devyn shoved Irn away from him and turned to fight. Irn moved to join the number against Devyn.

Scared and furious, Alix clenched her teeth. Not willing to stand by and see Devyn hurt because of her, Alix grabbed Irn's shoulder, pulled him around to face her, and caught him on the chin again. This time, she succeeded in knocking him unconscious. Her swollen fist throbbed as Irn fell to the ground.

In stunned awe, she watched Devyn finish the others with a precision that confirmed Zarina's tale of his military training.

After the last one crumpled, Devyn turned to face her. "Are you all right?"

Her throat tightened with a gamut of emotions—fear, pain, regret. She stared at his concerned eyes and wanted to hug him for his kindness. No one had ever stood up for her before.

But if he learned her secret, he'd hate her. That thought hurt more than her throbbing cheek or hands.

Biting her lip, she had only one choice. She must leave before he found out, too.

Without answering his question, she ran from the bay.

"Alix!"

She heard Devyn's call but didn't stop. Her thoughts tumbled over each other as she ran past the shops.

Devyn must never know her mother was a slave.

No one must ever know. If anyone ever found out, then they could claim her for their own or sell her.

She would never be owned again!

Alix choked on her sobs, but she refused to let her tears fall. All too well she knew how to control her pain, and she refused to cry.

She didn't know where she was going; she just had to put as much distance between herself and Devyn as she could.

Heading down a narrow corridor, she slowed to fast walk.

A hand grabbed her shoulder. Panicked, Alix turned around with her fist clenched to slug her assailant.

She paused.

Devyn placed his hands on her shoulders. A deep, concerned frown lined his handsome features. "What's wrong with you?"

Alix stared up at him, wishing she could tell him the truth, but she knew better. The truth would destroy him. "I quit. I can't stay on the *Mariah* anymore. Just leave my stuff in a locker in the bay and I'll pick it up later."

Devyn's frown deepened. "Tell me what's wrong. If I can help—"

"You can't help!" Alix twisted out of his hold with a sob. "No one can." She headed away from him.

"Alix, dammit! Don't walk away from me."

In spite of all her common sense, which told her to keep walking, Alix stopped and turned around. Her tears gathered in her throat to choke her. Her vision blurred. "Take care of your shipment and forget about me."

Devyn came to stand in front of her. "I can't. I don't know what your problem is, but I'm not going to leave you alone. I was taught that problems are best handled with friends and family."

His warm hand cupped her cheek, sending a chill down her back. No one had ever cared before when she had a problem, and she found his concern a welcome change. But she had no right to it, or to him.

A small tear slipped past her defenses. Devyn caught it with his thumb and brushed the moisture away with the back of his fingers. "Sway and I are your friends. Let us help."

Her lips trembled. If only they could help, but she knew they couldn't. The HAWC Universal Law Code would require them to either own her or sell her. And if Devyn ignored the Code, he could be enslaved, too.

He tilted her head up to look at him. Concern

burned brightly in his dark eyes. Alix wanted to stay with him more than she'd ever wanted anything else in her life, but she knew she couldn't.

"I have to leave," she whispered, the words stinging her throat.

A shadow of sadness passed across his face. He sighed. "I can't make you stay. But if you ever need us, call us and we'll come."

She offered him a trembling smile. They hadn't known each other long, but it had been the first time in her life she'd actually felt like she belonged somewhere, like someone wanted her to belong.

Devyn stroked her cheek, a sad smile on his face.

"You, there!"

Simultaneously, they turned their heads to see a group of Keepers approaching them. Alix bit her lip and hurriedly blinked back her tears.

Dropping his hand, Devyn moved away from her. "Is there a problem?"

The lead Keeper's gaze narrowed on him. "The two of you are wanted for assaulting the crewmembers of the *Prixie*."

Alix clenched her hands into fists. "Irn," she mumbled under her breath, her anger returning at the treacherous beast's actions. If he'd ever had one decent bone in his body, he must have sold it to the devil. "I should have killed him."

She exchanged gazes with Devyn, who appeared amused by the turn of events.

Grinding her teeth, she wished she were as carefree about jail, but the thought of spending the next few hours in a holding cell didn't amuse her in the slightest.

The Keepers surrounded them. "We won't gyve you unless you cause trouble."

Devyn shrugged. "No problem. I've done my fighting for the day."

Alix scowled at him. "You're not funny."

He responded with a charming smile.

Without any more words, they followed the Keepers through the station to the security area. They were searched for weapons, then taken to a small holding cell in the rear of the security office to wait until the station's judge had time to hear their case and fine them.

Alix looked around the cell, grateful they were the only two in it. A single cot lined the left wall, but other than that, the room was empty. Not even a window broke the simple, solid lines of the room.

With a sigh, she sat down on the cot.

Devyn joined her. "Guess you can't get away from me in here. Care to fill our next few hours with the details of what I interrupted?"

Alix leaned back against the wall, crossed her arms defensively over her chest, and closed her eyes. "Nothing terribly important. The man you grabbed in a headlock was the navigator on my father's freighter. We just had some unfinished business between us."

He grunted. "From the look of your cheek, I'd say it was more than business."

Instinctively, Alix opened her eyes, touched her throbbing cheek, and felt the bump forming over the bone. She clenched her teeth. Bruises had been a common enough occurrence while her father had lived.

Devyn took her injured hand in his. He unwrapped her bandage and studied the cut left by the crate. His warm touch thrilled her.

She steeled herself against the emotions whirling through her body, the pounding beat of her heart. She mustn't forget who she was, who he was.

"So are you going to tell me the story?" he asked, wiping the blood away with her handkerchief.

"I can't."

He sighed and rewrapped her hand.

The sudden silence hung between them like a pall. A knot closed her throat, and she wished for a time and place in which they could have met and been friends, or maybe something more.

"How long do you think it'll take before the judge can see us?" she asked.

"I hope not too long. There are few things I hate more than being locked up."

Alix widened her eyes in surprise. "For someone who hates jail, you seemed obliging enough with the Keepers."

A small smile curled his lips. "They're just

65

doing their jobs. I don't take it personally."

"Is that why you don't use weapons on your ship?"

He nodded. "Keepers and Probers aren't paid enough to die for my political views. I've seen enough killing in my life. I hope I never see any more."

His low tone echoed in the room. Alix thought about Zarina's words and for the first time, she realized Devyn wasn't quite as carefree as he appeared. "You told me runners were motivated by a lot more than money. What's your motivation?"

He stared at the wall in front of him, his eyes dark and tormented. "Have you ever seen what a child looks like when it's starved to death?"

Alix swallowed the lump in her throat. She'd never seen a child die, but she'd seen enough on the verge of death. She took his hand in an effort to soothe some of the pain on his face, and gave a light squeeze.

Devyn sighed, a frown creasing his brow. "They're so little, you know. Frail. They don't look real."

With a fierce curse, he pushed himself off the cot. Emotions played across his face: hatred, anger, disgust. He raked his hand through his hair, his back to her. "I went marching in like some great god to help our wounded soldiers. We were supposed to be fighting for right and justice."

He faced her with a sneer. "We were supposed to be fighting men, not starving entire families! The supply lines we cut were for the soldiers, but that didn't stop them from eating. Instead, they took the food from the civilians and left their own people to starve. What the hell were they fighting for, if not their families?"

Devyn slammed his palm against the wall, turned around, and leaned his back against it. He crossed his arms over his chest, and Alix ached for him. "The worst part was, I wasn't really fighting for justice or right. All I wanted was glory."

An angry tick beat in his jaw. "Some hero," he whispered, closing his eyes.

Alix went to him. She rubbed his rigid shoulders. Never had she seen anyone look so miserable. "It wasn't your fault. You were just doing your job."

He shook his head. "I took an oath to help the sick. To turn no one away from any medical care I could provide. You should have seen the mothers grabbing at us as we marched past, begging us for any tiny scrap of anything we could spare. My High Command wouldn't even let me give the starving children vitamins."

Alix's heart pounded in sympathy for him. She ran her hand over his firm biceps. "So you run blockades to feed the civilians?"

He nodded. "This way I know they get the food and supplies, along with enough weapons and ammunition to make sure they can keep the food for themselves."

She smiled at him. A warm rush filled her. "You're the only runner I've ever known who doesn't fly for profit. In my mind, that makes you more of a hero than anyone who's ever filled the history disks."

A tiny smiled played at the edges of his lips. He looked down at her with a strange expression she couldn't define, but one that quickened her heart.

"With the exception of Sway, you're the only person I've told this to," he said, his eyes liquid night. "He thinks I'm a fool for tossing away the HAWC."

Alix bit her lip. She stared up at him with all her admiration flowing through her body. "No one's foolish for following his convictions."

"Maybe, but I threw away six years of medical school for a tarnished reputation."

"Well, the universe is filled with competent doctors, but a decent runner is one in a trillion."

To her surprise, he placed his hands on her cheeks and tilted her head to look up at him. The care reflected in his eyes stole her breath and brought an ache to her chest. "You're the one in a trillion, not me."

Alix shook her head in denial. She wanted to tell him her secret, have him soothe her pain and insecurity away, but she was afraid to see hatred replace the gentleness in his eyes. She'd convinced herself that her father's disgust didn't really matter to her, but if Devyn looked at her that way, it would break her.

"What's wrong?" Devyn asked.

She blinked and shifted her gaze away from him. "How do you mean?"

"You look scared."

She tried to think of some excuse to keep from telling him the truth. She remembered Irn and decided to make use of the *prato*.

"Not scared," she said, glancing up at him. "I was just thinking about how my luck ran. Out of all the men in the universe, why is Irn the only one ever to give me a second look?" She gave a halfhearted laugh. "I wouldn't touch him even if he were made of taria stones."

Devyn leaned closer to her.

She swallowed, her heart racing in response to his nearness.

"He's not the only man to take a second look at you." He traced his finger over the lines of her lips, causing chills to tingle her face. "Your biggest problem is that you never notice when a man does look at you."

Frowning, she refused to believe his words and what they signified. "What?"

"You're a very attractive woman, Alix," he said quietly, his breath tickling her lips.

Before Alix could think of a response, his lips covered hers.

# *Chapter Four*

Alix's head swam at the contact. Firm yet gentle, Devyn's mouth caressed hers; then he slid his hands down her back to bring her closer to his warmth. She opened her mouth, welcoming the sweet taste and feel of him.

Never in her life had anyone been so tender. Never in her life had she hoped to receive a kiss from a man so handsome, so strong.

In that instant, she knew her fate. God help her, she wanted Devyn as she'd never wanted anything. Not her ship, not her mother. Nothing. Only Devyn existed, and only he could ease the longing that burned a pain in her heart sharper than any blow her father had ever given her.

Tears gathered in her eyes, and she knew she

should pull away and run from him, but she couldn't stop. Besides, she would only be running from herself, and there was no place to hide from your own soul.

No, she needed this moment. She would not run. Sanity would return only too soon. For now she would be a creature of passion.

Suddenly, the door slid up.

Devyn pulled back from her, his gaze narrowing as he rose to his feet.

Clearing her throat, Alix stood up to face the three Keepers entering their cell. Gyves dangled from the Keepers' hands, and they watched her and Devyn as if the two of them were monsters about to feast on their souls.

Alix lifted a brow. What in the universe would have three armed Keepers trembling so?

"Turn around," the captain said gruffly.

Devyn scowled. "Why?"

"Both of you are being extradited."

She and Devyn exchanged a puzzled look. In spite of the warm reassurance his eyes offered, Alix's mouth dried from her apprehension.

"Extradited?" Devyn asked with a hint of laughter in his voice. "By whom, and for what?"

"The HAWC. For murder."

Alix thought her legs would buckle. The HAWC? Devyn had mentioned having trouble with them in the past. But murder?

Coldness consumed her. This couldn't be happening. Everything had to be a dream. Definitely. Devyn wouldn't have kissed her. Any minute Sway or Devyn would buzz her room, and she'd wake up and laugh about it. Right?

"Turn around."

She stared at the Keepers, her cold hands trembling. "Devyn?" she asked, hoping he had an explanation.

Devyn shrugged. "Do it," he said, a note of resignation in his voice.

Alix opened her mouth to protest, to tell the Keepers that she knew nothing about the HAWC, but her voice wouldn't work. Her lips cracking from dryness, she allowed one of the Keepers to turn her around and cuff her wrists together.

She glanced at Devyn. A frown lined his brow as if he were trying to figure all this out, or remember what he had done to make the HAWC want him.

*Please*, she begged silently, *let this be a huge mistake.* She didn't want to die in prison for a crime she'd had no part in.

With a rough grip, a Keeper grabbed her elbow and swung her out of the cell and into the hallway. Alix took several deep breaths, warning herself to stay calm and trust in her innocence.

As they entered the main office, she came to a complete stop, her mouth falling open. Zarina lounged before one Keeper's desk like she owned the station.

Humor danced in Zarina's eyes as she met Alix's gaze and for a moment, Alix was certain every Keeper in the room had to know the whole thing was a ruse.

"You!" Devyn snarled in a hate-filled voice that set her heart pounding.

Zarina curled her upper lip in a ferocious snarl. "So, Kell, you thought you could escape us. That was quite a stunt you pulled on Kildara. Three Keepers downed and half a million *cronas* in damage."

Zarina shook her head like an angry mother scolding a naughty child, then looked at the Keeper in front of her. "I can't thank you and your people enough. If not for you, he would have probably escaped us again."

The Keeper looked like Zarina had just pinned a service medal on his fat chest. "My pleasure, Agent Kyrelle. We are always delighted to help our HAWC counterparts."

It was working! Dear God, how could they possibly believe Zarina?

Relief shot through Alix so rapidly she feared she might burst into laughter. Yet somehow she managed to control herself.

"Well, High Keeper," Zarina said, winking at the old Keeper officer who flushed a bright red, "we need you guys as much as you need us."

Her features hardening, Zarina turned and approached her and Devyn with the swagger of a trained killer. She stopped before Devyn and ran her gaze over his body in a disgusted manner. "I'm going to look forward to seeing you vaporized for your crimes."

Devyn lifted his chin and smirked. "Just try it."

"Agent Kyrelle," another woman said from behind Zarina. Alix looked over to her and noted the attractive dorjani female. "We'd better get our prisoners on board before they have another chance to escape."

There was no mistaking the warning in the woman's voice, and in that instant, Alix recognized the soft, lilting accent as the one that belonged to Sway's wife, Claria.

Alix also agreed with Claria. They needed to get out of here before one of them made a mistake and the Keepers realized they'd been duped.

Zarina nodded, then grabbed Devyn by the arm. "C'mon, space scab. It's time to pay the shuttle fee."

Claria moved forward and pulled Alix out behind Zarina and Devyn.

As soon as the four of them had cleared the building and several blocks of distance, Devyn broke into laughter. "Jeez, Rina, your brother will have your ass over this stunt."

"Don't laugh, flyboy," Claria said sternly. "Your charges really were upgraded to smuggling, espionage, and three counts of murder."

Alix's eyes widened and her heart lurched. What in the universe had she stumbled into?

Devyn stopped so suddenly she nearly ran into him. "What do you mean three—"

"Someone's out to get you," Zarina said, cutting him off.

Claria nodded. "I was trying to pay your fine when I saw the new charges being posted. If not for Zarina and her crazy ideas, you two would be headed out on the next shuttle to the nearest prison."

Alix watched as shocked disbelief etched itself onto Devyn's face. Just what kind of man was he, and what enemies hated him to the point of framing him for murder? Her stomach knotted. Then again, for all she knew he just might have committed a number of murders and the charges just might be earned!

Dear Lord, maybe she ought to abandon him now, before it was too late. But before she could move, a small tremor inside told her that she had already waited too long.

Besides, if she ran now the Keepers would find her again and lock her up. And if they did that, Irn would be able to claim her.

Her heart pounding in terror, she returned attention to Devyn.

"I don't understand," Devyn whispered. "Who would frame me?"

"Doesn't matter right this instant," Claria said, pushing him forward. "Get a move on it. If the Keepers find out about this, or check Zarina's stupid credentials, we're all cooked toggles."

Zarina laughed and draped her arm over Claria's shoulders. "Don't worry. If they run my numbers they'll come up with Jayce's HAWC file. I learned his serial number a long time ago."

She lifted her hand to her breast in a mock HAWC salute. "Agent Kyrelle, commander in charge of special assignments and proceedings. They don't even list his sex or age for fear of an assassin finding him." She winked at Alix. "I love my brother!"

Devyn shook his head at Zarina's incorrigibility and held his wrists out to her. "Ungyve us and let us launch."

While Zarina opened their gyves, he gave Alix an amused smile that somehow warmed her breast despite all the dangers facing them. "I can't believe she faked HAWC status to get us out. They'll burn her for this."

Zarina scoffed. "Pah-lease. Besides, you can't blame me for this trick; I got the idea from your mother."

Devyn looked down at Zarina and rubbed his wrists. "You should have remembered her whole tale, then."

Zarina lifted a quizzical brow.

"She almost went to prison for her stunt."

Zarina smiled. "But she didn't."

Devyn rolled his eyes and took Alix by the arm, his grip stern. "C'mon. We need to get out of here."

Before he could take a step, Zarina grabbed him. "You can't leave me behind," she said desperately. "Taryn's out tonight and he doesn't plan on leaving for two more days. If the Keepers find me here, they'll know I lied. And if they lock me up one more time my father will kill me. That is, if Taryn doesn't first."

Amazed by Zarina's panicked words and the knowledge that the princess had been locked up before, Alix watched emotions play across Devyn's face—anger, suspicion, tolerance, and finally resignation.

He sighed disgustedly. "All right, Your Highness. You've got your reprieve from Taryn, but I'm dumping you on the nearest outpost."

Zarina smiled, and Alix wondered if Zarina hadn't planned her escape along with theirs from the very beginning.

"Fine," she said. "Just don't call my dad."

Devyn narrowed his eyes. "If I had any sense at all, I would. You're lucky I owe you my life."

"You're welcome," Zarina said, planting a kiss on his cheek.

Devyn shook his head, then led them the rest of the way to his ship. Claria said a quick goodbye to Sway and in less than half an hour, they were back in space.

Alix sat at her terminal checking their equipment and cargo specs while Devyn and Sway programmed their new coordinates and destination into the ship's computer.

Zarina sat in the gunner's chair looking about as smug as the gimfrey who stole the freshly baked bread. Despite herself, Alix smiled at the princess's success. If only she could get things to work out for her as easily as Zarina managed to.

Devyn turned around and noted the look on Zarina's face. "Don't look so happy, Rina. You've got a choice to make. Your parents, my parents, or Uncle Calix. Who do you want me to call to take you home?"

Her smile faded into a black scowl. "You know, Alix, your boss is a real—"

"Rina!"

She stiffened and cast Devyn a glare that would have shriveled a lesser man. "Next time, bud, I'll let you stew in your sauce."

Devyn shook his head, a slow smile lighting his face. "You're right; I should be more grateful. Thanks for saving us, but you know I can't turn you loose. Your dad and mine would take turns beating me if I did something that stupid."

Zarina sighed, and Alix almost felt sorry for her. "Okay. Call your mom. She's the least likely to chew my rump sore."

Alix could swear Devyn paled at Zarina's words.

She looked back at Zarina and noted the triumph in her eyes. She stifled her smile. There was a wicked side to Zarina's humor and Alix warned herself to stay in Zarina's good graces.

Devyn pushed himself out of his chair. With every step that brought him closer to Alix, her heartbeat increased. He stopped at her chair and leaned over her to verify his coordinates with hers.

When he looked at her, all Alix could think of was the way his lips had tasted, how it felt to be in his arms.

"Do me a favor and double-check the cargo seals for leaks," he said, his voice barely audible.

Alix nodded, her gaze dropping to his lips.

He looked away as if embarrassed by her attention. "I'd better call my mom so we can dump Rina and get back to business."

"Uh, Devyn?"

Alix looked past Devyn's shoulder to see Sway cringing in his chair. He shook as if in fear for his very life.

"What?" Devyn asked, pushing himself away from her.

Sway glanced at Zarina, then at Alix, and finally his gaze settled on the floor. He chewed his lips. Alix couldn't imagine what had him so distraught.

Devyn took a step toward him and she thought for a moment the dorjani might actually manage to merge himself into his chair. And with each cringing action, Devyn's expression grew darker, more malevolent.

"Say it," Devyn demanded in a commanding tone Alix had never heard him use before.

Sway paled, took a deep breath, and spoke in a hurry. "The closest rendezvous point with

79

your parents will take us four days out of our way."

Devyn snarled in response. Eyes narrowed, he looked as if he were barely one step from murder. Alix swallowed. He clenched his fists so tightly at his sides his knuckles protruded. An angry tic beat in his jaw, and Alix felt her own apprehension and fear rise like a thermometer placed in hell. Never before had she seen a man so enraged. Not even her father in the height of a drunken rage could compare to Devyn.

Glancing to Zarina, she noted her fear as well. Now she believed every single story Zarina had told her about Devyn's temper.

"How many days to rendezvous with her parents?" he asked Sway.

"Six," Sway squeaked.

"Calix?"

Sway swallowed. "Seven."

Devyn turned about and faced Zarina. Blood lust darkened his eyes as if he were contemplating her dismemberment.

Zarina shrank in her chair, a trembling, placating smile on her lips. "Sorry," Zarina offered, her voice unsteady.

Devyn approached her like a beast after prey. Bracing one hand on each arm of her chair, he pinned her with his gaze. Zarina's eyes widened, terror shining in them brightly, while she slowly shrank away from Devyn.

Alix held her breath, waiting for Devyn to

strangle Zarina, wondering if she and Sway could prevent Zarina's untimely death. Instead, he kept his jaw clenched and he just stood there. Silent. Shaking.

"Sixteen people will die because *you* couldn't stand to have your brother take you home," Devyn finally said between clenched teeth. "Tell me, Your Highness, is your mental comfort worth the cost?"

Tears welled in Zarina's eyes. She shifted her gaze to the floor and said nothing.

"Answer me, Rina."

She looked up, her eyes filled with pain. "I'm sorry, okay? You guys never tell me anything until I mess up; then you all jump on me like I'm supposed to know what I did wrong. I didn't know. I'm sorry!"

Devyn just shook his head, his anger still tangible.

After several erratic heartbeats that had Alix fearing she'd have a coronary, Devyn pushed himself away from Zarina.

"Plot the course," he said to Sway in a low, deadly tone. "And keep Zarina out of my way."

Once Devyn had left, Zarina took a deep breath and pushed herself back up into a sitting position. She cleared her throat and straightened her clothes. "So, Sway, why are you guys going to Paradise City?"

Alix could have laughed at the question after what had transpired. Did anything intimidate

## Sherrilyn Kenyon

Zarina for long? Her own hands were still trembling and Devyn's hostility hadn't even been directed toward her.

Sway looked every bit as shaken up as Alix felt.

He stared at Zarina as if he, too, doubted the woman's sanity. "There's a HAWC blockade on Jarun Eight. Their governor sent a dispatch to the Kirovions begging for help. He said it's been three months since any supplies have come into any of their ports and that their government has scorched all their natural staples."

Alix's stomach twisted. A colony without food couldn't survive for long. "How many people are there?"

Sway looked at her. "A little over a thousand. Almost a third of them are children under the age of twelve. And our last readout said that at least four people die every day from starvation."

The words Devyn had spoken inside the holding cell drifted through Alix's mind. No wonder he'd been so angry. Those poor people were waiting for them and the supplies they were bringing. And she knew Devyn felt for each starving victim. Deeply. "What did the Jaruns do to cause a blockade?" Alix asked.

Anger darkened Sway's eyes. "They refused to release Glibben crystals to the Querilans, so the Querilans went to the HAWC and charged the Jaruns with treason against the Werthern Pact."

Alix shook her head in confusion. "Werthern Pact?"

Zarina sighed and sat back in her chair. "It's a pact that was drawn up three years ago by the eight Jarun colonies. The eight leaders wanted their home government on Queril to provide them with protection against pirates and smugglers. In order to get Keepers and Probers they had to sign a deal saying they would turn over any explosive compounds they mined to the Queril officials." She looked at Sway. "I take it the Jaruns didn't hold up their end of the agreement."

"They intended to, but when Prylar took the Querilan High Seat six months ago and started invading planets, the governor on Jarun Eight decided to boycott Prylar's activities."

Alix stared aghast at Sway and the blasé tone of his voice. "You sound like you think he should have minded his own business."

Sway nodded. "I don't think political views are worth the lives of children."

"What about the children on the planets they invade?"

"Whoa, guys!" Zarina said, interrupting them. "No heated political arguments. I get enough of this at home."

"Okay," Sway said, meeting Alix's gaze. "I'm sorry I got so excited."

"Me, too," Alix said with a smile.

She sat for a moment and thought over their words. Alix wanted desperately to ask them about Devyn's HAWC days and why starving children disturbed him so much, but she decided she shouldn't pry. The answer might only add to the attraction she already felt for Devyn, and she didn't need any more reasons to want to stay with him.

Instead she settled on knowing more about the Jaruns' situation, since her fate now seemed tied to theirs. "Explain to me why the governor didn't go to the HAWC and tell them what Prylar is doing. I thought the HAWC was supposed to protect the smaller planets."

"I think Rina can answer that best."

Zarina studied her hands. "The HAWC reeks like year-old garbage."

Alix's mouth dropped open. "But your brother . . ."

"Yeah, I know. Most of my family has been in the HAWC at one point or another. That's why I can make statements like that. I know firsthand how corrupt the Golden Council is. Jarun Eight is too small for the HAWC to mess with. If they had something the HAWC wanted or needed, then they could have all the HAWC protection they wanted, but so long as Prylar is stuffing the pockets of the HAWC High Command, Jarun is pretty much *tribbled*."

Alix shook her head at the reality of politics. She'd never much involved herself with such things. A political freighter was a dead one. And since her father had never identified himself with a planet or race, there was no need to worry about what emperor or governor controlled what or whom. Out in space, the fuel and oxygen levels and radiation shields were the only rulers a person had to heed.

"Well, now that we've bored each other with politics, I think I need to find something to eat," Zarina said, rising to her feet. "C'mon, Alix, let's see what we can discover."

Alix looked up at Sway. "You want anything?"

A strange look darkened his eyes. "Yeah, but we left her on Nera."

Zarina moved to Sway and gave him a tight hug. "I know, it's awful when they leave you."

Alix didn't miss the sad wistfulness in Zarina's voice.

Sway bristled under Zarina's care. "Go on and eat before you lose any more weight."

"All right," Zarina said, straightening up. "If Taryn calls, tell him you guys got tired of me and launched me out the air lock."

Sway snorted. "Sounds like good advice. I'll keep it in mind in case you start causing trouble. And stay away from Devyn. In his current mood, he might do that just to appease his sense of justice."

Zarina laughed before leading Alix down the hallway to the galley. Alix remained quiet while Zarina searched through the cabinets, dropping cans and making more noise than Alix had ever heard in her life.

"What do you guys live on?" Zarina asked as she sat back on her heels and yielded a disgusted sigh.

Alix frowned at her. "What are you looking for?"

"Anything sweet and decadent."

Why didn't that surprise her? "Devyn has some cookies stashed in the big brown toggle box."

Zarina gave her a suspicious look. "Oh, yeah?"

"I didn't find them on purpose," Alix said defensively. "I was looking for dinner one night when he came in and pulled them out."

Smiling, Zarina reached for the box in the cabinet, opened it, and let out a triumphant laugh. "Leave it to him. I should probably go through all the boxes. I'm sure Sway has something stashed away too."

Biting into a cookie, Zarina took a seat next to Alix. She tilted the box to Alix as an offering. Alix shook her head in denial.

"They've always been weird about sweets," Zarina said. "As kids, they used to scrounge all the sweets, then hide them in so many places they never could remember where everything was."

Alix frowned at her words. "Why?"

"Devyn is hypoglycemic and has to watch his sugar intake. When he was a kid, his mom would only allow him one treat a week. And Sway's mother didn't believe in a boy having candy. Some weird dorjani custom."

Her eyes faded as if she were drifting into the past; then she laughed. "I'll never forget the time Devyn's mother caught them wolfing down a box of candy. She was so furious. And poor Devyn shook for a week. I'm actually surprised he can eat anything sweet after that."

"Well, I learned not to take all my pleasure at once," Devyn said from the doorway.

Hesitantly, Alix watched him as he moved forward and grabbed the box from Zarina.

His anger had decreased and now he just appeared aggravated. "Stay out of these. If you eat them all, I'll have to strangle you. If you have to have sweet stuff, eat Sway's disgusting klanan syrup."

"Selfish." Zarina wrinkled her nose at him, but even so, Alix noted the cautiousness in Zarina's eyes as she watched Devyn. "I prefer your mom's recipe to that store-bought junk."

"Me, too," Devyn said as he closed the box and returned it to the cabinet. "But my mom only sends this stuff once in a gray rocket and there's no telling when she'll send me a new batch."

In spite of their teasing voices, there was a tenseness between them that unnerved Alix. She'd spent too many years living with explosive tempers to hang around for Devyn or Zarina's next outburst.

So before they lunged at each other's throats, she decided she ought to leave the room.

"I'm kind of tired," Alix said, pushing herself up from her chair. "If you two will excuse me, I think I'll go take a nap."

"Alix, wait," Devyn said, stopping her from leaving. "I need to talk to you for a minute."

Devyn noted the sudden spark of happiness that filled her eyes. His gut twisted. What he was about to do made him miserable. But he had no choice.

"Zarina, could you excuse us?"

Zarina lifted a curious brow. To Devyn's complete astonishment, she actually got up and left without making a comment.

Thank God she had the good sense to know not to push his already strained control.

Now alone with Alix, he felt his will started to fluctuate. *Do it*, he told himself, but even so he regretted what he had to do more than he regretted anything, including his days in the HAWC.

Not even an image of Onone could ease his conscience.

Alix stared at him with those incredible blue eyes, and he knew he lost a few inches of height.

Clearing his throat, he turned away from her. Maybe it would be easier to say it if he didn't watch her reaction. "I've been thinking about . . ." His voice trailed off. Stupid! He had practiced this a dozen times in the last few minutes, so why couldn't he recall the way he'd rehearsed it?

"Look, Devyn, I know what you're going to say."

He turned around to look at her, but the pain in her eyes made him regret the action.

Glancing away from him, she gripped the door frame. "It was the lighting, or maybe just an impulse. You didn't mean to kiss me, and you wish you hadn't."

She clenched her teeth and he swore he could see tears in her eyes. "I'm a grown woman; you can be honest with me." She cleared her throat before meeting his gaze. "I'm not looking for a lover either, okay? So let's just forget anything ever happened. You command the helm and I'll watch my gauges, and we'll just go our own ways."

*And I'll damn myself for it in twenty years.* He watched her leave and it took every ounce of control he had not to run after her and apologize, to tell her he didn't mean it, that he wanted her.

But dammit, he couldn't. She wasn't the type of woman a man would tire of in a few months. She was the type who forever haunted a man on lonely nights, made him regret the decision to leave.

And he had too many regrets already.

Besides, love made a man a fool. That was one

lesson he'd already learned and he'd learned it in such a way as to never forget it.

"You know, I don't understand you at all."

Devyn turned around, his heart pounding at the sudden voice intruding on his thoughts.

Zarina moved into the room and pulled a plastic bottle of water from the cooling unit. Her gaze raked him as if she were looking at something unclean.

"I thought you'd quit being such a selfish bastard, but I guess a verrago can't change its coat."

Devyn clenched his fists at his sides. He fought for the slipping control on his temper. No matter how angry Zarina made him, he couldn't strangle her.

But at the moment that was the only action he could think of that would give him satisfaction.

Devyn slammed the door closed on the cooling unit and invaded her personal space, pushing her back without touching her until she was trapped between him and the counter. "I find it odd that you of all people would dare castigate me for selfish behavior."

She lifted a shocked brow at him.

Devyn curled his lip in response. "I thought you had made your own oath to quit drawing hasty conclusions and to find out all sides of something before you started hurling insults."

Zarina pushed him away from her, her eyes blazing as she moved to the other side of the table. "All right, then, let's hear your reason for why Alix ran past me in tears."

All the anger drained out of him and left his soul deflated. He had never meant to hurt Alix or anyone else.

Zarina pulled out a chair and took a seat. "I'm listening. Explain to me why you stare after Alix like a gimfrey sniffing food, then you cut her heart out." She took a swig of water and Devyn wished she'd choke on it.

Guilt and pain ripped through his gut. He hadn't asked to be attracted to Alix. God knew if he could turn off his feelings, he would. But something inside him kept reaching out to Alix every time he looked at her.

Dammit, he couldn't allow Alix to invade his life, to make him care again. He needed to be unattached. His missions were the only thing he could do, the only way he could make amends. No one must ever come between him and his job.

"I don't really want to talk about this with you," he said, turning to leave.

Zarina gave him that old chiding look that was unique to her. "I bet you never thought Onone could cause you more pain dead than she did when she was alive."

His breath caught in his throat. He knew better than to ask how Zarina knew what had him bothered. She'd always had an irritating ability to read people. Just like his dad. "This isn't about Onone."

"Then what's it about?"

Sighing, Devyn pulled another bottle out of the cooling unit and took a seat next to Zarina. No use trying to leave; she'd only pursue him until he either told her what bothered him, or he killed her.

"Everything," he said.

By the skeptical look on her face, he knew she didn't believe him.

Devyn sighed and tried again. "All right, maybe I've just learned to leave things alone. For the first time in a long while, I like myself and my life and I don't want it to change. I have my freedom, my ship, and missions that mean something. If I tied myself to Alix, I'd lose everything I've built."

"Pah-lease!"

Anger burned raw in his throat. His vision darkened. "Don't act outraged. You know what I'm talking about. Both our fathers gave up their careers for our mothers. Calix, who swore he'd never allow any woman to rule him, stopped smuggling as soon as he met his wife. Name me one person who continued their old life once they married."

"My brother Adron."

Devyn almost spewed his water. "Bad example. Correct me if I'm wrong, but didn't his enemies kill his pregnant wife? And look at him now. Crippled, embittered, and living alone on an isolated planet." He shook his head. "Yep, show me where to sign up for that future."

Zarina punched him in the arm. "Don't forget cynical. You've already got that down to a fine art."

He rubbed his aching biceps. If only he could ease the pain in his heart as easily.

Zarina stood. She stared down at him with a pitying look that scorched his soul and made him want to push her back into her chair. "Unless you change your ways, you're going to be a lonely old man, Devyn Kell."

# Chapter Five

Devyn stared at the dull gray ceiling overhead. He knew the outline of each steel plate and rivet. For the last two hours, he'd done nothing but look up and think.

After so much time, he thought he'd have an answer to the three billion questions and concerns torturing him. Instead, he'd only uncovered more confusion.

Zarina's words haunted him. He didn't want to grow old alone. He'd give anything to have the kind of love his parents shared, but he wasn't sure he wanted to pay the price of such love. Adron was a prime example. And, of course, Sway. Every time Claria left, Sway fell into a deep depression. A depression made worse by the fact that Sway knew the two of them could never remain together no matter how much they loved each other.

That kind of love Devyn could do without.

The only alternative would be to leave everything behind and settle down as his father had done. After all, his father had given up a legendary career to go back to school and become a mundane surgeon who never got shot at or arrested. Even his mother had left her career as a bounder so that he would have a normal childhood with two parents. But Devyn just couldn't see himself following after them. Maybe he had too many Laing genes in him for that. The thought of giving up his missions tore at him worse than the fear of being alone.

No, he owed too many people a chance. As an officer in the HAWC, he had caused too many deaths, executed too many people. If he quit running humanitarian missions now, he'd never be able to live with himself.

"Do you love me?" Onone's voice taunted him from the past.

His stomach lurched from guilt and pain.

At the time, he'd answered yes, but now he knew the truth. Devyn almost laughed at himself and his stupidity. No one should be held accountable for what they think they want when they're young.

He had been attracted to Onone's beauty and sophistication. Too young to see through the shallow waters of her lies, he'd allowed her to use him right up to the last. He had been nothing to her except a distraction, a passing amusement.

Delusion's Gate. He remembered his father telling him stories about the lost civilization where nothing was ever what it seemed. On the one side everything was beautiful and pure, yet underneath the surface twisted darkness lurked, waiting to trap the unwary traveler. And he had walked right into it, eyes blind and heart open. His father had done his damnedest to warn him away from Onone, but he hadn't listened.

Slash a mark for Dad.

But Alix didn't play that game. She was different. He knew that. He couldn't forget her. Her goodness went deeper than physical beauty, and that scared him more than anything else.

*"I've never spent more than two weeks on a planet in my life."* Devyn closed his eyes, trying to blot out the image of Alix's face when she'd said the words. And he knew the truth. She wouldn't ask him to settle down; she'd be right by his side on every mission. Every time someone opened fire on their ship, she'd be there beside him, her life one plasma blast from ending. One little miscalculation and she'd disappear from his life as quickly as she'd stumbled into it.

Of course he could try a less dangerous career. Maybe captain a freighter like her father. Devyn nearly bolted off the bed. What the hell was he thinking? He could never be a freighter captain any more than he could allow Alix to die.

If he had one single brain cell capable of working, he'd dump Alix off the ship with Zarina. Before it was too late.

His stomach tightened at the thought of never seeing her again.

"Dammit!" he snarled.

He was in control here, not Alix.

She could be pushed out of his thoughts. He'd prove it. With that thought, he went to the weight room. A little exercise and he'd feel a lot better. He didn't need a woman he barely knew clouding his thoughts, making him rethink a life-shaping decision he had made a long time ago. An important decision he knew was right.

Alix glanced up as the door opened. Her heart lurched at the sight of Devyn and she wanted a big hole to appear in the side of the ship and suck her out into space.

He looked gorgeous in a pair of tight black exercise shorts. His naked upper body displayed perfection. Her gaze fell to the long, even, white scar that ran across his left side where a blaster had struck him, and she realized how just one mistake could ruin someone.

Devyn could easily be her one mistake. They didn't belong together. *Just look at yourself, Alix.*

She wore a baggy pair of shorts and a loose tank top. The combination only served to emphasize the boyishness of her body. Sweat dripped down her face, and odd pieces of hair had come free from her braid, no doubt forming a frizzy frame around her thin, boyish face. She knew she looked worse than she ever had before.

Why couldn't she just drop dead on the spot?

Devyn stopped as he caught sight of her in the shadowed corner where she sat working on leg lifts. "I'm sorry," he said softly. "I didn't know you were in here."

He appeared a lot calmer than before, almost mellow. She couldn't detect any of his earlier hostility. Now it seemed as if he had come to terms with their delay and her.

"It's okay," Alix said. "I was just finishing up." She reached for her towel.

Devyn came closer and grabbed the pull-down bar just over her head. The dim light of the room flashed against the small gold medallion he wore around his neck. He leaned so close she could smell the sweet musk scent of his after-shave. Her heart raced.

Alix did her best to ignore the bulging muscles of his arms and torso, but his stance only emphasized the well-defined flesh. She ached to run her hands over his body, to feel the rippling dips of muscles over his lean ribs.

If she could have one wish . . .

*Don't!* her mind screamed, and she quickly looked away.

He didn't want her; he'd made that plain enough in the galley. She might not be the most attractive woman in the universe, but she did have her pride and she refused to abase herself with lovesick glances for a man who had no use for her.

Alix raked the towel over her face and neck, purposefully scraping her skin in hopes of banishing him from her thoughts.

He pulled the towel from her hands.

Shocked by his action, she looked up into those wonderful dark eyes. A smile played at the edges of his lips, but it wasn't the mocking smile she'd expected. Instead he appeared almost enchanted, or maybe deranged.

Devyn cupped her chin with his left hand while he patted her burning cheek with the towel. Alix trembled at the warmth of his fingers against her skin. Her chest tightened, her pulse raced, and a demanding need scorched the very essence of her. Why did he have to affect her this way? Why couldn't she just get up and walk away?

She ignored the answer that echoed through her head.

"You haven't depleted too much body fluid, have you?" he asked, his low tone seeming like a shout in the stillness of the room.

"No," she said, her voice so breathless she wished she hadn't spoken.

A concerned frown lined his brow as he slid the cloth over her fevered skin. "You look flushed to me. Do you have a headache?"

Alix licked her lips, her gaze unintentionally gliding over his body. "I'm fine," she said past the lump that had appeared in her throat.

Devyn stared at her, his heart pounding so fiercely he thought it might actually break out of his chest and flop onto the floor.

Trying to alleviate the dryness of his throat, he swallowed. Alix watched him with a hooded expression he couldn't read. But she wasn't pulling away from him.

He told himself to leave, but for some reason his feet wouldn't listen. All he could do was stare at her.

Her tank top hung low over her breasts, which glistened from her exercise. Devyn had always been attracted to a woman flushed by a workout. He wanted her. From the core of his desperate soul a cry started, calling out to him not to turn and walk away from this. From her. Before he could stop himself, he leaned down and captured her moist, sweet lips.

Alix gasped at the contact of his mouth against hers. All thoughts fled her mind and left her sitting there like a fool. She knew she should push him away. Instead, she opened her lips, welcoming him into her lonely, isolated world.

Inhaling the warm, spicy scent of him, she wrapped her arms around his strong shoulders, drawing him nearer, closer. She felt like the mythological tyrilian girbeast who allowed itself to be lured by a lover, knowing that at the end of the act its mate would only incinerate it, its life sacrificed for a moment's pleasure.

But she didn't care. Instead, she wished she could melt with Devyn, become part of his beautiful world where her ugliness wouldn't matter. Where the slave girl could be forgotten. A place where she could be free.

He pulled her tightly against the molten, steely wall of his chest, his mouth driving her to the brink of madness with each deep, probing kiss. His mouth teased hers, his tongue tracing the contours of her lips in a sensuous path that caused her body to erupt in heat.

His small gold disk slid under her shirt between the crevice of her breasts, brushing against her taut nipples, sending chills down her arms.

And his torture continued as he shifted his head and traced her jawbone, his teeth gently nipping as he went. Unbelievable delight shot through her, scorching, sizzling every piece of her. She arched toward him.

He pulled back from her lips only to dip his head down to her breasts. Alix moaned in pleasure. His tongue slid over the swell of her breasts, electrifying her, while he massaged her arms, her back, her buttocks. Her stomach tightened in response, a heated throb spread through her, demanding him, and she knew she would never want another man this way.

"I want you, Alix," he whispered, lowering her to the floor.

Alix barely understood his words. Her head swam from giddy sensation as he lay atop her, pinning her against the floor. She reveled in the heavy feel of his body against hers. Running her hands down the muscled planes of his back, she smiled at the deep, throaty moan he yielded. He arched against her, sliding his body in an intimate caress that whetted her appetite for him all the more.

Oh, she wanted him. Only him.

Alix recaptured his lips with all the desperation inside her. No one had ever made her feel so desirable, so beautiful. Devyn was everything to her—all her childhood dreams of the handsome prince who would come rescue her and beat her father for all his abuse. Then the two of them would leave the rusty old freighter in a new, sparkling ship.

Now her dream was happening.

*Please, don't let me wake up. Not yet. Just once let me have the one thing I want.* Tears formed in her eyes and she wanted to cry. She tightened her grip on him, holding him against her.

Devyn buried his head in her neck, where he teased the flesh behind her ear. Alix shook all over from the chills that formed. She closed her eyes, surrendering herself to the erotic ministrations of his hands.

He smiled at her in sensual delight, then pulled at her tank top.

Like a cold splash of water on an electrical fire, reality snapped and hissed through the haze of her mind. This wasn't a dream. If Devyn saw her back . . .

"Devyn, no!" she shrieked, pushing against him. Her body trembled from sudden fear, her passion forgotten. He must never see her slave mark. What had she been thinking?

He stared at her in dazed confusion.

"Let me up," she demanded, scrambling to her feet.

"Alix—"

"Just leave me alone!" she said, her voice betraying her hysteria.

Devyn watched her run from the room, his body still burning. Damn! What had he done wrong? She'd welcomed him, hadn't she?

Rolling over onto his back, he groaned on the floor like a dying verrago. Now what was he going to do? He ached for a release Alix had denied him and he wanted blood. His body throbbed and burned in a contracting need that tore through him with each beat of his heart.

*Cold shower, cold shower, cold shower,* his mind repeated, and he knew that would be the only thing to return him to a seminormal state. But where the hell did someone get that much water on board a ship?

Devyn kicked his feet and groaned even louder. Someone shoot him and put him out his misery!

Pushing himself up from the floor, he knew he couldn't stay there a moment longer. Images of Alix working out kept flashing before his eyes like a great strobe light.

He had to get his mind off her. There might be someone trying to capture them. There might be a hundred probers out there about to take them. Yeah. Something was bound to be wrong in the control room. Something that could take his mind off his aching frustration.

And Alix's beautiful face.

Before he could make the distance to the bridge, Zarina cornered him. "Hey, Dev, I was wondering—"

"Out of my way," he snarled.

Zarina frowned. "Now what's wrong with—"

"Woman, leave me alone!"

Zarina snorted and made a grand gesture to pass him. "Jeez, you act like you've got a case of the rock-heavies."

Devyn ignored her crude comment, which unfortunately was exactly what had him upset, and made his way onto the bridge. Sway looked up, his brows cocked in question. Heading straight to him, Devyn grabbed him by his shirt collar. "If you're a real friend, knock me unconscious."

Alix stepped out of the waterless shower, her body still trembling from Devyn's near discovery. She must be more careful in the future. One stupid mistake like the one she'd almost made and Devyn would know the truth.

Then where would she be? The nearest slave auction, no doubt.

God, how she hated her father. She could still see him gloating the day he had taken her to Overley and had her branded a slave. That had been her birthday present when she turned thirteen.

Her back had stung for a week afterward, and it had seemed that every day after that he had threatened to sell her off just as he had done with her mother and brother. Every time money got scarce, he'd look at her with a sadistic gleam in his eyes as if weighing her worth.

How many times had he cursed her for being ugly? But that had been her only saving grace. Had she been born beautiful, she had little doubt her father would have sold her off to pay for the alcohol he loved so much.

A knock sounded on her door.

Grabbing a long shirt, she threw it over her tank top. "Come in."

The door opened to reveal Zarina.

"Hi," she said, stepping into the room rather hesitantly. "I just wanted to check on you. You looked really upset earlier and I thought you could use some cheering up." Zarina pulled Devyn's box of cookies out from under her shirt. "I've even brought sweets!"

Despite herself, Alix laughed. "Devyn's already mad at you. What are you trying to do, get yourself killed?"

Zarina flopped on her bed. "As long as he doesn't look like he did in the control room, I'm not worried. He's got his father's temper, you know. Real quick to flare up, but equally quick to die out. You just have to be sure you can make a hasty retreat until he calms down."

Considering Zarina's words, Alix walked to her cooling unit and pulled out a bottle of juice. She crossed the room and sat at the head of the bed. "I don't know. He gave me quite a scare when he turned on you."

Zarina smiled. "Yeah, but he's a good guy most of the time. I've never known him to hit anyone other than my brother Jayce. And Jayce really deserved it."

Alix cocked a brow.

Zarina set the box down on the bed and turned around to face Alix, her features deadly serious. "Look, I like you a lot and believe it or not, I don't usually like strangers. I also have a suspicion Devyn likes you a lot, too, and he could really use someone like you by his side."

"If you're trying to play matchmaker—"

"Wait," Zarina said, holding up her hand to silence Alix. "I know what you said on Nera, but I also know you didn't mean it."

A lump constricted Alix's throat to the point that she feared she might suffocate. And actually she wished that she would suffocate. It would make her life a whole lot better. "Rina, you don't understand my life. I can't stay with Devyn as anything more than an engineer."

Zarina frowned, disappointment burning in her eyes. "It's really a shame you two are so stubborn. You'd make a great pair."

Alix gave a wistful smile. If only dreams really did come true. "Yeah, but you have to admit Devyn deserves someone a whole lot better than me."

"Better?" Zarina gasped. "Honey, they don't come any more sincere than you."

Alix looked down at herself and gave a short, ironic laugh. "But they do come a whole lot more attractive."

"Pah-lease!" Zarina rolled her eyes. "Come here," she said, sliding off the bed.

Unsure what Zarina wanted, Alix followed her to the mirror.

"Tell me what you see," Zarina said, standing just off to the right.

Alix sighed, disgusted with the image. "What's the point?"

Zarina shook her head and Alix wished she could wipe the pity off Zarina's face. She didn't need anyone's pity.

"I'll tell you what I see, what Devyn sees, is an attractive woman who holds her head up. Look at you. Your eyes are stunning."

Alix shrugged. "Maybe, but my lips are too full, my forehead too high, my nose too fat, and—"

"And you're impossible."

Alix turned away and headed back to the bed. She just wanted to crawl beneath it and stay there for the duration of her life.

She could never have anything more than her own ship. So why entertain foolish hopes and dreams?

Maybe she'd wait until she had enough money for a fully automated ship; then she wouldn't be surrounded by people who would only make her yearn for things she couldn't have.

Zarina stood over her, hands on hips. Her stance brought a smile to Alix's lips despite her sadness. "C'mon, Zarina, don't scold me anymore. You act like you should be my mother."

Agitation draining from her eyes, Zarina sat on the bed. "It's funny how many people say that to me; then when they find out my age, they gape like fish."

Alix stared at her. She figured Zarina to be around her age, maybe a little older, but a little twinge inside made her suddenly suspicious. "How old are you?"

"Don't gape. Remember I look Deucalion and Deucalions always look older to humans than they are."

"Okay," Alix said. "I promise I won't gape. How old?"

"I'm seventeen." Zarina frowned and crossed her arms over her chest. "Now look, you said you wouldn't gape."

Alix closed her mouth, her head reeling over Zarina's disclosure. "I'm sorry, I just had no idea."

Zarina shrugged. "No matter. It always happens."

Suddenly, Alix burst into laughter.

"What?" Zarina asked, looking around the room as if she sought a source for Alix's amusement.

Alix sobered. "It's just strange to me. People always think I'm about half my age, and here I thought you were almost double yours."

A wide smile broke across Zarina's face. "Yeah, I couldn't believe it when Sway told me how old you are."

Alix nodded. "Maybe people shouldn't pay so much attention to what's on the outside of a person."

Zarina sat back and eyed her like a kelfrey scoping out a verrago. "Devyn doesn't look on the outside. Not anymore."

# Chapter Six

Alix came awake with a scream lodged in her throat. Her heart pounding in her chest, she scrambled from the bed and looked about wildly trying to find Irn. The automated lights sensed her movement and came on, momentarily blinding her.

Nothing greeted her frenzied gaze except her meager furnishings. Realizing she'd been asleep and it was only a nightmare, she gave a shaky laugh and went to the cooling unit to get a bottle of juice.

"Lights dim," she said, and they instantly became a soft, dull glow that didn't burn her eyes.

She took a drink of juice, her hands trembling

to the point that she spilled several drops on her T-shirt.

"Ugh," she groaned, dabbing at the spill with a cloth. Nerves. Who needed them?

Would she ever feel safe? Alix paused in the center of her room and tried to peer into the shadows around her. No. She'd never know the security that came so easily to most people. Her life had been spent looking over her shoulder in fear, wondering what terror her father or his crewmen would visit on her next.

Yet when she thought of Devyn and the way he had protected her, a warm wave crashed through her, telling her that here, at least for now, she had safety. Devyn would never harm her.

But how long could it last?

Irn was out there. Despite the infinity of the universe, she'd learned a long time ago that the same people continually crossed paths. It never ceased to amaze her how many times her father would run across men he owed money to, and how many of those people had shown up after the funeral demanding she pay them.

She would meet Irn again, she had no doubt.

Then what? What would she do? If he ran to the authorities and claimed free rights, she would be his forever. Her stomach twisted to the point that she feared she'd be ill. An image of him pawing at her breasts, his fetid mouth sliding over hers, the remembered feel of his chafed, cold hands on her flesh scorched her.

She couldn't allow Irn to own her. Dear God, she'd rather die.

"Don't think about it!" she said adamantly, but still the thoughts twisted through her, making her body quake, her eyes water.

Suddenly, the room seemed to shrink. The stale air clogged her nose. She had to get out of here. Find someone, anyone who could talk to her and get her thoughts off the waves of panic that narrowed her vision and suffocated her lungs.

She grabbed her robe from her closet and shrugged it on.

Swallowing the heavy lump in her throat, she ran to the control room.

When the door opened and she saw Devyn sitting in his chair, she almost rushed to him and hugged him. Relief swept away the remnants of her fear and she knew he would help her fight her monsters.

"Hey," he said, looking over his shoulder at her. "What are you doing up so late?"

Nervously, she fidgeted with her robe, drawing the fold up higher on her neck, hoping he wouldn't think it was a ploy to make him desire her. But part of her did wish he would take her in his strong arms and hold her until all bad thoughts were forever banished.

Alix licked her dry lips and moved forward to sit in Sway's chair. She took a minute to study Devyn, and the first thing she noticed was the air of tenseness around him.

Was he upset over what had happened in the exercise room, or had he misread her current intent?

Guilt hung heavy in her breast like an asteroid trapped by gravity. She didn't want him to hate her; she wanted to draw him into her arms and have him hold her, but she was afraid of what she might do if she touched his warmth.

"I had a nightmare and didn't feel like sleeping for a while," she said, stifling a small yawn. "What about you? Why are you still awake?"

He clenched his teeth and looked out at the darkness surrounding them. Alix noted the pain burning in his eyes and she wondered if he'd had a similar nightmare.

Finally, he sighed. "I don't usually sleep well." Some of the tenseness seemed to drain out of him.

"Which monster stalks your sleep?" Alix asked. "Regret, fear, or anxiety? I call mine by the last two."

He gave a halfhearted laugh that brought a small glimmer of humor to his eyes. Again the need to reach out consumed her, but she knew this time she would deny the piece of her soul that yearned for him.

"Mine would be the first. I suppose the two of us together form the whole triad."

She watched him as he made minor adjustments to their course, the booster rockets hissing

113

a response. Staring at the glowing lights on the console, she thought over all the questions she had about her captain. Why regret haunted him.

"Do you ever miss the HAWC?" she asked, thinking that maybe that was what bothered him most.

He froze. No emotion showed from any part of him. It was almost as if she'd pressed a button that turned him off, and too late, she remembered Zarina's warning about mentioning the HAWC. Her throat tightened. Would she ever learn to think before she spoke?

Then suddenly, Devyn swung his chair around and focused a probing stare on her face. "No, I don't miss the HAWC," he said, his voice dull, lifeless.

Silence encompassed them, yet it oozed and throbbed with a thick intensity that broke through the barriers of her heart. Agony burned in his eyes.

He looked back at the control panel and sighed. "What would you say if I told you I was discharged from the HAWC in disgrace?"

Surprise tore through her like a cold wave of ocean water. She found it hard to believe that her brave captain could do anything disgraceful.

Dumbfounded and confused, Alix didn't know what to say. "Were you?"

He nodded, his eyes darkening with each furious beat of her heart. Agony simmered in the black depths, reaching out to her with a need she couldn't define, but one she wished she could answer.

"Why?" she asked. "I can't imagine you doing anything—"

"I was stealing supplies."

Disbelief washed over her, and again she felt as though she were sinking beneath a cold wave. Devyn a thief? "Why?" she asked again.

Devyn took a deep breath. "It's a long story."

Alix sat forward and took his icy hand into hers. He glanced at their entwined hands, then looked back at her face.

"I've got all night," she said, giving him a reassuring squeeze.

Devyn swallowed and pulled his hand out from under hers. Alix almost gasped as her palm touched his hard thigh and a jolt of desire burned through her.

Jerking her hand away, she sat back and waited to see if he would explain.

A cloud of sadness around him, he braced his elbow on his armrest and leaned his chin against his palm.

She waited.

"I was . . ." His voice trailed off and he instantly straightened up in his chair.

Alix frowned.

"Brace yourself!" Devyn shouted an instant before something struck their ship.

The ship lurched sideways and rocked.

Warning sirens blared, deafening her ears. Devyn switched them off, but the warning lights on the control panel continued to flash and dance.

Alix tightened her grip. "What the—"

A flash of color illuminated the darkness of space, blinding her. Someone had fired a flare directly into their visuals in an effort to knock out their scanners and video.

Alix blinked the tears from her eyes, trying to see again.

"Pirates," Devyn snarled, his own eyes tearing.

Alix closed her eyes. Terror settled over her body. She'd never faced pirates before, but she'd heard enough stories about their cruelty to know that most liked to launch their victims out the air lock without spacesuits. And the last thing she wanted was a firsthand view of a vacuum.

Breathing deeply, Alix made herself calm down. She should have considered this possibility sooner, but usually pirates left independent freighters alone. It was only company freighters, or newer ships like Devyn's, that they attacked.

"Drop your shields," a gruff voice demanded over the hailing channel.

Devyn scoffed, but didn't answer them.

"What are we going to do?" Alix asked, her mind completely blank. "Should I get Sway?"

"No," Devyn said, his gaze scanning readouts

and gauges. "Sway won't be able to help." He stopped at one gauge and anger furrowed his brow. "They've got shieldings. *Karistium marki!*"

Confused, Alix clenched her hands into fists. "What are shieldings?" she asked. Never in her life had she heard of such a thing.

"It's a new weapon. It strips off prinibben shields and leaves a craft exposed to cosmic rays."

What little blood was left in her face drained down her body to her toes. No one could survive without prinibben shields.

"Drop your defense shields!"

A trickle of sweat ran down her cheek. "There wouldn't happen to be a wormhole around here?" Alix asked, grasping at the hope that there was a hyperspace opening through which they could escape.

Devyn shook his head.

"What are we going to do?" she asked, her voice trembling.

Devyn punched in data too fast for her to read. "I'm open to any and all ideas."

"Can we outrun them?"

"Where?" he asked incredulously. "Look out there. We've got an asteroid field in front and on starboard. They've got two ships: one on our stern, the other to port."

Her fear turned to anger. By God, she wasn't going to let some mysterious group of space rats gnaw on her bones, not when she flew in a ship as new as the *Mariah*. "Will the disrupters help?"

Devyn raked his hands through his hair, but his eyes lightened a degree. "It's risky. They might have a countering device that could turn it back on us."

Alix stared out into space.

There had to be some way to get out of this unscathed, and she was going to find it. After all, pirates were as infamous for their stupidity as they were for their cruelty, and she refused to be bested by idiots.

No sooner had her thought finished than the solution appeared like an heir at a funeral. "I have an idea."

Devyn lifted a brow. "What?"

"Have they scanned us?"

"No," he said slowly, his brows knitted. "I've got a blocking device."

Once more the hailing channel buzzed. "You have one minute to drop shields before we vaporize your ship!"

Alix smiled despite the threat, her heart rate finally beginning to slow. Her idea just might work. It had to work.

Running to her chair, she began frantically typing in weapons specs.

"What are you doing?" Devyn asked.

"Reprograming our specs," she said with a laugh. "This way, they'll think we carry full firepower."

She punched in the last code. "Okay, drop the first-level defense shields and your blocking."

His eyes firing with mischievous humor, he smiled. "Damn, woman, I think you're more of a gambler than I am."

"Do we have a choice?"

Devyn laughed. "No, but I think I know a way to up our ante."

Clearing his throat, he opened the hailing channel. "This is Captain Devyn Kell of the Bracken Class Five starship *Mariah*. We are on an imperial mission from Tryphonius Three to Drymon. Our cargo is Class A and we are directed to self-destruct before surrender."

Crackling static filled the channel.

Devyn dropped the first-level shields.

"Son of a—" The channel closed. Almost instantly, the warships turned around and fled the sector.

Devyn faced her with a frown, disbelief filling his eyes. "What exactly did you do?"

Thank God, it had worked!

Laughing in relief and triumph, Alix sent her faux specs to his console. "I just made the disrupters appear to be Class A nuclear reactors."

Devyn returned her laugh, scooped her up in his arms, and swung her around. "You are absolutely brilliant! We must be functioning on the same wavelength."

Sobering at the contact, Alix stared down at him, holding her breath, reveling in the feel of

119

his strong arms wrapped around her hips.

The familiar throb began inside and she ached to taste the sweetness of his lips. She ran her hand through the soft strands of dark hair that had flopped into his eyes, brushing them back.

His laughter died. His eyes turned to liquid night and burned with an intensity that stole her breath. Alix's heart pounded. Her resistance melted and left her vulnerable.

Why must she always feel this way around him? Why must he affect her so?

She watched his eyes darken and turn dreamy with his passion. She knew he wanted her as much as she wanted him and her entire body responded with a demanding need she couldn't deny.

He slid her down the length of his body, the rough material of his clothes rubbing against her thin robe, caressing her stomach, her breasts, until she nearly moaned from the unexpected pleasure.

*Kiss me, Devyn*, her mind begged, knowing she couldn't allow herself to utter the words aloud.

Just as he dipped his head to hers, the control room door opened. The sound of the hydraulics sliced through her passion and nerves like sandpaper across fine china.

Devyn released her so quickly she nearly fell.

"What's going on up here?" Sway demanded,

scanning them. "The safety shields had me locked in my room."

Zarina entered a step behind him. "Yeah, what hit us?" she asked, then yawned widely.

Devyn looked at Alix with a smile on his face that warmed her heart. "Thanks to Alix, we just missed a visit from the local pirating committee."

"What!" Sway roared. "There aren't supposed to be any pirates in this sector. The HAWC patrols this whole area. Who would be dumb enough to attack here?"

Devyn shook his head. "Beats me, but I saved the scan I did on their ships. We shouldn't have any trouble figuring out who they were."

Devyn and Sway moved to the control panel to run through the scan.

Her hands trembling, Alix pulled her robe tighter around her, still somewhat embarrassed at being almost caught in willful abandon with Devyn. But from the conniving look on Zarina's face, she knew her newfound friend wouldn't censure her behavior. No, Zarina would encourage it. Something that might prove even worse in the long run.

After a few seconds of silence, Devyn let out a curse.

He turned to face Alix with a stare that chilled her blood. "The smaller ship was called *Prixie*. I think you and I need to have a talk about your friend Irn."

Alix's sight dimmed. She grabbed onto the back of the chair beside her, fearful her quaking knees would send her to the floor.

Dear God, had her dream been a premonition? Why was Irn after her now? Nothing about her should warrant his pursuit. And the money she owed him was negligible.

Surely he had better things to do than chase her across the universe. Granted she had ordered him about on her father's ship, but she'd never been rude or offensive. Why was he doing this to her?

Sway gave her a parting, sympathetic look that only added to her discomfort.

Zarina stepped forward and patted her shoulder reassuringly. "Don't worry about Irn. Devyn can handle him."

When the two of them were alone again, Devyn motioned for her to retake Sway's chair.

"All right," he said sternly, like a parent talking to a child. "Why is this guy after you?"

Frustration tore through her. She rubbed her hands down the armrests, her heart pounding. "I don't know. I wish I did. I've done nothing to him. Ever. I, uh, I—"

"Okay," Devyn said, interrupting her. He laid his hands over hers to keep her from clawing the upholstery. "Don't get so upset. There are a lot of weirdos out there. We'll just have to keep a closer guard in the future."

Alix nodded, her stomach burning. Once more,

she felt as though the room were shrinking, as if she couldn't breathe.

Why couldn't she just have her freedom? Was that so much to ask?

"Where are we stopping to meet your parents?"

Devyn frowned. "Phrixus. Why?"

She nodded, her heart tearing into small pieces at the mere thought of what she had to do. "I'll get off there. This time of year there should be several ships looking for help."

"Alix—"

"Look," she said, placing her hand on his forearm to cut him off. She tried not to think about the muscles that corded underneath her fingertips and sent a chill up her arm. "I appreciate what you've done for me, but I can't put you and Sway in any more danger. What you do is risky enough without you keeping me on board knowing someone is out there trying to capture me and doesn't mind killing you in the process."

His stare bored into her. "What if I said I didn't want you to leave?"

Tears gathered in her eyes.

Alix looked up at the ceiling overhead, forcing her emotions back into restraint. She had waited her entire life to hear someone say that and never in her most vivid dream had she ever hoped for it to come from a man like Devyn Kell.

But it couldn't be. Her past would never allow her the fairy-tale ending she wanted.

Meeting his gaze, she sighed. "What's the point, Devyn? We both know I'm not the type of woman you want or need."

He cupped her face in the palm of his hands. Dark torment filled his eyes. He stroked her cheeks with his thumbs, his touch burning her, sending wave after wave of desire through her. "It's been so long since I've wanted anyone around me," he said, his voice a ragged whisper. "Then you appear one day out of nowhere, and now all I can think of is you."

His words tore through her, shattering every barrier she'd ever constructed.

No! She couldn't let this happen. She lived in the world of reality, not the make-believe, perfect sunshine of childhood fantasies.

"You don't need me," she insisted.

A sad smile curved his lips, tugging even more forcibly at her heart.

"That's what I keep trying to tell myself," he said. "But as soon as I see you, I forget every reason my mind comes up with that tells me why I can't have you."

She covered his hands with hers and forced herself not to give in to the pleading in his eyes, the warmth of his touch. "There's so much about me that you don't know. That you don't want to know."

He shook his head. "No. I want to know everything about you."

Alix clenched her jaw, making herself not cry. She pulled away from him, hoping a little distance would rectify the damage already done to her defenses, knowing nothing would ever repair the damage done to her heart. "I can't stay," she whispered, and left the room.

Devyn watched her leave, his heart splintering. Like her, he knew all the reasons why the two of them should go their separate ways, yet inside he knew he couldn't stand letting her go.

The door opened. He spun around, hoping it was Alix returning.

Instead, Sway came forward and took his chair. "Did you find out anything?"

Devyn shook his head and forced himself not to think about his feelings. He still had a little while left to try to convince Alix to stay. "Irn was her father's navigator, but she has no idea why he's after her."

"And you believe her?"

"I guess so," Devyn said. "Why would she lie?"

Sway shook his head and sighed. He glanced out the window. "Are they following us?"

Devyn lifted a surprised brow. He hadn't dared tell Alix about the tiny blips on their scanner that signified the pirates. "How'd you know?"

Sway smiled. "If they've gone to this much trouble, it would only seem natural they'd continue after her." He pulled up the blips and made a few calculations. "So what's she planning to do?"

Devyn sighed, his stomach churning. "Get off at the next stop."

"Are you going to let her do that?"

Devyn stared at him, wondering how Sway knew about his feelings for their engineer.

"C'mon, Dev. I'd have to be blind not to notice the way you look at her like you're a starving man and she's a nine-course meal." He looked back at the scanner. "About time, too, I might add."

"What do you mean?"

Sway looked back at him and took a deep breath. "I know we've always had an unspoken understanding not to meddle in each other's personal stuff, but I owe you one meddling. And right now, I'd like to know when you're going to let go of the past and start living again."

Devyn stiffened. "I am living."

"*Vriska*. You're still trying to prove to the universe that you've earned the right to live. Your whole life you have felt guilty for having so much. I know you too well, Dev, so don't try to deny it."

Anger clouded Devyn's sight. "You don't know what you're talking about."

"Yes, I do."

Devyn glared at him.

"All right," Sway said, throwing his arms wide. "If I'm wrong, then tell me why you're so maniacal about running these missions? Why have we been risking our asses for the last three years?"

Devyn clenched his jaw as a wave of pain and raw fury tore through him, almost driving him to attack his best friend. "You know why."

"Oh, yeah," he said, then sneered. "Onone."

Devyn's anger intensified and all the emotions he'd done his best to bury came to the surface. It seemed no time had passed since Onone had pulled her gun out and shot him straight in the chest. Too bad her aim had been off. A little higher and she would have ended his uselessness.

"Look," Sway said, his voice soothing. "I know she put you through hell, but you've got to get over it. You killed her. You had no choice, you know that. So why can't you forgive yourself and go on?"

The knot in Devyn's throat closed and all the fury died, leaving him numb, empty. "That's easy for you to say. You're not the one who blew a hole in her head."

"She shot you first and she'd have killed you if you hadn't pulled the trigger."

Maybe she should have killed him.

Sway snarled. "Dammit, Devyn, give me a break. Give yourself one."

Devyn sat there in silence, not willing to discuss this any further. He locked his jaw, and by the darkening scowl on Sway's face, he knew his friend realized he had retreated into himself.

"Fine," Sway said, pushing himself out of his chair. "Sit there and sulk. I just hope you realize all the supplies you run aren't going to bring back any of the lives you took when you were in the HAWC."

Sway towered over him, his entire body shaking from fury. "What do you intend to do, Kell? Run supplies until the day you drop from old age? You used to want more than that."

Devyn listened to Sway make his way out of the room, his stare focused out the window on the darkness that used to soothe him like a mother's touch. It had been so long since he felt at peace, so long since he could sleep at night and not be tortured by screams and pleas.

But as much as he hated to admit it, Sway was right. He did remember a time when he had wanted more out of life than temporary relief missions. A time when he had thought he could do anything.

Idealism of youth. Funny how life stripped it from everyone. He clenched his fists, his stomach twisting.

All he had ever really wanted was to be worthy of the life his parents had given him. His father and mother had grown up impoverished orphans. By their intelligence and diligence, they had pulled themselves out of the filthy streets and built a life together.

He, on the other hand, had been born with only the best life had to offer. The best schools, the best house, the best toys.

He shouldn't feel guilty, but he couldn't help it.

Devyn tensed as a wave of pain tore through him. Rubbing his eyes, he tried to banish the old, torn picture of his father at age six. He'd been snooping in his mother's picture box looking for a picture of himself to send in with his HAWC application. And there it had been on the very bottom. A frail, malnourished child with haunted eyes that bore the pain of an aged man.

Even now he had a hard time assimilating that child's picture into his image of his father, an intimidating man who refused to bow down before anyone or anything.

From the moment he'd realized who the child was, he'd decided never to forget how fortunate he'd been. He must never forget.

And he was certain Alix had grown up the same way as his parents—alone, abused. No one had ever watched after her. Her mother hadn't been there to cradle her against her breast and rock her to sleep when she had a cold or was scared by nighttime shadows.

Her father hadn't tossed her up in his arms, stroked her hair from her face, and told her that he'd kill anyone who ever threatened her. So many nights he'd lain awake trying to imagine what it must have been like for his parents, and now those thoughts centered on his engineer.

His gut tightened. Alix didn't deserve her past any more than his parents deserved theirs. If he could change it, he'd gladly do so.

Tomorrow she would leave him and venture into God only knew what dangers. He clutched his fists together, his mind shouting a denial. Could he change her mind?

Maybe if he swore to leave her alone, she'd stay.

Devyn almost laughed at himself. What use would his promise be? Where she was concerned, he couldn't maintain his normal control. He'd been trying to avoid her since she first stepped on board his ship and what had it gotten him? Rock-heavies.

No, she wouldn't listen to him any more than he'd listened to his father when his father had warned him about Onone. All he could do was offer her friendship and a promise that if she ever needed him, he would be there.

"Good-bye, Alix Garran. I hope you at least find what you're looking for," he whispered, knowing for him the search would never cease.

# *Chapter Seven*

Irn sat in the captain's chair, eyeing the tracking scanner. The *Mariah* continued to blink on screen and he altered his course to make sure his prey didn't leave his range. A smile curved his lips and he felt like laughing. Of course he never laughed, not anymore.

"Captain?"

He looked over at his second-in-command, Frinskey, an Yrprian reject who reminded him of a fuzzy shoe. Worse than his appearance and whiny, hissing speech, the alien's skin stank to the six corners of Perulia. But after the last few months, he'd grown almost accustomed to it.

Frinskey squirmed in his chair. "Werren wants to know if we're to maintain pursuit. After seeing the *Mariah*'s weapons spec, he thinks we should—"

"He thinks?" Irn snarled. "Open the channel."

An image of Werren's handsome face flashed onto his screen. He hated handsome people almost as much as he hated life.

"Captain," Werren said in greeting.

Irn curled his lip. "What's this about your thinking?"

Werren turned a strange shade of green. "Nothing," he said, his voice as breathless as a cornered virgin.

Narrowing his eyes on the space scab, he knew Werren would desert him at the first opportunity, but he had no intention of losing a pilot with Werren's skill. He'd kill him first. "You'll follow my lead without question. That is unless you want to end up like your *former* captain."

Werren's face paled.

Satisfied that he had quelled the moron, Irn cut the channel. "Anyone else want to question me?" he asked sadistically, delighting in the way his own crew cringed.

Once more he felt like laughing.

Triumph would soon be his. At long last he would have his vengeance against his enemy's seed. Still, it seemed small compensation for thirty years of hard prison labor and the loss of his younger brother—the only person he'd ever given a damn about.

Aye, he'd make Malena's son squirm. He

wouldn't just open Devyn's main artery and watch him die. No, he intended to cut him into pieces, film every incision, and make sure Malena Laing Kell received a copy of her son's death. He'd tear Devyn apart just like the inmates had done to his brother, and she'd watch, helpless to stop it.

Irn drummed his fingers against his armrest, all the while watching the screen's blip.

When he'd finally gotten out of prison, he'd wanted to go after the *jarlia* and kill her, but that took more money than he'd had. And no one wanted to hire a man who had just done thirty years for murder, rape, drug running, and child molestation.

No one other than Alix's father. That old, stupid, drunken bastard hadn't thought twice about checking his faked credentials. Garran had earned what he got.

Irn's sight dimmed. He could still remember the first time he'd seen Garran's daughter and her stuck-up ways. If he hadn't needed the money so bad, he'd have humbled her the first week on board their rickety old freighter. But he'd waited, knowing eventually he'd have enough money to get back at Malena and Alix.

He growled low in his throat. But he'd waited too damned long. After he killed Alix's father, she'd escaped him. But not this time. First he'd finish his business with Devyn; then he'd take

## Sherrilyn Kenyon

pleasure in making the haughty bitch serve every
want and need he'd ever had.

Alix left the closet with the last of her clothes.
Sighing wistfully, she took one final look around
her room. Would she ever again have anything
so nice?

"I really wish you'd reconsider," Zarina said
from the plush chair next to the porthole.

"What's to consider?" Alix said with a confidence she didn't feel. She'd give anything to
stay, but she knew it was impossible.

Zarina held the blue choker she'd bought for
her on Nera, lacing the sparkling jewels between
long, graceful fingers. She met Alix's gaze and
Alix immediately noticed the sudden calculating
gleam in her eyes. Trepidation filled her.

The princess was planning something. Heav-
en only knew what she'd come up with now.

Zarina smiled. "If you really are leaving, could
I buy you one last going-away present?"

She hadn't known Zarina long, but she'd
already learned to be wary of Zarina when she
had that mischievous gleam in her eyes. "I don't
know."

Zarina smiled so sweetly Alix felt awful for
questioning her intentions. "Please? I want to
do one last thing. I promise no one will get hurt,
nor will any Keepers be involved."

Despite herself, Alix smiled. Part of her wanted
to run the moment the ship's ramp was lowered,

but the other part of her didn't want to leave at all.

She would never again see Zarina, Sway, or Devyn. Pain coiled inside her like a vicious snake sent to tear her insides apart.

Breathing deeply, she tried to think up reasons why she couldn't do what Zarina asked. She couldn't find one single reason not to give in to Zarina's wishes.

"Okay," she said at last. "But remember you promised no jail."

Zarina laughed. "No jail."

She rose to her feet and grabbed Alix by the arm. "Come on, let's go annoy the guys while they try to land us."

Alix's throat tightened. Could she stand seeing Devyn one last time? If she saw him again, could she leave him? "I don't know if that's such a good idea."

"*Vriska!* Of course it's a good idea."

Reluctantly, Alix allowed Zarina to pull her down the corridor and into the control room. As soon as she entered, she wished she'd listened to herself and had stayed in her room.

Devyn stood with his back to them, but even so she ached for him. Biting her lower lip, Alix suppressed the wave of tears that threatened to spill down her cheeks. How could she leave him? *Why* must she leave him when all she really wanted was to stay and be near him forever?

Sway turned around to face Devyn. "I've got the landing bay controller."

Devyn nodded his head and for the first time,

Alix realized he wore the communications head-set and was talking privately with someone over the hailing channel.

"Uh, Dad," he said as if to interrupt some-one. He turned around and glanced at Alix and she noted his frustration. He clenched his jaw and rolled his eyes. "Dad," he repeated. "No!" he said emphatically. "Don't put Mom on. Dad! Don't . . . Hi, Mom," he said, then sighed.

Alix gave a small laugh. Devyn folded his arms over his chest, looked at her, and, smiling, shook his head.

Alix could hear excited chatter even from her distance, but couldn't make out any of the words.

"No, Mom, we're . . . She's . . . But . . . If you'll . . ." Devyn shook his head. "Here," he said, tossing the headset to Zarina. "Talk to her so I can land this damned thing."

Alix laughed.

Devyn cast her a menacing glare. "I'm glad someone's amused."

Sway leaned back and eyed Devyn. "Actually, we're all amused."

"Ha, ha," Devyn said, sitting in his chair and taking the controls.

Alix took her chair and belted herself in.

"He's been a beast to me!"

Shocked by the words, Alix turned to look at Zarina, who cast Devyn an evil smirk as she sat in her own chair.

"No, he didn't do that. But still—" Now Zarina looked flustered.

"Just wait," Sway said to Alix. "You'll see how hard it is to say a word around Devyn's mother."

Alix smiled again. She could just imagine what the woman who had given birth to a man like Devyn must look like. No doubt gorgeous, his mother probably towered over them all, and as far as her being protective, well, Alix couldn't blame her in the least. If Devyn belonged to her, she'd be the same way.

With all the longing swirling inside her, she watched Devyn, trying to absorb every part of him into her memory so she could recall his image on future lonely nights when she couldn't sleep. Her lips trembled.

She loved every minute detail of him—the way his hair flopped down over his eyes, the shape of his mouth, those dark, wonderful eyes.

An image of him in his exercise shorts scorched her. She gripped the arms of her chair and fought against her surging desire.

If she could go back, she'd have her one night with him, consequences be damned.

"Aunt Malena," Zarina said, "I think we just landed. Okay, I'll tell him. Yes. Okay, bye."

Zarina set the headset down and gave a heavy sigh. "Boy, Devyn, your mom sure can talk."

"You should be grateful she's never lectured you. If not for my dad, I guarantee I'd be deaf by now."

Despite his humorous remark, a lump constricted Alix's throat. She'd miss Devyn, Sway, and Zarina. In fact, it was harder to leave them than it had been to sell her father's freighter and leave her so-called home.

Devyn locked down their gear, then moved to stand next to Alix. "My parents have invited all of us to dinner. I was wondering if you'd like to join us before you leave."

Alix swallowed to clear her throat and ignored the excited voice in her head that begged her to say yes.

She couldn't bring herself to meet Devyn's gaze. Instead, she kept her eyes focused on the center of his chest. "I'm not—"

"C'mon, Alix," Zarina said. "You've got to eat anyway."

Frowning, she knew she should deny both of them, but she couldn't. Devyn and Zarina had been too kind to her.

As Zarina had said, she had to eat anyway, so why not have a few more hours with the only real friends she'd ever known?

"Okay," she said, looking up at Devyn.

Relief shone in his eyes. He offered her a smile, then turned to release the ship's ramp.

She followed Sway, Devyn, and Zarina to the center of the ship where the door was located. As soon as Sway pushed the controls, Devyn's mother rushed in and grabbed him in an embrace that had Alix flinching at its tightness.

Dazed by the sight of his mother, Alix stared at the tiny woman who barely reached above the middle of Devyn's chest. From the way they all acted and talked, she'd been certain his mother was over forty feet tall.

Dark brown hair had been swept up into an intricate coiffure that hung around his mother's face and shoulders in soft, shiny ringlets. Never in her life had she seen any woman more beautiful. Not even Zarina.

His mother certainly didn't look like any bounder Alix had ever beheld.

"My baby!" she cried, clutching Devyn to her. "I've missed you so much." She pulled back from him and quickly scanned his body.

Alix squelched her smile at the blush that spread over Devyn's cheeks and the way he blustered under her scrutiny.

Looking at his face, his mother gave a cry of dismay, cupped his chin in her hand, and brushed his hair back from his eyes. "You look like you've not been sleeping well."

She glanced over her shoulder. "Valerian, look at him. His eyes are bloodshot."

His mother turned back to Devyn and touched his cheek and forehead as if feeling for a fever. "Have you been eating right? I brought more cookies, but if—"

"Malena, please," Devyn's father said, pulling her back against his chest and encircling her waist with his arms. A wide smile curved his lips, and Alix was amazed at how much father and son favored each other. "Devyn can take care of himself. He looks fine to me."

Malena lifted her chin and pouted. "But his eyes—"

Valerian shook his head. "If you didn't call him in the middle of the night, he might be able to get more rest."

Alix hid her smile at the way his mother shifted indignantly.

Elbowing her husband, Devyn's mother pushed herself away and went to hug Zarina and Sway.

While his wife was preoccupied, Devyn's father hugged him, and Alix didn't miss the way his father's hands tightened around Devyn as if he wanted to duplicate his wife's embrace and never let go of his son.

All too well, she understood that need.

His father released him, then turned to face her. "You must be the new engineer, Alix," he said, extending his hand out to her.

"Yes, sir." She took his hand and shook it.

"I'm Valerian Kell," he said with a smile. "And the worry rat is my wife, Malena."

Malena lifted a finely arched brow and swept a look over Valerian that spoke more of her irritation than any words. "I wouldn't worry so much if Devyn took after me and not you and Calix. I swear the three of you are on a crusade to shorten my life."

Alix glanced at Devyn to see how he was dealing with their presence. Humor danced in his eyes and she knew he didn't mind his parents at all.

Malena finally turned her probing amber stare to Alix. "Aren't you a pretty little thing," she said, bringing a stinging heat to Alix's cheeks. "No wonder Devyn's voice softens when he speaks of you."

"Mother!"

Alix's eyes widened in shock over Malena's disclosure.

Malena waved a hand at Devyn's outrage as she disregarded him. "Now, Devyn, I'm too old for you to chastise me. If I can't speak my mind, then why was I given one?"

Devyn's face flushed a shade that Alix was sure matched her own.

"Dad, can't you muzzle her?"

Valerian smiled. "I could, but I happen to enjoy her comments. Besides, when you're around, she's not picking on me."

Alix laughed, which brought an angry glare from Devyn. "Sorry," she said, but his features didn't soften.

"Hey, I've got an idea," Zarina spoke up, breaking them apart.

She moved to stand between Valerian and Malena and took each one by the arm. "Why don't you two take Devyn and spend some time by yourselves for a while?"

Sherrilyn Kenyon

At least Devyn's glare went to a new target. He cleared his throat. "I don't really have—"

"What a great idea," Malena spoke up. "We hardly ever get to see him anymore and we could use a few hours."

Devyn looked to his father for help. "Dad?"

Valerian shook his head. "I love you, Dev, but I also love your mother and she's the one I have to live with. You're on your own."

Malena turned to Devyn, her face that of a guileless angel, and Alix wished she could learn how to be so manipulative while looking so beautiful and sweet. "You wouldn't want to hurt my feelings, would you, Devyn?"

Devyn's frown melted into a smile and he hugged his mother. "No, I could never do anything to hurt you."

Zarina gave Alix a conspiratorial wink. "Well then, you go along now and—"

"You're coming, too," Devyn said, his face stern.

Duplicating Malena's beguiling look, Zarina batted her lashes. "I would just be intruding."

Valerian cocked his brow in a way that reminded Alix an awful lot of Devyn when he was irritated or thoughtful. "I think I agree with—"

"I won't get into any trouble," she promised. "I'll stay right by Sway and Alix, and they can watch over me until dinner."

Alix bit her lips to keep from smiling. She didn't know what Zarina was planning, but she

142

was learning a lot by observing the way Zarina got what she wanted.

"Now look who's being overprotective," Malena said. "She can take care of herself."

Valerian's mouth dropped.

Disregarding his shock, Malena turned to Zarina. "You'd better show up at dinner. If you try to escape again, I'll hunt you myself."

For once, Alix saw trepidation in Zarina's eyes. "Yes, ma'am."

Alix watched them go, a lump in her stomach. They were such a handsome, loving family. What she wouldn't give to have grown up in such a home, surrounded by that kind of love and laughter.

If only she could give such a life to her children. But who was she fooling? Any child she bore would automatically be a slave and she refused to bequeath that status to anyone.

As soon as they disappeared into the crowd, Zarina turned to face Sway. "Batten down the hatches, flybaby. We're going shopping."

"Shopping?" Alix and Sway asked simultaneously.

Alix swallowed; she hated shopping.

Zarina pushed Sway toward the control room. "I'm going, and if you let me out of your sight, Devyn will have your head. So lock up and join us."

Alix shook her head. "I don't think this is such a good idea."

Hands on hips, Zarina faced her. "No complaints. You said I could give you one last present, and you're not about to disappoint me!"

Alix opened her mouth to argue, then thought better of it. No one argued with Zarina. Rina always got what she wanted. But what in the universe could she have planned?

She and Sway exchanged a wary glance.

"I hate shopping," he muttered, pressing the buttons to seal up the ship.

"No more than I do," Alix said, contemplating what it would take to outsmart Zarina. She doubted anyone could ever keep the princess from anything she set her mind to.

"No more whining, you two," Zarina said. "Trust me."

Over the next hour and a half, Alix was pushed and pulled until she thought she might actually strangle Zarina herself. She should have asked what Zarina wanted to give her before she agreed to this hellish trip.

They visited over a dozen clothing shops until Zarina finally found a blue dress to match that stupid choker.

And what a dress! Cut low in front, it barely held Alix in, but at least the back was high enough to hide her mark. Though the hem fell at her ankles, a giant slit opened the right side up to midthigh. Just thinking about it made Alix's cheeks burn.

She couldn't possibly wear that to bed, let

alone dinner, where people might actually see her.

Now she sat in a hair salon, with Zarina and some unknown hairdresser discussing her as if she were the main dish for a feast. She pulled at her wet hair, wondering if there were enough gel and makeup in the universe to make her anything other than plain.

"Quit fussing!" Zarina scolded, putting her hair back in her eyes as she talked with the hairdresser.

Alix bristled under the sharp reproach, tempted to tell Zarina what she could do with all this, but at least someone was trying to help her. Who was she to complain?

"I think we should take six inches off the length," Zarina said while the stylist combed Alix's hair.

Leaning over, she opened a slit so Alix could see her. "Is that okay with you?"

Alix lifted her brow, amazed Zarina had even asked. "Does it matter?"

Zarina frowned as if she'd slapped her, and a wave of guilt tore through Alix. "I'm sorry," she said. "I just didn't expect all this."

Zarina's frown wilted. "You could use a little makeover. No need to hide all the beautiful aspects of yourself."

She moved to Alix's side and pulled several wet strands of hair around Alix's face. "I was thinking of a style that came in a little around your face. Something soft and alluring. Maybe a couple of highlights?"

"I know just the thing," the stylist said, and Alix knew her opinion didn't matter in the least.

Yet she really didn't mind. No one had ever told her about fashion before. She'd never had anyone teach her how to wear her hair or makeup, and she welcomed Zarina's lessons.

On board her father's ship, she'd spent most of her time trying to look unappealing. But just once, she wanted to feel glamorous, to look like the type of woman who might turn Devyn's head.

And if Zarina actually thought she could transform her, then Alix was willing to give it a try.

While they worked on her hair, she imagined meeting Devyn and rendering him speechless. An image of him holding her flashed through her mind and she knew if she could have one wish, it would be to go back to that night in the gym and make love to the only man who had ever made her feel beautiful, womanly.

Her heart heavy, she realized all she was leaving behind. Damn Irn and his interference. If not for him, she could stay with Devyn and maybe find what she really wanted.

Why couldn't things work out for her as they did for Zarina? She sighed, knowing the answer only too well. It was just her awful luck. It would never change.

Once her hair was cut and styled, Zarina moved

her to the makeup counter. Alix listened as the cosmetologist explained each step and how to wear every item.

The cold, liquid makeup felt strange against her cheeks, but if it would leave a lasting impression on Devyn, then she guessed it would be worth it. Besides, a little color never hurt.

When the woman finished and held the mirror up to her face, Alix gasped. She almost turned around looking for the woman in the mirror. Surely it couldn't be herself.

"I told you!" Zarina said with a triumphant laugh. She took the mirror from Alix and handed it back to the cosmetologist. "I'll take one of everything you used on her."

Alix wanted the mirror returned. She wanted to make sure it really was she and not some other person.

While Zarina finished with the cosmetologist, Alix stepped down from her chair and went to the full-length mirrors nearby. Hesitantly, she studied herself. No one could mistake the drab beige pantsuit and ugly black boots, but from the neck up, she looked like someone else.

True to Zarina's words, the stylist had lightened her hair a couple of shades to a pretty honey blonde. He had swept it up off her neck into an intricate braid and soft wisps of hair curled around her face and neck.

The makeup hid the tiny scar under her eye and somehow, the cosmetologist had made her eyes appear larger, darker, her cheekbones more defined. Breathless, she stood in awe of the temporary miracle and wished that she could freeze herself like this forever.

"Are you ready?" Zarina asked, stopping at her side.

Alix was speechless.

Zarina laughed and took her by the arm. "Just wait till you get that dress on. Devyn will be on his knees to keep you."

In spite of herself and the tiny voice that said she could never stay with Devyn, Alix liked the sound of Zarina's words.

Following after Zarina, she left the shop.

Zarina went straight to Sway, who sat in the center of the plaza reading a small book. When he looked up, Alix got the biggest compliment of her life—his mouth dropped open.

"Alix?" he asked in disbelief, rising slowly to his feet.

A thrill rushed through her. No man had ever looked at her that way and she couldn't wait to see Devyn's reaction.

"C'mon," Zarina said, grabbing her by the arm. "We have a date I don't want to miss."

# *Chapter Eight*

Devyn tried listening to his mother's discourse on his family's health and well-being, but despite his best effort, his thoughts kept drifting back to Alix. Checking his watch, he sighed. Alix and Zarina were twenty minutes late, which for Zarina was typical, but he found himself more anxious than normal as each second ticked by.

He could kill Zarina for this. He'd never intended to stay so long here, but his mother was insistent and he had no desire to hurt her. But he had to leave soon.

Where could Rina and Alix be?

Though his parents always preferred a private dining room in restaurants, he now wished they'd chosen a table in the main hall. At least

149

in the public area, he could have watched the door for Alix's arrival.

What could be keeping them?

A hundred thoughts went through his mind—Zarina insulting the wrong person and ending up in jail again, or worse, Zarina running away and taking Alix with her. Maybe the two of them had tied Sway up and were even now boarding a shuttle off-planet.

He should have never left them alone. Zarina could manipulate anyone into anything.

He fingered the tiny box in his pocket and a lump settled in his gut. If Alix left without his going-away present . . .

Dammit, he couldn't stand this any longer.

Just as he slid his chair back to check outside, the door dilated. Devyn looked up, relief spreading through him.

Zarina stepped in first, her eyes glinting mischievously, and by that he knew she had been up to something.

Sway came in behind her, a smug look on his face. What had they been up to?

Suddenly, Alix stepped forward. Devyn's stomach lurched as if he'd been punched in the solar plexus.

His mind vacant, he could only stare. Curves he'd never guessed she possessed were outlined by the daring cut of her gown. She walked forward like a shy schoolgirl, but her body left no doubt that this was a woman full-grown, and

still, somehow, she maintained her competent
air. A dangerous combination.

All his control dove south and his body
burned with a painful need. If not for his
parents, he'd toss Alix over his shoulder, bolt
from the restaurant, and make sure she never
left him.

Slowly, Devyn rose, his throat more parched
than the arid dunes of Mallisor. Moving forward, he pulled out a chair for her. Alix looked
up at him with adoring eyes, and he'd never felt
so gallant, so masculine. For the first time in his
life, he understood his father's behavior where
his mother was concerned.

"Devyn, you're so rude! You could at least hold
my chair, too." Zarina's voice broke through the
fog clouding his thoughts.

Sudden realization struck him, and he flushed.
How could he have behaved that way with his
mother present?

His father seated Zarina, then turned to face
him. "Why don't we exchange seats? I'm sure
you want to sit next to Alix."

Devyn wanted to crawl beneath the table and
hide. He looked at his mother, who hid her smile
behind her glass. It'd be a long time before he
lived this down.

Clearing his throat, Devyn took his father's
chair.

*Don't look at her.* But still his gaze drifted
back to Alix.

"So, Alix," his mother said, and Devyn braced himself for her probing questions. "Devyn tells us your father owned a freighter?"

"Yes, ma'am," Alix said, twisting the napkin in her lap around her shaking fingers.

Devyn started to reach out to comfort her, but caught himself before his hands left his lap. Clenching his own napkin, he warned himself not to intervene anymore. His mother didn't bite and Alix could handle herself.

"Isn't it awful growing up on a tiny ship?" his mother asked, setting her glass back on the table. "My father was a smuggler, and he refused to buy a house until after he had three children scavenging in his cargo. He probably never would have bought one at all had he not been stopped one day by HAWC Probers. They were about to let him go when my brother, Calix, showed up with one of the boxes they were scanning for and asked my father what prinibben crystals were used for." Her eyes twinkled and Devyn smiled, proud of his mother and her charm.

Then her gaze turned calculating and his throat tightened. Don't let her go into her match-making program. Anything but that. Please, no cute Devyn baby stories. He'd have to leave if she started those.

His mother propped her elbows on the table, leaned her chin on her folded hands, and turned Alix one of those guileless yet perfect looks that won her a place in most everyone's heart. "But the worst thing about ships are those horrible fumes and stuffy noses." She shuddered and directed a conniving glance at him, Sway, and his father. "Men can be so unobservant. I swear I think most of them are born without olfactory glands."

"Mom," Devyn warned, but as expected, she just patted his hand and continued.

"Not that Devyn's like that. I made sure he learned how to care for a woman. He'd never subject his wife to such tortures."

Okay, so it wasn't the baby stories, but it was almost as bad. Devyn tightened his hand around his fork to keep from strangling his mother. When would she learn?

"Malena, maybe Devyn's not ready to settle down. He's happy the way he is."

Devyn could've hugged his father for those words.

"*Vriska*," his mother scolded. "You men think you know what you want." She smiled the coy smile that never failed to bend his father to her will, and Devyn knew his reprieve would soon end right along with his father's interference. "Until you meet the right woman."

His father's eyes glowed. "Let's just hope when Devyn meets her, she doesn't try to kill him."

Pain tightened Devyn's chest. He'd never told his parents the whole story about Onone, and he hated when his father brought up the fact that his own mother had tried to kill his father the

153

first time they met. But his mother had acted out of desperation and fear, not the cold-blooded maliciousness that had spurred Onone's attack.

Frowning, his mother stabbed at her appetizer. "You're never going to let me forget that, are you?"

His father smiled. "How could I? The guilt from it has served me well all these years."

She snorted. "I should have aimed better. If my hand hadn't been shaking so badly, I could've shriveled your callous heart."

Alix listened to their playful banter. Her parents had seldom spoken. What few words passed between them had been coarse, direct orders from her father and submissive, mewling responses from her mother.

Yet all Valerian and Malena's teasing was good-natured. There was no malice lurking beneath their words.

She spent the entire dinner listening to them, picking up tidbits about Devyn's past, speaking only when someone asked her a question.

All too soon, dinner passed and Alix knew her reprieve had ended. Once more, she would be on her own, with no one to trust, or confide in. Alone. She closed her eyes against the despair that gathered in her heart.

Devyn's parents walked them back to Devyn's ship, where they said their good-byes.

When Malena stepped forward and gave her a hug, Alix thought she would finally succumb to the tears lurking beneath her cheerful facade.

"Take care, Alix. It was nice meeting you."

Alix nodded, afraid to use her voice. One word and she was certain she'd crumble.

Zarina also gave her a hug. "Watch yourself, *shanna*. Remember you've always got us if you need us."

She squeezed Zarina tightly, wishing she could repeat the last few days. "Thank you, for everything," she whispered.

Stepping away, Zarina smiled.

Alix stood beside Devyn and watched the three of them leave. Soon, she would be leaving as well. Tears gathered in her eyes, dulling her sight.

*Don't feel sorry for yourself.*

But still, her grief and sadness choked her. Just once she wished luck would befriend her.

"I guess you want to change," Devyn said, pulling her attention to him.

One last time, Alix admired the expensive cut of his suit, the way the black fabric emphasized the muscles she knew lay beneath the silk.

She cleared her throat. "I guess it'd be the prudent thing to do." She swept her hand over her dress. "It'd be hard to find an engineering job looking like this."

Devyn gave her a devilish grin. "I doubt that. In fact, I'll double your salary if you stay."

Alix gave him a sad smile. She liked his teasing. "Don't tempt me."

"And if I did?"

His eyes told her the earnestness of his words.

What was he thinking? She'd give anything to know. But what could they have?

If she'd learned anything in her life, it was that everything caught up to you in time. Her father's brutal murder attested to that. He'd died as he'd lived—cold, brutal, and callous. A knife sliced through his heart the way his words had always cut through hers.

The past. How long could she run from what she was before fate caught up to her as it had her father?

And yet there before her stood Devyn, his dark eyes warm with concern. It would be so easy to stay. So easy to forget, to hope.

Dare she?

Before she could stop herself she stepped into his arms. A wave of excitement tore through her when he didn't pull away. There was one thing she wanted, one last thing she would ask of him before she left. One dream she would still fight for.

"Love me," she begged, every bit as afraid he'd turn her away as she was that he would agree.

Devyn's answer came as an impassioned kiss. Alix opened her mouth, welcoming him, reveling in the taste of sweet wine on his lips. She needed this. For once in her life, she would not be denied.

Devyn shook from desire and the fear that she would pull away one final time and leave him more desperate. He knew he needed to leave, to finish his mission, but he also needed her. She was his life, his breath, and the thought of her leaving cut through his soul like a lason knife.

"Don't leave me," he whispered against her lips, holding her closer.

She didn't answer him with words, but her arms wrapped around his shoulders and he sensed that this time she wouldn't pull away. And with that came the knowledge that afterward he wouldn't be able to let her go. All his intentions be damned.

Resigning himself to fate, Devyn scooped her up in his arms and carried her to his room.

Alix laid her head on his shoulder, no longer willing to fight herself. The future stretched out before her like a giant black hole—lonesome and cold, sucking all the light out of her life.

There had never been anyone in her life who made her feel like this, and she knew there would never be anyone else. She needed this night with Devyn. Maybe this one memory would be enough to take some of the misery out of the lonely nights to come.

He pushed the controls to his room and she gasped at the luxury surrounding her. No expense had been spared, and she doubted if even a palace could have finer furnishings. His bed, like hers, was a bunk against the far wall. But there any resemblance to her room ended.

# Sherrilyn Kenyon

A rich, dark blue, down-filled silk comforter covered his bed, and it molded against her body like a flimsy cloud as Devyn placed her upon it. She closed her eyes to savor the feel of both the soft mattress and Devyn's strong arms.

Before Alix could speak, he kissed her deeply. She welcomed his taste, his scent. No other man had such a rich, heady smell of leather and musk, of raw male sexuality. It whetted her appetite for him more than a prime steak set before a starving beggar. No other man would ever satiate her.

A wave of embarrassment engulfed her, but she shook it off. She had dreamed of this for so long, and she knew this would be her only opportunity to hold him, to love him. Tonight she would surrender herself to the world of make-believe and love him just as she had done a hundred times in her head. Only this time, it would be real. Devyn would be real.

Alix pulled him closer, running her hands over him, groping at the buttons that separated her hands from the hardness of his chest, the feel of his skin. She wanted to touch every inch of him, to hold him until dawn.

Gasping, Alix remembered the light. "Could you darken the room?" she asked, her voice breaking with her nervousness.

Devyn pulled back, his eyes glowing warmly. "Bashful?"

She nodded, swallowing the lump in her throat. In the dark, he'd never see her mark, and she wouldn't have to worry about him being disappointed with her missing feminine curves.

She watched him manually adjust the light.

"All the way down," she said when he started to leave it partially on.

He frowned. "I won't be able to see you."

Her heart hammered and she wished she could see him unclothed. But she would settle for just being able to feel him. "I know, but I prefer it that way."

He flipped the switch. Alix listened to him cross the room, then curse as he stumbled and something slammed against the floor.

"Damn stupid chair," he growled; then the bed dipped beneath his weight.

Smiling, Alix rolled over and grabbed him about the waist, pulling him closer. Tonight he belonged to her and her fantasies.

He lay on his back and she untucked his shirt, then gently began unbuttoning it from the hem up, kissing each inch of his warm flesh as she went. She inhaled the clean scent of his skin as she worked her way up the hardness of his belly, the solid planes of his chest, and over the tendons of his neck. Never had she tasted anything more delectable, more sweet.

Pausing over his hardened nipples, she licked the soft ridges, inhaling the scent of his flesh. He quivered beneath her and she laughed, unable

159

to believe her boldness, but unwilling to stop. She rose above him, dragging her breasts over his chest. Heat consumed her.

Devyn moaned, the sound vibrating his throat under her lips. Her body throbbing, she straddled his hips, delighting in the power she had over him, the foreign feel of him beneath her. Finally, she was glad Zarina had chosen a dress with a long slit.

Devyn slid his hands over her buttocks, her back, and up to her hair, where he pulled out the pins and let it fall over the two of them. Shaking her head to loosen the curls, she leaned into his hands. He caressed her scalp, sending a billion tiny electric shocks through her.

She licked his neck, delighting in the chill bumps that spread across his chest under her hands. Her lips brushed something warm and hard. Pulling back, she lifted her hands and searched the darkness until she held the small medallion she'd seen him wearing in the gym. Unable to see it, she traced the etchings with her fingertips and noted the raised, encircled cross.

Devyn's hands closed around hers and even though she couldn't see his face, she sensed his smile. "It belonged to my father," Devyn whispered, taking one of her hands to his cheek, where he brushed the back of her knuckles against the prickly stubble. "It's the symbol of St. Tirus, the Gelfarion patron saint of thieves."

"Of thieves?" she asked, remembering what he'd said about his expulsion from the HAWC.

Devyn's soft laughter echoed around her while he nibbled her fingers and sent deep waves of pleasure straight to her stomach. "My father has always been a very religious man. As a child he used to pray to St. Tirus for protection and one day an old priest gave him the medallion with a blessing. My father swears wearing it will keep me from harm."

"Do you believe it?" she asked, wondering if he shared his father's faith.

His teeth stopped their nibbling and his grip tightened. She wished she could see his face. But her only clue to his mood came as a gentle kiss in the palm of her hand. "I believe he believes it, so I shall always honor his faith by wearing it."

Pain burned inside her chest. Here was the type of man she'd always dreamed of, always wanted. A man who stood by those he loved, who would protect and love her. Why must she let him go?

Alix blinked back her tears. Tonight she would stay. No more denials. For once she would have what she wanted, conscience and fate be damned.

Devyn reached for her zipper, his warm hands touching her back as he slid the dress slowly off. Biting her lip, Alix arched against his hands, allowing him his way as he caressed her breasts.

Wherever he led her tonight, she intended to follow.

Devyn returned to her lips, claiming them fully. He stroked his hands over her body and she shivered from the demanding waves of pleasure pulsing inside her.

Hesitantly, timidly, she reached down to unbutton his pants, her knuckles grazing against the soft curls between his legs. Dare she continue?

*You've only got one night.*

The words echoed in her head. She peeled back the soft, silk pants. He sucked his breath in as she touched him. Caressing his hardness, she delighted in his moans.

Suddenly, he reached down and captured her hand. "If you don't stop that, you're going to be terribly disappointed."

Alix laughed at his breathless tone. She found it hard to believe that she could excite him so completely. Who would have imagined that someone as beautiful as Devyn could ever want someone like her?

Reaching up, she traced the roughened edge of his jaw. His whiskers prickled the palm of her hand, sending chills up her arms.

"You are incredible," she whispered.

He responded with a kiss. She opened her lips to taste him. She ran her hands through his thick hair, reveling in the strands that slid between her fingers.

He left her for a moment and removed his pants.

She gasped at the warmth of his naked body against hers. A wave of fear gripped her, but she pushed it away. There was nothing to be afraid of. Devyn wouldn't hurt her.

"Your skin is so soft," he mumbled, tracing the length of her waist. "Like the fur of a newborn verrago."

Alix smiled. Running her hands over his broad shoulders, she pulled him to her.

"Love me," she said with all the yearning inside her. She needed this proof that he cared for her, that at least for the moment he did love her.

Devyn separated her legs with his body and slowly started kissing a path from her belly to her neck. Alix arched against him, her body on fire from each touch of his tongue against her skin.

He kissed her breasts, running his tongue over them until she thought she'd die from the pleasure. And when he nibbled the sensitive flesh behind her ear, her body ignited.

Suddenly, he slid into her and pain stole all traces of her pleasure. Alix gasped.

He tensed. "What the—"

She stopped his words by placing the tip of her finger against his lips. "Love me, Devyn."

He took her hand from his lips and held it against the pounding beat of his heart. Tracing the tense lines of his muscles, she sensed a sadness inside him.

"Am I hurting you?" he asked.

Alix closed her eyes at the note of concern in his voice, and a small tear ran from the corner of her eye. "No," she lied, knowing the worst, most enduring pain she felt wasn't from his body inside hers, but from her own soul.

Slowly, he began to move against her hips. Alix ran her hands down his back, reveling in the muscles that rippled beneath her palms.

She'd had no idea that he would know this was her first time. Maybe she should have told him, but now it didn't seem to matter.

Besides, Devyn was the one man she would always love. The only man she would ever love, and she wanted to experience the most intimate of actions with him alone.

Devyn buried his head in her neck and inhaled the fresh scent of her hair. Never in his life had anyone offered him what Alix had given him this night, and he felt like the lowest of life-forms for having taken it. If only he'd known. But now it was too late.

She nibbled on his ear, sending waves of pounding pleasure through him, and he surrendered himself to the feel of her body wrapped around him. He'd waited so long for someone like Alix. Someone honest he could believe in. Someone who would never lie, deceive, or use him.

Her hands felt so good against his skin, like warm velvet sliding over him. He wished he could freeze this moment in time, relive it over and over again.

Gone was the emptiness inside him, the guilt and pain. Peace enveloped him like a warm cocoon and he knew Alix was the source. If he let her leave, he'd return to the misery that had become his life these last few years.

But how could he keep her? She wanted to go, and there was nothing he could do to prevent it.

Alix stroked the taut muscles of Devyn's neck. Her pain had melted into a new pleasure that demanded more of him. Arching her hips, she brought him deeper inside.

Never had she dreamed of such pleasure. Her body burned and throbbed, demanding more and more. Suddenly, her body tensed, pulling at him; then all her nerves exploded into waves of pulsing, blissful release.

She moaned with delight.

In the next instant, Devyn's body shook and his grip on her tightened. Alix smiled as contentment assailed her. She'd give anything to stay forever in his arms like this, with his breath caressing her cheek, sending chills down her neck.

Devyn withdrew from her, pulled her into his arms, and gently stroked her soft hair. Her head lay upon his chest and he could feel the beat of her heart against his stomach, her breasts against his ribs. Never before had he known such contentment. But how much longer did they have? Was she even now thinking of a way to tell him good-bye?

"Devyn?" she asked quietly.

Pain coiled in his stomach. He didn't want to hear her next words. "I know," he whispered, his throat closing.

Before Alix could say anything more, a whistle rent the darkness. "Yo, Dev, get to the ramp *now!*"

Despite the anxiousness of Sway's voice, Devyn couldn't help but feel somewhat relieved. Maybe this new crisis could keep Alix here awhile longer.

Leaving the bed, he felt around the floor until he found his pants, but before he could pull them on, Alix's voice stopped him. "No regrets, right, Captain?"

Devyn ached to touch her. He almost turned around and reached for her. But he mustn't. To touch her now would destroy his control and if that happened, he'd do whatever it took to keep her on board his ship.

"No regrets," he said, the lie catching for an instant in his throat. There was one regret he had, one that would forever gnaw at his soul— letting her go.

Throwing his clothes on, he left the room, refusing to look back.

*Concentrate on Sway,* he told himself. *Forget Alix.* Yeah, but how the hell was he going to manage that feat?

Devyn sighed disgustedly.

"Stop dragging your feet!" Sway snapped, pulling him forward. "This is really serious."

He frowned as he stepped out onto the ramp and faced a group of stern-faced Keepers. Scanning each one independently, his gaze locked on Irn standing at the rear of them, a smug smile splitting his ugly, greasy face.

Rage darkened Devyn's vision. What the hell had that *skagen* done now?

"Captain Devyn Kilaro-Maur Kell?" the lead Keeper asked.

He hated when people used his full name. It reminded him of his mother scolding him. Devyn clenched his teeth, trying to control his wrath until he learned more about the situation. "Yes?"

The Keeper handed him a wad of papers. "By order of the Grand Governor, I am impounding your ship. You and your first mate have been harboring a runaway slave and treating her as a freewoman. According to the HAWC Universal Law Code, I declare both you and your said mate slaves."

# Chapter Nine

"Do what?" Devyn asked, his anger snapping to the foreground. "What the hell do you mean—"

"There's been a mistake!" Alix said, cutting his words short.

Wearing her old, faded brown pantsuit, she stepped forward, her hair still tousled as she tried to comb it with her fingers. "I haven't run away from anyone. I belong to Captain Kell."

Devyn's mouth opened in stunned surprise, but he quickly caught himself and shut it. Could the Keeper's accusations be true? Had Alix been lying to him all this time? Putting his life, Sway's life, in danger? Bitter fury twitched his jaw.

*Don't jump to conclusions,* he warned himself. For now, he'd best act as if he knew what was going on and figure the rest out later.

The Keeper eyed him and Alix. "Do you have ownership papers?" he asked Devyn.

Steeling himself for the lie, Devyn nodded. "I filed them on Pikara with Emperor Calixei."

"Do you have a copy?"

Devyn looked at Alix, his sight narrowing. "No, but if you call the emperor and give him my name, he'll verify it."

Alix bit her bottom lip, her heart hammering against her ribs. Dear Lord, if the Keepers didn't buy this bluff, she, Devyn, and Sway would be headed for the nearest auction block.

This was all her fault! Why hadn't she left? Her lungs closed and she struggled for air, her panic making her legs shake. An image of Devyn's naked body being poked and prodded by potential slave buyers flashed before her eyes and she hated herself for jeopardizing him.

Glancing at Devyn and Sway and their unconcerned stances, she calmed a tiny degree. Maybe Devyn did know what he was doing. At least he had the brains to play along with her lie, but she'd never dreamed he'd go so far as to mention an emperor as a reference.

"He's lying," Irn said, elbowing his way past several Keepers to stand before her. His hate-filled gaze scorched her. "I own that *jarlia*."

Alix stepped back, her heart regaining its frantic beat.

# Sherrilyn Kenyon

The look on Devyn's face would have stopped any sane man from persisting. Alix quickly learned the extent of Irn's madness when he stepped forward, grabbed her arm, and pulled her toward him.

"Let her go!" Devyn snarled, catching hold of Irn's forearm. His eyes turned black as death. "Or do *you* have ownership papers?"

Hatred crackled between them, reminding her of a current of electricity dancing between two conductors. Almost tangible, its intensity reached out to all of them, and the Keepers stared in indecision.

Anger and vengeance smoldered in Irn's eyes, but he held his tongue. His grip tightened on her arm, numbing her hand, making her fingers burn and throb.

Alix trembled. She wanted to slap or fight him, but a slave was forbidden ever to strike a free person, no matter the provocation. As long as the Keepers watched, she was powerless to resist.

Curling his lip, Irn released her and jerked his arm away from Devyn's grip. "This isn't over, Kell."

Devyn raked him with a look that sent chills of fear all over Alix. "Don't try to intimidate me, *borixum*. It takes a hell of a lot more than the threat of a rat like you to fray my edges."

Irn spat on the ground next to Devyn's shiny boots. "Watch for me."

170

"Yeah, I'll keep an eye on my back, since it's what cowards prefer to attack."

Alix watched Irn's hands clench and unclench and she was pretty sure he imagined Devyn's neck under their pressure.

Certain only the Keepers' presence kept Irn from attacking, she still marveled at his control. She'd never seen him deny his primitive urgings before, at least not until a weapon dissuaded him. During the time Irn had spent on her father's freighter, he'd attacked their gunner at least once a week, usually over nothing more than the boy breathing out of turn.

Devyn and Irn continued to stare at one another in a typical game of male intimidation. Had the lead Keeper not stepped forward and pulled Irn away, they would have probably continued the game indefinitely.

The Keeper's gaze swept over her dishabille and Devyn's hastily donned shirt. By the condescending sneer on his face, she figured he had deduced what they had been up to before the disturbance. "Well, it looks like she does belong to you," he said slowly, giving Irn a warning glare. "We're sorry about the misunderstanding, Captain."

"No problem," Devyn said.

Holding her breath, Alix watched them depart.

Irn paused at the edge of her vision, and the glare he gave her made his intentions more than clear. He would be back.

171

She shuddered, her hands shaking with dread.

As soon as the Keepers and Irn had left, she turned to face Devyn and Sway. In Devyn's eyes she met her worst fear. Hatred glowed in the darkness of his eyes, flashing at her with such an intensity that she thought she might collapse.

"I'll collect my things and leave."

Devyn grabbed her by the arm, his hold so tight she was certain a bruise would form. "You're not going anywhere."

Sway stepped forward. "Devyn—"

"Leave it be, Sway. This is between me and Alix."

Alix looked at Sway, who offered her a sad smile, shook his head, and walked back inside the ship.

She swallowed the lump in her throat and faced a man she knew wanted to beat her. Would he? Could he be the same caliber as her father? Had he only been gentle in the past because he thought her a freewoman, not a slave?

"Devyn, please, you're hurting me."

Her words shocked him. Devyn loosened his hold a degree, but not enough to allow her to escape. No, she'd lied to him, deceived him, almost cost him his freedom, and he wasn't about to let her get away. "Why didn't you tell me?"

She wrenched her arm from his grasp and frowned. "Why?" she repeated, her voice heavy with sarcastic disbelief. "Isn't it obvious?"

Devyn wanted to throttle her, to tear her apart for not telling him the truth.

Was there not one woman alive who didn't manipulate men? Or was he just the unlucky buffoon who kept finding the ones who weren't trustworthy? "Get inside your room and stay there until after we've cleared orbit."

Anger leapt into her eyes. "You can't keep me!"

"No?" he asked, his fury making him more than unreasonable. "By your own words, you belong to me. Or would you rather run back to Irn?"

Panic flashed across her face a moment before she could recover herself, and a twinge of guilt tore through him. He stifled it.

"You bastard," she snapped.

Devyn grabbed her shoulders, pinning her back against the wall. "You've never seen me really pissed off, but if you don't get inside right now, you're about to learn why the HAWC called me a piece-hacker."

Alix's eyes widened and Devyn knew he'd finally found something that could bring her under heel. At least now she knew what his job in the HAWC had been—military executions. Granted, it wasn't the hands-on killing of an assassin, but either way the victim ended up dead.

Tears welled in her eyes, but she blinked them back and didn't even so much as sniff. Lifting her chin with pride, she cast him a menacing glare, then pushed him away, turned around, and sauntered into the ship.

Tempted to rush her along, Devyn knew it would be best to leave her alone for a while. He had to sort through this whole mess—and his feelings—before he could deal reasonably with her.

Pain tearing through his heart, he secured the ramp. Why was it every time he cared for a woman, she ended up lying to him, using him?

"When are you going to open your eyes, Kell?" he sneered. "At least this time you didn't get shot." His scar itched as if in reminder, not that he needed it. He'd more than learned his lesson the night Onone had called him a fool and aimed her blaster at his heart.

But the wound Alix had given him ran much deeper.

He *was* a fool. Twice he'd let a woman get to him and twice he'd been deceived. There wouldn't be a third time.

Sighing, he raked his hands through his hair. What was he going to do? He had three months' supply of food and medicine for the Jaruns in Paradise City who were in desperate need of his help. If he didn't get there soon, more people would die and it would be his fault.

He ground his teeth as guilt slashed at his conscience. He never should have stayed here this long. If only his mother hadn't been so insistent. If only Alix hadn't been so beguiling. For a few hours' pleasure, how many people had died? His gut knotted.

No more delays.

But Alix needed him. He cursed the wave of protectiveness that ran through him. How could he still want to protect her? "What is wrong with me?"

He clenched his fists, impotent fury running through him. Alix a runaway slave. Who would have thought?

Did Irn really own her? Had every single thing she told him been a lie?

He slammed his hand against the wall, pain slicing through his soul. Why had she made love to him? He remembered her smell, the way her hands felt sliding down his back. Closing his eyes, he trembled from the force of his memory. And once more he asked himself if it had been a lie, too.

Onone's face flashed before him and he damned himself multiple times for a fool. At least with Onone he'd had the comfort of being young and stupid. Now he was old and stupid.

Women. None of them was worth a damn. No doubt they were born with the skills of an accomplished liar.

If he had any sense at all, he'd hand Alix over to Irn and get on with his mission. But he couldn't. No matter how much he told himself to let her go, he knew he had to help her.

Growling low in his throat, he made his way to the bridge. First he needed to get them out of here; then he'd deal with Alix.

Alix stared at her face in the mirror. She'd scoured her skin until all traces of makeup had been removed. Gone was the temporary beauty Zarina had provided along with her tentative safety.

"You should have listened to yourself," she sneered, wringing out the rag, wishing she'd left on their arrival as she'd originally intended.

Now Devyn hated her and she was trapped.

Her gaze focused on the scar under her eye and anger burned through her. Damn it! She was a human being, a sentient creature, not a piece of property or cattle. She would not be owned. Not anymore.

No one would ever again hold her down and beat her, tell her what to do and when. No one would ever again have final say over her and her life. So help her, she'd kill Devyn if she had to.

Suddenly, bright, horrifying images tore through her—her mother begging her father to stop beating her, her brother's face the day her father sold him on the block, the way the buyers groped her brother's naked body and degraded him, the laughing face of her father while he allowed potential buyers to fondle her.

Hundreds of memories spiraled through her head in a dizzy kaleidoscope that brought pain, despair, and rage. The bathroom walls around her seemed to close in, to force the very air from her lungs. Panic dimmed her sight and she knew she'd lost control of her life.

"No!" she screamed, throwing her washcloth aside. "This is my life. You can't have it."

She had to get out of here. It didn't matter where she went so long as she was in control. No one could be trusted. No one. She must have her freedom!

Light-headed, Alix ran from the room toward the ramp.

Before she reached the hatch, Devyn grabbed her from behind. "What are you doing?" he asked, his arms wrapped around her like thick ginjy vines she couldn't escape.

"Let me go!" she shrieked, trying to kick and squirm from his grasp. "I'm not staying here anymore. You don't own me. I won't let you!"

Devyn swallowed at her hysterical tone. She acted as slanted as the worst lunatic he'd ever seen. "Calm down," he said gently, trying to soothe her with his voice. "You're all right."

"No!" she said. "I want to get off this ship. Now."

She elbowed him in the throat. Devyn let go with a curse, his Adam's apple throbbing. Grabbing his neck, he was tempted to knock sense into her.

What was wrong with her? She was acting every bit as psychotic as Onone.

She ran to the ramp, pushing at the controls.

Devyn caught her hands and pulled her away. "We've already launched. If you want to eject yourself into the outer atmosphere, fine. But don't smear blood and guts all over my air lock. I don't want to clean up after you."

Alix wrenched her arms away from him and slapped at the hatch, her panic melting beneath a wave of defeated tears. She was trapped.

Dear God, would she ever escape? Why had she signed on with Devyn?

Leaning against the wall, she sobbed into her hands, all her dreams shattering. Why was freedom too much to ask?

She should have run the first time she saw Irn on Nera. After her father had died, she should have sold their ship and settled for working in a small shop, or some other job that kept her out of space and out of Irn's reach.

She should have . . .

Sliding to the floor, she allowed her tears to fall unchecked. She was tired of fighting. So very tired. And why should she even bother? Where had any of it gotten her?

She wiped at her tears, hating herself for the weakness. Tears accomplished nothing; she'd learned that long ago during the nights she'd cried after her beatings. Tears hadn't brought back her mother or brother; they hadn't healed her bruises. All they did was swell her eyes and make them burn, and point out the fact that she was utterly alone and vulnerable.

Alix drew a trembling breath. Like it or not, this was her fate. A slave to be bought and sold on the whim of whoever owned her. And at the moment, that person was Devyn.

Devyn knelt beside her, but she refused the gentle touch he offered.

She curled her lips, and pushed him away. "I don't want your pity, *laigron*."

"I'm not your master," Devyn whispered.

She looked up at him, his face blurry through her tears. "Then what are you?"

"I used to be your friend."

She scoffed. "Slaves don't have friends. Oh, I forgot. You wouldn't know about that, would you? No one ever beat you or had your back branded. You grew up in your wonderful little family with all the money and freedom you wanted."

He couldn't have looked more shocked or hurt had she reached across and slapped him. "I don't know why you worry about my pity. You've got enough for both of us."

He rose to his feet, his eyes guarded. "Sit and wallow in your grief. When you're ready to talk this over, I'll be logging in my cargo."

Alix watched him leave, her heart heavier than it ever had been before, and she wished she did possess the courage to open the air lock and toss her useless self into space. No one would even miss her.

Why couldn't someone just hold her once? Just love her for one tiny moment? Must she always be alone?

Devyn checked the logs and did his best to ignore Sway, who sat on a nearby crate eyeing him.

"They're all counted. I don't know why you're still down here," Sway said.

"I want to double-check the seals."

Sway snorted. "You only want to double-check the seals when there's something you don't want to think about."

Devyn set the computer ledger down and glared at him. "Thank you, Dr. Porrish, and to think I might have paid an analyst several hundred *cronas* for that type of deduction."

"Don't be sarcastic. I'm not Rina or Alix."

Devyn tensed; he knew Sway's next words before the dorjani spat them out.

"The least you could do is talk to her. You know I don't like to meddle, but—"

"But you *are* meddling."

Sway smiled. "Yeah, I know. But you've got to understand how much I hate seeing you tear yourself apart for something you couldn't help. I remember how much you used to enjoy life. Ever since Onone, you walk around like a corpse looking for its grave. The only time you're happy anymore is when you've got a squadron of

Probers on your tail, or when you're around Alix."

Devyn looked up at him, his heart hammering over the fact that his emotions were so obvious. His mother had always commented on how easily anyone could read him. And he'd always hated himself for that.

Sway cleared his throat in an attempt to regain Devyn's attention. "Do you remember what you said to me eight years ago when I almost made the biggest mistake of my life?"

Devyn closed his eyes. He remembered his words only too well. *When there's something you want, you should go after it no matter how impossible or difficult the journey seems. Better to be defeated trying than to grow old wondering if you gave up too soon.* His father had said the same to him too many times to count, and he had relayed the message to Sway when Sway had walked out on Claria during their first year of marriage.

"This is different," he said, tugging at the seams of the nearest crate.

"Dammit, Dev, I don't know why you're being so stubborn. You need Alix, you know you do."

Devyn snarled and turned to face Sway. He noted the wariness in Sway's eyes, but not even that could quell his temper. "She lied to me!"

"She's a slave. Think of how she felt, what she must have gone through."

Devyn clenched his fists, wanting to tear something apart—like Alix's black, conniving heart.

181

"She should have told me. I had a right to know what I had taken on board my ship!" *And into my bed*, he added silently. "She used me like Onone did and now she can't even face me."

"I'm not a coward, Captain."

Devyn turned around to see Alix standing in the doorway. Restrained anger glowed in her eyes as she moved forward with that competent grace that still had a way of unnerving him.

"I think I'll go check the helm," Sway said, pushing himself off his crate.

Devyn returned to checking the crate seals, his soul torn between wanting to kill Alix and wanting to protect her. But what he really wanted was just to block her completely out of his mind and get on with the mission he needed to finish.

She moved to stand on the opposite side of the crate he was checking. "I'm ready to answer all your questions."

He looked up at her, but couldn't stand to see the emptiness of her swollen eyes. "Does Irn own you?"

"No."

Retrieving his ledger to make notes, he snorted. "And how can I believe you now? You lied to me."

"I had no choice."

Devyn paused in his writing and looked up at her. "Just like you have no choice but to lie if Irn really does own you."

Her gaze narrowed. "Believe what you will. I can't control your mind."

"Right," Devyn scoffed, finishing his tally and setting the ledger on top of another crate. "Now that I think back on it, it looks like you've played up to me from the very beginning. You knew which buttons to push to bring out my protectiveness. That simpering little smile, the way you keep your head cocked like you're afraid of cruel words. You really should give lessons."

Her lips trembled. "I never played games with you."

He slammed his ledger back on its peg. "Save it for the next fool you find. This one has retired."

Grabbing his arm, she turned him to face her. "How can you say that after what we've shared?"

The bittersweet memory almost sent him to his knees. She had done him far more damage than Onone. Onone had been the first woman to show him desire. Alix had restored his belief in the goodness of people. She had given him hope, then brutally snatched it away.

Now she brought up the brief time when he had actually thought she might care for him. He wanted to hurt her, to make her feel the pain that pounded through his body with every beat of his heart. "No doubt that was part of your hoax, too. What, did you have your virginity restored before you signed on board my ship?"

Alix tried to slap him, but Devyn caught her hand before she could strike his cheek. Blue eyes blazed at him and he almost felt guilty for his words, but the agony of betrayal kept the guilt at bay.

Dropping her arm, he curled his lip. "Don't ever try to hit me again. The way I feel, I might tear your arm off next time."

She lifted her chin, her eyes swimming in tears, and Devyn's control slipped. God help him, he still wanted to protect her, care for her, pull her into his arms and make love to her.

Once more he had the impression that she stood ready to take whatever slings life threw at her. "Don't worry, Captain. I'll keep myself out of your way."

She started to move away, then stopped and turned back toward him. "May I be excused?"

Her supplicant voice tore through him, wrenching his gut. "Yeah," he whispered.

When she reached the door, Devyn spoke the words that had been stinging his throat since the moment he realized she really was a slave. "You know, I could have helped you if you'd told me the truth when we met."

She looked back at him with the steeliest stare he'd ever received. "And now that you own me, your desire to help me has faded. How typical."

Angry with himself and the universe in general, Devyn glared at her. "I was—"

Something hard struck the ship and rocked them to port. Devyn caught himself against a crate, but the impact sent a wave of pain down his ribs. He pushed himself to his feet and started for the door.

Alix lay on the floor where she had fallen, her face pale, her eyes closed. Fear ripped through Devyn. Had she struck her head?

Devyn knelt beside her, pulling her closer. He cradled her head, but something warm and sticky covered his hand. Brushing her hair back, he saw the blood seeping from a gash just above her left ear.

"Alix?" Devyn asked, his voice cracking.

Her eyes fluttered open. "What happened?" she whispered.

Relief washed over him, tearing at the barrier he had tried to construct to keep her out of his heart. "I don't know. Something hit us and you fell and struck your head." He pulled the tail of his shirt out of his pants and tore off the bottom. He wrapped it around her injury, then helped her up. "Are you dizzy?"

"No," she said, her face still too white for his comfort. "Other than a ferocious headache, I feel fine."

Devyn smiled. "Okay. C'mon, I need to check Sway."

His anger forgotten, Devyn helped her to her feet and supported her against him.

In the hallway, he paused at a wall link and buzzed the helm.

"Yeah?" Sway asked, his tone worried.

"What hit us?"

"Don't know. It looks like we might have a small leak in the primary shieldings, but I can't find a trace of what collided with us."

Devyn looked at Alix. Her features were pinched and he figured her head must really be giving her hell. "Probably just space debris. Try to lock down the leak and I'll look—"

"I'll check the leak," Alix said. "I remember how well you checked the last one."

Devyn bit back the caustic response he yearned to make. She was right. "I need to check your injury."

She pushed him away. "My head can wait; the leak can't."

Devyn wanted to argue, but he knew it would only prolong her stubbornness. "Fine, you know where to go."

"Yeah," she said with an odd note in her voice. "I know *exactly* where to go."

He stiffened. "I didn't mean it that way."

Alix knew she shouldn't be so snappish, but for her life, she couldn't help herself. He didn't trust her. Probably never would again. So be it. She had too many other important things to worry about. Like how she planned to escape once they landed. Devyn would follow her, but there were ways to vanish that could elude even the most diligent trackers.

Irn paced behind his gunner's chair. "Did the tracker make it?"

"Aye, Captain," the gunner said, his whiny accent grating on Irn's ears. "Caught them just to starboard."

A slow smile spread across Irn's face. "Fall back," he ordered his navigator. "Give them plenty of room. There's no need to keep them in scanning range, and I don't want Kell to know he's being followed."

The tracker would signal Kell's whereabouts as well as feed him the full specs about the ship and its weapons systems. He'd find Kell's tender parts and when he did, he intended to amputate them.

Irn smiled at the thought. A few well-placed malfunctions and his prey would land right where he wanted. With a little patience, all his dreams of vengeance would come true.

And he had waited a long time already. He could wait longer.

His smile widened. By the end of the week, he'd serve Devyn Kell's head to Malena and take his leisure with Alix.

# *Chapter Ten*

Two days later, Alix lay on her bed, staring out her porthole and into the darkness surrounding their ship, the same darkness that now seemed to have settled in her heart and blotted her future.

At her father's funeral she'd been so naive, thinking all she had to do was find a new freighter to sign up on, and freedom would be hers. She'd thought her father's murder a godsend that liberated her from her past, but her life now was no better.

Devyn no longer spoke to her. The best she could hope for from him was a nasty glare. Each time he looked at her, a part of her heart shriveled. Maybe she should have told him the truth from the beginning. But she hadn't, and there was no way she could undo that now.

Looking back, she much preferred her father and his abuse. At least there had never been a time when her father pretended to care for her. She and Devyn had shared so much. He had been her friend, and now she sat alone and forgotten like an old toy during a child's birthday.

A knock sounded on her door. Alix sat up, her heart pounding. Maybe it was Devyn. Maybe he hadn't forgotten her after all.

"Come in," she called.

The door opened and Sway stepped inside. Deflated by disappointment, Alix lay back against the wall.

Sway came forward with a tray and set it on the table beside her bunk. "I thought you might be hungry, so I brought you some stew. It's not the best in the universe, but it hasn't killed me or Devyn yet."

Alix gave a halfhearted laugh. "Thanks," she said, taking the bowl. She wasn't hungry at all but she didn't want to hurt his feelings. These past few days, Sway had been unusually kind.

"You want me to get you something to drink?"

"Sure," she said, amazed when he crossed the room and pulled a bottle of water out of her cooling unit.

After handing it to her, he sat in the chair across from her bunk. "How's your head?"

"Better," she said, taking a bite of stew.

"Good."

He sat for several heartbeats staring at the floor while Alix ate her food. Her stomach was so knotted she had a hard time eating, and the silence didn't help any.

Finally, he met her gaze. "You know, I really miss seeing you in the control room. Devyn does, too, but he won't admit it."

Alix spooned the stew around the bowl. "Maybe he won't admit it because he doesn't miss me."

Sway laughed. "Nah, I know him too well."

Turning to face her, he watched her with such curiosity that heat slowly crept up her neck. "What?" she asked, wiping her chin in case some gravy had spilled on it.

He rubbed the back of his neck, a deep frown lining his brow. "I've been talking to Devyn for three days straight trying to make him see your side of this mess. Since he's ignoring me, I thought I might try you."

"Great. You sound like Zarina." Alix set her bowl aside, her stomach no longer able to handle any more. "I appreciate what you're trying to do, but it's a waste of time and energy."

He cocked a honey-colored brow. "Is it?"

"I think so."

"Then tell me what you want."

"What?" she asked in shock, staring at him. Why would he want to know something that personal?

He sat forward and leaned his elbows on his

knees. "Tell me what you want and I'll do my damnedest to get it for you. If it's freedom, I think I can arrange it. If it's Devyn, I *know* I can arrange it."

Alix stared at him in disbelief. No one had ever asked her such a thing, nor made such an offer. Devyn would have his head if he knew Sway was in her room trying to set them up for a relationship. And she had no desire to break up their friendship or cause a fight between them. "Forget it."

"Why? Are you afraid?"

"Yeah," she said, her voice cracking from the pain inside her. "I'm afraid. I'm tired of having nothing but disappointment."

He smiled, and despite her mood, a strange warmth spread through her. "Well then, you're due for a change of fortune. What have you got to lose?"

"Hope," she whispered, unsure if she could stand another loss where her heart was concerned.

Sway rubbed his legs. Watching him, she had a feeling he was wiser than either she or Devyn gave him credit for.

"You know," he said, "there's only a fine line between hopeful and hopeless. The one who keeps trying is hopeful. It's the person who gives up who becomes hopeless. Once you've accepted hopelessness you might as well be dead."

Pulling the pillow from behind her and settling

it in her lap, Alix scoffed. "Like you would know what it feels like to be owned."

Sway arched his brow. "Don't I? You've never been around dorjanie. A male has no rights or powers except those granted to him by his wife or mother. You have far more freedom as a slave than I do as a man."

Alix shook her head, sympathetic pain coiling in her stomach. She couldn't imagine anyone having a worse life than a slave, but from what Devyn had told her, Sway really did have it hard. "How do you deal with it?"

Sway laughed and tucked a braid behind his ear. "As a kid, I didn't even realize how much control my mother had over me. It wasn't until I started spending time with Devyn and his family that I realized his father had final say, not his mother."

Alix shifted, pulling her knee up to rest her chin on it while she listened.

"When we were fifteen, Devyn and Adron Kyrelle decided to join the HAWC. I wanted to join more than I have ever wanted anything, but only female dorjanie are allowed into the military."

She glanced up at the pain his voice betrayed and saw the sadness in his eyes.

He looked away. "That was the first time I realized how little control I had over my own life. Talk about feeling hopeless. Off they went to train and I was sent home on the next shuttle."

He sighed and stared at the floor. "A year later Claria decided she wanted me as her husband."

Alix looked up at him. "But you're happy with her?"

He smiled, his strange eyes warm and mellow. "Now I am, but our first year was hell."

"Why?" she asked with a frown. "Didn't you love her?"

Sway nodded, his smile turning wistful. "More than life."

"Then why—"

"Why do you think?" Sway sat forward, his gaze capturing hers. "I had to stay with her parents and I couldn't do anything without her permission. I couldn't even be left alone. Every move I made was watched, noted, and reported to Claria. After six months, I couldn't take it anymore. I ran and would have kept on running had Devyn not found me."

Alix smiled at Devyn's kindness. It was such a typical thing for him to search for a friend and help him. "He took you home?"

"No. Devyn talked sense into me and after I decided to try it again, he went with me and offered guardianship."

"He did what?" she asked, her eyes widening at his disclosure. "How could he do that while he was still in the HAWC?"

"Well," Sway said with a smile, "he had to get permission from the High Command first, and after his father donated a little money to their cause, they didn't seem to mind." His smile widened. "It was really weird to be the only civilian around all the cadets, but I got a free medical education out of it and I didn't even have to study."

Alix laughed.

Sway reached out, took her hand, and held it in his, his eyes probing hers as if he searched her soul for something. "So you see, Alix, I do understand how you feel. I can help you, if you'll let me."

Alix closed her eyes, her throat tightening. Devyn was the only person she'd ever trusted and look what had happened. Should she trust Sway?

Then again, what did she have to lose? If he could help her, wasn't it worth the risk of disappointment?

What did she really want?

Opening her eyes, she frowned. "I'm not really sure what I want anymore. Part of me still wants Devyn, but I also want my freedom." She stared into his eyes and spoke the truth. "I don't want to be owned. I can't allow myself to be owned."

Sway nodded and released her hand. "Devyn wouldn't keep you as a slave. He's got too much honor for that. Whether you two have a relationship or not, you'll get your freedom."

"How?" she begged, needing an answer. "What is he, a mythical god in disguise, or a fey who grants wishes by flapping his ears?"

Sway smiled. "It's not quite that dramatic. Devyn's the nephew of Emperor Calixei of the Trakerian Galaxies, and the godson of Zarina's father, who's the Kirovion Emperor. He will get you your freedom. If you had told him about this before we had traveled this far, he could have probably already freed you."

Alix sat still, her body going numb. Could her freedom be that easy, that close?

No. It was too simple. Nothing ever worked out that easily for her. Something would happen and she'd never get her freedom.

"Why would Devyn help me now?" she asked with a sigh. "He wants my head."

Sway frowned, confirming her suspicion. "Well, that's a harder problem. You never should have lied to him."

Frustrated, Alix lifted her arms. "How was—"

"I know," he said, putting his hand up to stop her angry flow of words. "I understand why you did it, but Devyn's not so easy to convince. He thinks you used him."

A lump of guilt constricted her throat. She had used him, but not the way he thought. She'd never lied about anything other than her status. "I didn't mean to use him," she whispered.

Sway nodded. He cupped her chin and forced her to meet his gaze. "Do you care for him?"

Her heart pounded, warmth flooded her body, and she knew she loved Devyn Kell, but she didn't want to admit that to Sway or anyone else. Admitting it was the best way to lose him.

Yet before she could stop herself, her mouth said, "Yes."

"Do you want him?"

The lump in her stomach tightened. "Yes."

"And are you willing to fight for him?"

Pain slashed through her soul. Was she?

Before her mind could think, the answer came from her heart. Devyn meant more to her than anything, and she'd do whatever she must to make him believe in her again. "Yes, I'm willing to fight."

He sat back. "Good, 'cause you're going to be up against the bitterest memories you can imagine."

His seriousness sent a shiver down her spine. What memories? Were they the same ones that kept him up at night, saddened his gaze when he thought no one watched him? "What do you mean?"

Sway chewed his nail and frowned as if debating what he ought to tell her. "How much has Devyn told you about his military career?"

Shrugging, she glanced up at the ceiling. "Only that he was a physician and he was discharged for theft."

Sway laughed. "Good old Dev, he always leaves out the best parts."

Alix scratched her ear, more confused than ever. "So what happened? I can't imagine Devyn as a thief."

Sway's eyes darkened. "Oh, he stole, all right, and I helped. We were taking military supplies and giving them to starving, sick civilians."

"He felt guilty about being a piece-hacker?" she guessed.

Sway cocked his head. "He told you about that?" he asked in disbelief.

She nodded.

"Incredible," he whispered breathlessly. "Normally he won't even talk about that with me."

Alix wasn't interested in that at the moment. She needed to find out what had happened to Devyn. "So the HAWC caught you two while you were leaking supplies?"

His face tensed. Alix held her breath, knowing this was what she had waited for.

"No, we were betrayed by Devyn's lover."

Her breath left her as if she'd been struck. Pain coiled through her at the thought of Devyn being with someone else. Part of her wanted to put her hands over her ears and block out the rest, but the other part of her knew she had to listen, to understand.

Unaware of her feelings, Sway continued, "Onone pretended to share our concerns about the civilians. While Devyn broke codes and accessed files, she wrote down the alarm sequences, then went in after we left and stole classified information and weapons. When Devyn found out, she tried to kill him."

Horror filled her, dulling her sight. Who could do such a thing to Devyn?

"No," she breathed.

"Oh, yeah," Sway said, nodding. "She shot him and in reflex, he returned her fire. Luckily his aim was better than hers."

"He killed her?" she squeaked, remembering the scar on his chest, the one that barely missed the bottom half of his heart.

Sway nodded. "And he hasn't been near a woman since. Not until you."

A knot formed in her stomach. Everything fell into place and her heart sank. "And I lied to him," she whispered, all her good intentions dying. "He'll never forgive me."

"Yes, he will. But it won't be easy."

"Alix!"

Both of them jumped at the shout over the link. Alix's heart pounded against her breast. "What in the universe?" Getting up, she crossed the floor to the link and switched it on. "What?"

"Get to the control room, now." The heated tone of Devyn's voice could have defrosted meat.

"I think I'll go with you," Sway said, and she was more than grateful for his offer.

By the time she reached the control room, her knees were knocking from fear. What had she done now? Her palms were so sweaty, she couldn't even access the door to the control room.

"I've got it," Sway said, stepping forward and placing his palm over the plate.

The door slid open and they walked in.

Devyn faced them, his eyes piercing her. "Cute trick."

Alix frowned in confusion. "What trick?"

He approached her, backing her up several paces, dwarfing her with his size. If he was trying to intimidate her, it worked.

"You turned down the atmosphere in my quarters. I almost froze solid before I could get dressed and get out."

Her mouth fell as disbelief washed over her. "I didn't do it."

He curled his lip and raked her with a sneer. "Then I guess Sway did."

"I didn't do anything," Sway said.

Devyn looked at Alix and she almost took a step back in reflex. But this time she held her ground, knowing she was right and hadn't done anything wrong. "I didn't do it."

His eyes turned even chillier. "I guess the computer is holding a grudge against me. Maybe it wants new chips."

"Very funny," Alix sneered. "It could be a glitch in the system."

"All right, Madam Expert," he said, sweeping his arm out like a majordomo. "Run the diagnostic."

Alix moved to the terminal and typed in the diagnostic sequence.

After several minutes, the system came up clean. "I don't understand," she whispered.

Devyn came to stand so close beside her, she could feel his breath fall against her cheek, smell his warm, clean scent. Goosebumps spread over her arms and neck.

"I understand," he said, his voice low, lethal. "But next time, you'd better curb your pranks. I don't appreciate them."

She glared at him. "I'll stay up and run a few more tests. Maybe the diagnostic is malfunctioning, too."

His menacing glare didn't change. "Yeah, you do that."

Alix clenched her teeth, wanting to throttle him. He could be so damned unreasonable.

After Devyn left, Sway scratched the back of his neck. "You want me to hang around?"

"No," she said with a sigh. There was no need for both of them to lose sleep. "I've got it under control."

"Okay. I'll see you in the morning."

For the next hour, Alix ran through test after test, but couldn't find anything that would cause the temperature in Devyn's room to fall. Sighing, she decided to give up for the night. She left the diagnostic on, hoping it would uncover something while she slept.

With each step that took her closer to Devyn's room and her own, her stomach drew tighter. Memories assailed her and she wished she could return to the day they'd made love. He'd been so gentle and caring. Not at all like the man who

200

accused her of playing pranks, who threatened her with bodily harm.

What would become of her? Was Sway right? Would Devyn free her? But then what would she do?

Grab a ship and start over. It was what she'd always wanted, but why did that thought now sear a pain in her heart? She knew she couldn't stay. Devyn would never forgive her for what she'd done. Sway's words were proof of that. She couldn't even blame Devyn for not wanting her around.

*Are you willing to fight?*

Sway's words echoing in her head, she stopped outside Devyn's door. The only thing to lose was hope, and she'd lived without that for so long that its loss didn't seem to be much of a deterrent anymore.

Too bad Zarina wasn't here. She'd know what to do to make Devyn drool. Alix smiled. On second thought, she was just as resourceful as Zarina and she had listened well.

She touched Devyn's door, the smooth steel icy to her touch. The wall Devyn had erected around himself seemed every bit as solid and unbreachable. But just like the real door separating them, all she had to do was find the right control to push and the door would slide open.

"I'm not giving up, Devyn Kell," she whispered. "Good luck setting your alarm against me. You're going to need it."

# *Chapter Eleven*

Devyn pounded against the door for the eighth time. His patience had long worn thin. "Computer, unlock the door!"

Still no response.

"I'm going to kill her!" he snarled, knowing only Alix could reprogram the computer to ignore his commands. Sway had never given a damn about technical things. Besides, it was Alix who had a reason to want to play havoc with his life and comfort. And after being locked in his small, cramped bathroom for half an hour, Devyn was more than ready to play a little havoc with Alix's health.

Suddenly, the door hissed and slid open.

Devyn stepped out before it had a chance to

close again. He'd had enough of this. Last night his room, today his bath. Snatching up his pants, he promised himself that this time she would regret her mischief.

After pulling on his tunic, he headed down the hallway.

Halfway to Alix's room, a strange feeling came over him. He couldn't explain it, but he had an immediate need to check their heading. It wasn't like him to be paranoid, but drifting off course happened quite often. Since he hadn't spent the night in the control room as usual, he had a strange urge to verify their position.

Turning around, he'd started toward the bridge when a whistle sounded.

"Devyn?" Sway asked.

He stopped at the nearest link. "Yeah, what do you need?"

"You're not going to like this. I need you at my nav station. Now."

Devyn frowned. Was Irn hailing them? Or maybe a Prober. What else could go wrong?

He growled low in his throat, tired of their delays. He just wanted to get to Paradise City, dump their cargo, then get Alix off his ship and out of his life.

So why did his stomach lurch at the very thought of her leaving?

"Because you're a fool," he muttered.

Sprinting the rest of the distance, he quickly joined Sway at the helm.

"What is it?"

Sway pointed to his tracking screen. "Last night when we went to bed, we were here," he said, indicating the coordinates on the outer right edge of the screen. "Now, we're here."

Devyn's sight dimmed. Disbelief ran through him, only to be quickly replaced by rage. "We're eight hours off-course?"

Sway nodded.

His breathing ragged, Devyn wanted blood. Minor drifting was normal, but their ship had turned around and was now heading toward the Skjold Sector. "Alix," he snarled.

Sway looked at him as if he'd lost his mind. "She wouldn't do—"

"No?" Devyn asked, his vision darkening. "If we'd slept two more hours, we'd be in orbit around Twrdr."

Sway's mouth dropped. Looking back to the screen, he made a few calculations.

"Sonovabitch," he whispered.

"Exactly," Devyn said, slapping him on the back. "She rerouted us so she could jump ship on the one planet that allows runaway slaves freedom from prosecution or extradition."

Sway shook his head. "And I left her here alone last night. I didn't even think about her doing something like this."

"That's because we're both too trusting," Devyn said between his clenched teeth. "But not anymore. I've had it with women and with Alix in particular."

"Wait," Sway said, grabbing his arm as he started to leave. "Maybe she didn't do it."

"Oh, then who did? The Tourah beast? Maybe we should conduct a search looking for little fey creatures who have decided to play games."

"You don't have to be so damned sarcastic."

Devyn narrowed his eyes. "I'm going to be a lot more than sarcastic when I get my hands on Alix."

Devyn grabbed a set of gyves from storage and headed to her room.

By now she should have known he didn't take well to delays. Every second that passed killed more Jaruns. Damn it, how could she be so selfish?

His gaze narrowed. He'd make sure she got her precious freedom all right, but she was going to wait until he'd finished his mission even if he had to tie her down.

Women! And to think he was stupid enough to believe Alix was different. She was every bit as petty as Onone had been. Right down to her little pranks to get back at him.

No more. She'd long regret her viciousness.

Opening the door, he walked into her room intending to shower her with the full barrage of his anger. But the sight of her curled up on her bed in peaceful sleep stopped him.

She lay on her side, her lips parted. Her cheeks

were flushed and her soft, tangled brown hair fell across her pillow like a shiny piece of satin. All too well, he remembered how the strands felt sliding between his fingers, brushing across his naked chest, the sight of her beneath him while her hands clutched him closer, driving him beyond slanted with their gentle caresses.

His body burned and his breath caught in his throat. How could he want her after all she'd done?

Dear God, it was Onone all over again. Just like her, Alix had him wrapped around her finger, a toy to manipulate at will.

But not this time. No. He'd learned his lesson when Onone's blaster had seared his side. Alix would not control him. He could block her from his thoughts and he could control his errant body.

Regaining his anger, he crossed the room in three strides and jerked the covers from her.

"Get up," he snarled, doing his best to ignore how angelic she looked as she blinked her eyes open and stared up at him in confusion.

"What is it?" she asked with a yawn.

Before he'd seized the blanket, he hadn't realized she wore nothing but a thin, short shirt. Now he couldn't think of anything except the way the flimsy white material displayed the curves of her body, the delicate, delicious pink tips of her breasts. His mouth dried.

The hem of her shirt stopped midwaist, and

from there down the only covering she had was a tiny, tiny pair of underpants. Underpants he wouldn't mind sliding off her soft, curving hips to explore what lay beneath.

His loins tightened and all he wanted was to pull her into his arms and make love to her.

Finally, she woke up enough to realize what he was staring at. Gasping, she sprang from the bed, grabbed the blanket out of his hands, and wrapped it around her.

"What are you doing here?" she asked, her voice indignant.

Devyn took a deep breath to steady his nerves and bring his body under control. He forced himself to remember why he had come.

"Did you think me so stupid that I wouldn't check our heading?" he demanded.

Her eyes widened. "What?"

"Or was locking me in the bathroom supposed to keep me occupied until you had a chance to escape?"

"What are you talking about?" she asked, trying to position the blanket over her to form a lopsided dress. "Have you been sniffing delutants?"

His breathing ragged, he wanted to take her over his knee. "No, I'm sober and I'm one step away from launching you out the air lock."

She crossed the room, nearing him like a professional fighter meeting an opponent. "At least give me a trial before you convict me. What crime are you charging me with now?"

Why was she playing dumb? Could she be innocent?

No. The ship was too new to have the type of malfunctions plaguing them. A human had to be behind it, and the only suspect was Alix.

"Did you or did you not alter our course to take you to Twrdr?"

Her mouth dropped. Shock and confusion darkened her eyes, but whether from surprise at being caught or honest astonishment, he couldn't guess.

Deciding on the first, he closed the distance between them. "I don't give a damn what you do, but you're going to wait until after we reach Paradise City. If you want to live on Twrdr, fine. I have no intention of stopping you. Hell, I'll even bring you back here. But you will leave this ship alone or I'll see you launched HAWC style."

The blood drained from her face.

"Do you understand me?"

Her lips in a tight line, she glared at him. "I didn't do it, you dense-headed slug."

Devyn pulled the gyves out of his back pocket. "Fine. I'll just make sure you don't *not* do it again."

Grabbing her right arm, Devyn snapped a gyve onto her wrist.

"Stop it!" she shrieked, reaching to claw him, but he held her hand away from his cheek.

Panic dimmed Alix's sight. She tried her best to push him away, but he dragged her across the floor and secured the loose gyve to the bar in the closet.

Screaming in fear and degradation, she slung her arm out to hit him, but he stepped back before she made contact. She had to get free. She couldn't stand the thought of being left in the closet.

"Calm down," he sneered. "No one's going to hurt you, but you won't mess with my controls again."

"I didn't do anything!" she insisted, hoping he would see the truth. Why was he being so stubborn?

"We'll see. If the malfunctions continue, I'll come back, let you go, and apologize. If they stop . . . then I guess I'll know your true nature."

Fury clouded her sight; her chest heaved with each ragged breath she drew. "You'll know my true nature all right, Kell. I don't take kindly to being bound. If you have any sense at all, you'd better send Sway to release me."

He moved to stand before her. "Don't threaten me."

She wanted to claw out his eyes. "I can't believe I ever cared for you. That I thought you were different."

A trace of pain drifted over his face so briefly she thought she might have imagined it.

"I'm the one who was lied to," he snarled, his eyes cold. "You used me to escape Irn and now you've tried to use my ship. If I had any sense

209

at all, I'd hand you over to that bastard and let him deal with you."

She pulled against the gyve, wanting to be free long enough to kick him.

Instead, she struck out at him with the only weapon left: her words. "Then do it. I'd rather be with Irn than you."

This time, there was no mistaking the pain his eyes reflected.

"Enjoy your rest," he snarled, and left her gyved in the closet.

Alix closed her eyes, letting her frustration flow through her. What was she going to do? She stared at the metal gyves, a wave of panic rushing through her. In her childhood, her father used to chain her to keep her out of his things. He'd leave her for days without food. Forgotten.

Hot tears fell down her cheeks, but she angrily brushed them away. She had to escape. Somehow there had to be a way out of this mess. Leaning her head against the wall, she allowed her anger free reign.

"I'll get you for this, Captain," she swore to herself. No one would bind her and leave her ever again.

Devyn glared at the light screen, his vision dimming. "Half our logs are erased," he muttered, pushing himself away from the terminal, disgusted with his failure. "Can you retrieve them?"

Sway laughed in response and looked at him as if he were slanted. "Sure, if I had a manual and a year. I can't believe that you, the only son of *the* Valerian Kell, infamous computer hacker, can't even figure out minor retrieval."

"Arr," Devyn said, raking his hand through his hair in frustration. "My dad didn't like me messing with this stuff. He was afraid I'd take after him and start hacking systems."

Sway sighed and punched a few keys, which did nothing. "Yeah, well, I do know one person on board who can fix all this."

"Right," Devyn said snidely. "The same person who erased them. No, thanks. I'll keep trying."

Sway drummed his fingers against the console. "Why don't you call your dad?"

"I tried, but there's interference. I couldn't get through."

A slow smile split his face. "I wondered why we hadn't heard from your mom."

"Don't bother me with your humor," Devyn muttered, rerunning the start-up program.

Sway gave him a look that let him know how much his friend wanted to say whatever was on his mind.

Sighing, Devyn knew he'd hear it sooner or later. Why wait? "All right, let it out."

"I think you're a real *prato* for what you did to her. When I took her lunch in, I couldn't believe my eyes. It's not like you to do something like that. You used to be fair."

211

"I used to be a fool." Devyn slammed his hand into the terminal and turned to face Sway. "Besides, I didn't shut her up in the closet; I did leave the door open. I just made sure she couldn't access any more computer terminals! And I can't believe you'd defend her after what she's done."

"You don't have any proof."

"What proof do I need? A huge sign—Alix Garran lied to you, *cotched* your files, played pranks, and altered your course?"

"You really should bottle that sarcasm. I bet you could get a fortune for it. Remind me to tell your mom she should have beaten your ass more while you were growing up."

Devyn snorted. "Why? I get it from her."

Sway shook his head. He opened his mouth to say something else, but before he could, the ship's engines sputtered to a stop.

"What the . . ." Sway said, flipping the backup power switches. "The engine's resource generator is out along with the main supply."

Suddenly, all power went out except life support and the dim emergency lights. Devyn's body grew hot as his temper exploded. "What has she done now?"

Sway looked around like a penitent receiving a sign from his Maker. "I don't think she did this," he said, drawing each word out.

"Bet me."

Devyn moved to the door, but there wasn't enough power left in the line to raise it. He opened the control panel under the switch and used the manual release.

"Wait," Sway said, following behind him. "I'm not going to let you make a fool of yourself. She couldn't have done this chained up."

"No, but she could have timed the engines to stall last night."

"Forget the sarcasm," Sway said, helping push the door open. "I think you should bottle your paranoia and offer it to government officials. Uh," he breathed as the door slid open.

He straightened up and pierced Devyn with a glare. "Here, ladies and gentlemen, never mind those rational fears that come with your job, take Kell's special dose of psychosis and you'll never again feel safe, even in the privacy of your own mind."

Devyn shook his head and headed down the hallway. "Maybe I'm due a little paranoia."

Sway grabbed him and turned him around. "Just remember, a little goes a long way. And you're about due a mental breakdown at this rate. Maybe I should section off a room and pad it."

"Keep it up and you'll find yourself bound next to Alix."

"Fine with me. She has to be more optimistic than you. Or at least I know she can't be any worse."

Devyn growled under his breath and started back down the corridor.

After forcing open the door to Alix's room, they found her huddled in the rear corner of her closet, her face so pale she looked like a specter.

"Are you okay?" Devyn asked, touching her forehead to see if she was feverish.

The eyes that looked up at him were filled with anguish, terror, and accusation, and they cut him deeper than a lason knife. He'd never seen such horror on anyone's face and he couldn't imagine what had her so distraught.

"Do you intend to take even my light?"

His gut twisted at her whispered words and the pain they betrayed. He felt lower than the bottom kriston fish. "I didn't do this. We have a power failure."

She sighed and looked so deflated he wanted to beat himself. Tears glistened in her eyes, but none fell. "And I guess I did this, too."

Devyn caught the I-told-you-so look from Sway. "Did you?" he asked.

"Sure," she whispered weakly. "I detached my hand while you were gone, belly-crawled to the lower deck and rewired the computer, then crawled back up here and locked myself up so you'd never suspect me."

Rolling his eyes, Devyn unclasped the cuff on the bar. "Do you two give each other lessons when I'm not around?"

Sway laughed.

Devyn inserted the key into the gyve on her wrist. A loud explosion sounded outside. The ship

214

rocked sideways, throwing the three of them into the closet.

"Ion cannon," Sway said, verbalizing Devyn's thoughts. "We're under attack."

Alix and her gyves forgotten, Devyn ran for the helm. Without power there wasn't much they could do, but he had to know who was out there.

Deep inside, he figured it must be Irn. Once more, Alix had dragged him into the middle of her fight.

The three of them took their stations.

"Alix," Devyn called, trying to pull up stats, "can you give me any power?"

"Not from here," she said, her face even paler. "I'll go below and see what I can do." She ran from the room.

Sweat dripped into Devyn's eyes. "Sway?"

"I can't do *merkid* unless Alix gives us some power. We don't even have defense shields."

"Can we open the hailing channel?"

Sway punched in keys, but nothing happened. He shook his head. "The only channel we have is the one to your Maker. I suggest you use the prayers your dad taught you and ask for a miracle."

Devyn lifted a brow, surprised by the words. "When did you turn atheist?"

Sway looked up at him, his face white. "I started praying to my God after the first shot. I just thought you might want to consult yours.

Between the two of us, we ought to be covered."

They sat in the stillness of the control room, waiting for something to happen, the power to switch back on, another blast to strike them. Anything.

But nothing else happened. The ship stood eerily quiet, not even the walls creaking. Only the sound of Devyn's racing heart filled his ears.

The lights came on so quickly, Devyn jumped.

"Good old Alix," Sway said, a smile curving his lips.

The hailing channel crackled. "Greetings, Kell. It would seem we meet again."

Hatred tightening his stomach, Devyn stared at his intercom, wishing he were this close to Irn.

Another blast struck their ship and set it rocking.

"Come now, Kell, where's your fight, your resourcefulness? I expected more from a Laing spawn. Don't you want to make your mother proud?"

Devyn clenched his teeth. *Stay calm,* he warned himself. Irn was just trying to make his anger override his intelligence. An old ploy, but a very effective one if he allowed himself to succumb to it.

Another blast. The ship spun about.

Devyn slammed into the console, bruising his thigh and hip.

"Aren't you going to fight me for the *jarlia?*"

Sway gripped his chair. "Another incoming!"

Devyn tensed, but this one sped past their ship.

He stared out the window, unable to see Irn or his ship, but he could feel the evil presence, smell the man's pungent odor every bit as well as if Irn stood before him.

He ran through his options, but without power, nothing worked. They were floating primmons waiting for the shark's bite.

He flipped on the ship's link. "Alix, do we have any power yet?"

"Just the lights. The last shot knocked out preliminary shields."

Clenching his fist, Devyn struck the console, his hand throbbing, but he didn't care. So help him, he'd get Irn for this and tear him into so many pieces no one would ever be able to tell he had ever been human. Not that he really qualified as human even whole.

"Give it up," he said to Alix. "Get back up here before you're hurt."

"But—"

"Do it!"

Sway looked at him. "You're not going to surrender?"

Despair engulfed him. If only he could think of something. Anything. "Do we have a choice? We have no way of escape or of fighting."

Devyn flipped on the channel, but before he

could offer peace, Irn's voice blared, "Prepare for boarding."

The *Prixie* pulled up in front of their visuals like a leech attaching itself to its victim's leg.

Sway shook his head. "I'm not looking forward to this dance."

Devyn snorted. "You think he'd believe our dance card is full?"

Alix stumbled into the control room, her breathing hard. "Quick, fire the rail guns."

Devyn made a split-second command decision. "Do it!" he ordered Sway.

Sway hit the release. A stream of gas shot out of their ship and into a nearby piece of debris. The impact sent the junk straight into Irn's ship and knocked it sideways.

"Yes!" Sway shouted, rising to his feet, his fists lifted in triumph.

Without thinking, Devyn grabbed Alix up into his arms and swung her around, laughing with relief. "What was that?"

She smiled down at him and he'd never seen anyone more beautiful, more creative. "I diverted the rail guns to project outside."

Her laughter lifted a weight from his chest and for a moment he forgot all their anger and remembered how she used to make him feel.

"Dev—"

Another blast struck them. Fire exploded throughout the room and all hell burst loose.

Devyn tried to shield Alix, but the impact tore her from his arms and slammed him beneath the console. Equipment erupted into flames. Wires and rods hissed and popped all around them. Irn must have hit them with a particle beam.

Devyn tried to move, but pain engulfed him, stealing his breath. He rolled over onto his side. The fire's stifling heat and the fire extinguishers' stench weighed against him until he feared he'd lose consciousness.

Forcing himself up, he looked about for Sway and Alix.

Through the flames, he saw Alix struggling to rise near the door. "Are you all right?"

She coughed and nodded. "I think so."

Relieved, Devyn scanned the debris until his gaze fell to Sway. He blinked.

No. It was the smoke; it had to be. Horror filled him, and he wanted to drop to the floor.

"Oh, God, no!" Devyn shouted, fighting his way to his best friend, his brother.

He knelt beside Sway, who lay under Alix's chair. A long piece of twisted metal protruded from his chest. Blood covered him and leaked from his nose, eyes, and mouth. This couldn't be happening. Dear God, please. No!

"Sway?" Devyn asked, praying for a miracle as he pulled Sway into his arms. He couldn't die. Not Sway, not over a mistake he'd made. *Please, don't do this to me!* his mind screamed.

Sway opened his eyes, and Devyn knew his friend had accepted the inevitable.

"It really h-hurts," Sway gasped.

Alix crouched beside them. "Oh, Sway," she said, her voice cracking as she brushed his braids away from his face. "Don't talk."

Sway looked at her, his face contorting from his agony. He reached out to Alix. "No more stew, huh?"

Devyn's heart wrenched. He'd eat that wretched stew for every meal if Sway survived. Pulling off his shirt, he wrapped it around the steel. "Hang on, buddy. I'll—"

"No," Sway said, grabbing his hand with the weakest grip Devyn had ever felt. "Get to safety. I'm dead, you know that."

Agony filled Devyn's soul, bringing tears to his eyes. Before he could move or deny Sway's words, Sway hooked the open end of Alix's gyves to Devyn's wrist.

"What the hell are you doing?" he asked, his voice mixed with confusion, rage, and grief.

A sad smile curved Sway's lips. "I owe you for Claria." He coughed, sputtering blood over Devyn's chest.

"Sway!" he shouted, wiping at the blood, frantic over what that blood signified. And there wasn't a damned thing he could do!

Devyn unbuttoned Sway's shirt. Maybe he could pull the rod out and staunch the blood before it was too late. "Fight this for me," he begged, unable to accept reality.

Sway looked up at him. "Tell Claria . . ." The light faded from his eyes and his hand fell away.

Light-headed, Devyn just stared, helpless, furious, hurt. This couldn't be happening. Tears fell down his cheeks, but he didn't care. He reached for Sway's neck, trying desperately to feel a pulse, any sign of life.

Devyn touched Sway's cold cheek, his soul on fire from guilt and agony. He couldn't even revive him; the metal was embedded right where he needed to push.

"You can't do this!" Devyn snarled, wiping at the blood on Sway's face. "Oh God, please. *Please!*"

Alix reached out to comfort him. She pulled him into her arms, amazed he didn't resist. He sobbed against her shoulder like a babe, and her heart pounded in sympathetic pain, her chest tightening to the point that she could barely breathe.

The ship lurched.

Loud hissing seeped into the control room along with the bitter smell of melting steel. "They're coming aboard," Alix said, pulling back. "We've got to get out of here."

Devyn stood up so fast he almost wrenched her arm out of the socket.

"Careful," she snapped, pushing herself up.

Devyn looked around the room, then jerked furiously at the gyve on his wrist. "Damn it,

221

where's the key to this thing?"

"I don't know; you had it in my room."

He closed his eyes and clenched his teeth. "We'll worry about it later. C'mon."

Leading her into a narrow corridor off the helm, he pushed her down into an escape pod. She heard the loud snap as the control room door gave way to Irn's torches. Devyn closed the pod's door and jettisoned them.

They drifted away from the *Mariah*. Devyn fired the engines and they ran, dodging the shots Irn directed toward them.

Alix stared at the *Mariah* as it faded out of sight and her thoughts turned to the friend they'd left behind. Poor, sweet, kind Sway. He didn't deserve what had happened.

Why couldn't it have been her?

Devyn's grief reached out to her as he programmed coordinates. She touched his rigid shoulders, knowing he wouldn't find any solace in her touch. No doubt he hated her even more for this. If not for her, Irn wouldn't be after them and Sway wouldn't have died.

She choked on her tears, refusing to let them fall. For now she'd be strong for Devyn and help him. There was no telling where they were headed or what new threat they would face.

She just prayed that somewhere nearby, there was a life-sustaining planet.

# *Chapter Twelve*

In a bright flash of light that blinded Alix's sight, the *Mariah* disintegrated and Irn's two ships headed toward them. Flipping the controls, Devyn flew them into a wormhole and out of Irn's reach.

She closed her eyes, drawing a deep breath of relief that at least for the moment they were safe. Yet Devyn sat before her more silent than the dark space outside, his grief hanging like a weight upon her shoulders.

"Is there a place we can land?" she asked, her voice seeming like a shout in the quiet stillness.

Devyn pressed keys, scanning the sector. "Sure," he said, his voice weary. "Placidity is within range."

"Placidity?" She smiled at the name. "It sounds nice."

"Great place," he grumbled. "We'll be lucky if the inhabitants don't shoot us on sight."

"Excuse me?"

He sighed and leaned his head into his hands. He looked so sad, so hurt, she ached. "They're religious refugees from Gelfara. They founded the planet's first colony almost two hundred years ago, and since then they've cut most contact with outside worlds for spiritual reasons."

She forced herself not to touch him and offer him solace. At the moment, he wouldn't welcome her touch. *Concentrate on his words.* "If they're so isolated, how do you know so much about them?"

"Zarina's brother, Tiernan, was assigned there a couple of years ago as a diplomat."

He tugged at her arm as he lifted his head and continued to type in coordinates.

His movement caused her breasts to graze up against his naked back and desire scorched her. *Don't think about those muscles.* But how could she not? Every time he moved, they rippled. And he was so close, so very close.

Her breathing erratic, she swallowed. She had to distract herself. "Why was he stationed there?"

"How the hell should I know? I'm not privy to Kirovion secret politics."

The anger in his voice cut sharper than a lason knife, but at least it curbed her desire. Alix sighed, her throat tight. "I'm sorry about Sway."

He faced her with a sneer that tore at her. "Don't offer me your pity or sympathy. Sway meant nothing to you."

Pain and shock consumed her. "You're wrong."

He snorted.

"Devyn," she begged, "I . . ." Her voice trailed off. What could she say?

He and Sway had grown up together. For the little time she had been with Devyn, she'd witnessed their close friendship. She couldn't imagine losing anyone that dear to her. "It must be like losing part of yourself," she said, then cringed as she realized she'd said the words aloud.

His body went rigid. "I was supposed to protect him," he whispered. "My God, I took an oath before his wife, his mother." His voice cracked. "How can I look Crill in the face and tell her that I let her eldest son die?"

Alix reached out and touched the hair at his nape, running her fingers through the silken strands. She wanted to ease the agony that drew his body tighter than a spring. "Devyn, it's not your fault."

He bowed his head and she sensed the tears that gathered in his eyes. "Yes, it is. If only I'd carried weapons on board. One Gellon torpedo and I could have blasted that bastard straight to hell." He slammed his hand down on the console. "If only we hadn't fired that damn rail gun."

She wiped the single tear that slid down his cheek, his stubble gently scraping her fingertips. "It wasn't your fault. Irn would have probably killed both you and Sway anyway."

His face contorted by rage, Devyn pulled at the gyve on his wrist so hard, Alix feared he'd sever his own hand. He turned to face her, his gaze accusatory and hate-filled. "If you had told me the truth about Irn and you from the beginning, none of this would have happened!"

"What?" she breathed, unable to believe what he had said.

"Don't look so shocked," he snarled. "Had I handed you over to Irn as I should have, Sway would still be alive."

Pain and guilt consumed her. "It's not my fault!"

"Then whose is it? Irn's after you, not me."

Alix clamped her jaw closed to bite back the words she ached to release. He was grieving. Just as her mother had done after her father had sold her brother.

Her mother had said horrible things to her, had blamed her for being born ugly and being worthless. Granted her mother had always preferred Piran to her, but it had still cut through Alix that her mother had blamed her for Piran's loss. That her mother would have grieved less over her being sold.

Tears gathered in her eyes, but she shook them away, refusing to feel sorry for herself.

Now Devyn blamed her for Sway. Maybe he was right.

She should have been honest with him from the beginning. Had she only known what her lie would do, she would never have approached Devyn that fateful day.

She looked down at her herself, her guilt gnawing at her conscience. Suddenly, she realized what she wore. Her eyes widening, horror engulfed her. She pulled at the hem of the T-shirt, trying to stretch it farther down over her stomach, at least enough to cover her underwear.

Oh, it was no use!

In the heat of battle and fighting with Devyn, she had completely forgotten to dress. Even so, how could she have forgotten something so important? How could it have taken her so long to notice? Her cheeks flaming, she looked up at Devyn's naked back.

She cleared her throat, wondering how to broach this matter. "Uh, Captain?"

"What?" he snarled.

She bit her bottom lip, apprehensive over disclosing this. "Didn't you say the planet we're headed for was founded by a religious sect?"

"Yeah, why?"

She swallowed, a bad feeling settling in her stomach. "And it's still very religious?"

He looked at her, his features disgusted, or highly irritated. "What are you getting at?"

She clutched at the neck of her T-shirt and braced herself. "How do they feel about nudity?"

"How do they . . ." His voice trailed off. Devyn looked down at himself, then at her. "*Mekra tionora frikalo.*"

Alix didn't recognize the words, but the tone said they were in trouble. "I take it they don't care for it."

"If they cared any less, they'd be Toryani."

Her eyes widened. Toryani were renowned for their strict moral and dress codes that demanded no amount of flesh ever be exposed other than their faces. And neither male nor female could wear any piece of clothing that in any way displayed the lines or curves of their bodies.

Her stomach knotted and she wanted a hole to crawl into. "What are we going to do?"

Ignoring her question, Devyn set the controls on autopilot, then tried to move past her. The gyve jerked, wrenching the flesh of her wrist. Alix hissed from the pain.

"Careful," she warned.

"Sorry," Devyn said to her utmost shock before moving more slowly, taking care not to hurt her again.

He opened a small panel just beside the hatch and pulled out a large, dark gray backpack, which he opened and dug around in. Finally, he produced a thin blanket, a black pair of pants, and a shirt.

Alix frowned as he dropped the musty-smelling clothes in her lap. "How am I supposed to put these on with my hand secured to you?"

Devyn glared at her, but his anger faltered as he scanned her scantily clad body. Just the sight of her drove his thoughts in one direction—south. No wonder the Toryani and Placidians deplored exposed flesh. It did have a way of distracting people.

"Do the best you can," he said, sitting down next to her with the blanket.

Alix sighed and began pulling on the pants, his arm brushing up against parts of her he'd rather not have touched in his current mood.

Strange how his anger gave way to other thoughts, especially when she reached around to adjust the waist, leaving his hand dangling over her buttocks, brushing against her soft, supple skin, and it took all his control not to remove her freshly donned pants.

Devyn's body burned. His mouth watered and he longed to run his lips over every inch of her and taste her smooth, sweet flesh.

"Why are these inside an escape pod?" she asked as she finally finished buttoning her pants and easing some of his discomfort.

He cleared his throat and lowered his gaze to the blanket. "There's a couple of days' worth of supplies kept in here, including a change of clothes and two blankets, just in case of an emergency like the one we're in."

She nodded and reached for the shirt.

Devyn tried to ignore the way his hand brushed up against her breasts while she struggled into the top. His breathing labored, he swore to keep his hand still.

But it wasn't easy and his body wasn't happy.

Her face flushed by frustration, she looked up at him, her eyes large and pleading. "I can't get my left arm in."

She reminded him of a little kid trying to tie her shoes for the first time. Hiding the smile that threatened to break, he draped the material over her shoulder.

She struggled with it for several minutes before heaving a disgusted sigh. "This is never going to work."

Devyn studied the way her entire left side stood exposed. He attempted to wrap the sleeve around her arm, but still too much flesh showed. "All right, I'll slit the seams and we'll sew you into it."

Happiness lit her face. "You've got a needle and thread?"

"Yeah," he said, digging in the backpack until he found the small sewing kit. He handed it to her. "But you'd better play seamstress."

She cocked her brow and looked as if she wanted to give him a lecture.

"It's not sexist. I'm right-handed," he said, holding their gyved hands up to remind her which hand was bound to her, "and I really don't think you want me that close to your body using a needle with my left hand, especially since I'm not handy with a needle to begin with."

"Fine," she said with a small smile. "Split the seam."

Which he attempted, but he quickly learned he couldn't do that left-handed either. He handed the knife to Alix, realizing as he did so just how much he was going to need her until they found a way to separate themselves. Great, just great.

"Do you think Irn will follow us?" she asked, her voice shaking as she severed the last seam.

"Probably." Devyn checked their coordinates and pushed his emotions out of the way until he had more time to deal with them. All except his grief. The loss of his best friend weighed on him like the thousand-ton Rock of Kiravar.

Alix reached to scratch her cheek, but stopped as she tugged against the gyve. "Sorry," she said, scratching with her right hand instead. "This really is a nuisance."

Devyn gave a short, sad laugh. "Leave it to Sway. He always did have a twisted sense of humor." Bitterness closed his throat. He'd sell his own worthless soul to have his friend back, to have Sway tell him one more time what a spoiled fool he was.

Alix fingered the gyve, and he sensed her sadness. He started to reach for her, but decided it wouldn't be a good idea.

"Sway told me how the two of you went through medical training together."

Devyn smiled at the memory, which tightened the lump in his chest. "Yeah, it took us almost a month to get HAWC approval. From that point on, I was joined to him pretty much the way I'm gyved to you."

The hurt look on her face tugged at his breast. "But you enjoyed yourself a lot more with him, I'm sure."

Devyn opened his mouth to speak, then shut it. Did he? Though he loved Sway like a brother, the dorjani had always had a way of getting under his skin like no other person. Over the years, there had been plenty of times when he had wanted to revoke his oath and send Sway home.

Now he wished he had. At least Sway would have been safe. Miserable, but safe.

He closed his eyes and let the pain wash over him, stealing his breath, breaking his heart. He had led his friend straight to death. No matter which way he thought it over, or how much he wanted to blame Alix or anyone else, he knew the full blame rested on him alone.

Looking at Alix, he studied her frown and the tiny dimple in her cheek as she threaded the needle, then began her awkward, uneven stitches.

The conversation seemed to make her uncomfortable, but he felt her desire to cheer him up and that alone went a long way in making him feel better.

Though why she would want to help him, he couldn't imagine. These last few days he'd been far from kind to her.

She looked up and he glanced away, ashamed she had caught him staring at her like a worshiping fool. "I'm surprised the HAWC let you have Sway along. He said dorjani males weren't allowed in the military."

Devyn slit a hole in the blanket's center, inadvertently jerking the gyve.

Alix hissed as she stuck her finger.

Frowning, Devyn pulled her hand to him and examined the tiny drop of blood on her fingertip. That small touch sent an electrical current through him that went straight to his loins and set fire to his blood.

He glanced up and caught the desire in her eyes, and for a moment he stood immobilized by it.

Never in his life had anyone made him feel like she did. Even angry, even sad, all he wanted was for her to hold him, to pull him into her arms and make him forget everything, to return him to that wonderful, contented feeling he'd had the day they'd made love.

*Love me, Alix,* his mind, heart, and soul begged. *Say the words aloud, you damn fool.* He opened his mouth to comply, but his throat tightened.

She didn't love him. She might desire him, but that was all, and that just wasn't enough

233

for him. He needed more than a physical lover. He needed a woman he could trust, a woman he knew would be there fifty years from now.

Closing his eyes, he let go of her finger and turned away.

He took a deep breath and returned to their conversation, ignoring the disappointed look on her face as she returned to her sewing.

Forcing himself to be still, he watched her hands weave the needle through the fabric. "Sway was lucky," he said, then paused to clear his throat and steady his voice. "I couldn't pass the physical to become an assassin, like I wanted. Since doctors don't see much front-line activity, the High Command decided it wouldn't hurt to have Sway tag along."

She knotted the thread, then bit it, her white teeth flashing in the dim light. Devyn's groin tightened. Too easily, he remembered those teeth nibbling his flesh.

She put the sewing kit away. "You wanted to be an assassin?"

Devyn smiled at the memory and fought his hormones. "Yeah. My father's best friend was a HAWC assassin."

She lifted a shocked brow. "Really?"

He nodded. "Sway, Adron, and I grew up listening to my uncle tell us stories of his exploits. Incredible stories about how he flew missions and returned as the sole survivor. Of how he could slip into a room, execute his mission, and leave so quickly that not even a monitor could trace him."

Her gaze returned to his and once more he had to squelch the need to kiss her.

"So you wanted to follow in his infamous footsteps?" she asked, her nose wrinkling in a most adorable way.

Devyn nodded. "Adron passed the physical and I—well, my hypoglycemia kept me out."

Her hand shifted beside his, jiggling the metal chain. "Were you close to Adron?"

He lifted a curious brow at her question.

"I've heard you and Sway talk about him before."

"Oh," Devyn said, wondering what she'd overheard them say. "Yeah, the three of us were very close. Adron and I were born two days apart and Sway was born a month later. Growing up, the three of us got into everything together."

Alix smiled. She'd give anything to know that type of camaraderie or belonging. Her only friend had been a small stuffed dog she'd found sitting on a dumpster one day when she went to pull her father out of a tavern on Kildaria. "What happened to Adron?"

Devyn's eyes darkened, his mood turning black. "Six years ago, his partner botched a mission and killed the wrong target. The victim's father retaliated by tearing Adron's partner apart. He wanted to kill Adron, too, but Adron wasn't home. So instead, he killed Adron's pregnant wife."

"Oh, my God," she breathed, unable to believe anyone could do something so horrible.

Anger burned in Devyn's gaze before he looked away from her, and Alix realized how much the matter still bothered him. "True to his upbringing and training, Adron went after the man, and he cut Adron apart, then dumped his body outside HAWC headquarters."

Her breath caught in her throat as her stomach heaved. No wonder Devyn looked so sad. Good Lord, he'd lost both his best friends to murder. "What an awful way to die."

"He didn't die," Devyn said, his gaze snapping back to hers. "I've never understood how he survived, but he did."

She shook her head, unable to believe anyone could survive something so horrible, so brutal. "Where's he now?"

"Holed up on his father's private planet. He survived the attack, but it left him crippled, and his wife's death left him insane. I tried to see him once not long after he'd been released from the hospital, but he lunged for my throat and swore he'd kill me."

"He what?"

"He said he never wanted to see me again and that if he did, I wouldn't live to regret it."

Her mouth dropped in stunned disbelief. "Why?"

He looked down and studied their hands. "I have no idea. I guess he blames me for not helping him go after her killer, but I was stationed on a battlefield fifteen light years away when it happened."

She reached out and touched him, brushing his hair out of his eyes, sliding her hand down his prickly cheek.

He looked up and the grief she saw on his face tore at her heart. "I guess Sway's better off dead than becoming what Adron is," he whispered. "I never thought I'd ever see our triad broken up, especially like this. God, how I miss them."

Alix pulled him closer. Just as she opened her mouth to kiss him, a signal beeped on the panel.

He jerked away so quickly she felt like an idiot.

"We're nearing Placidity."

Alix held her breath while Devyn landed the pod, her arm constantly jerked and pulled as he struggled with the controls. Though the pod bucked all throughout the atmospheric entry, Devyn managed a soft landing beside a picturesque lake.

"How beautiful," she said breathlessly, staring out the window at the greenery around her.

It appeared to be late afternoon, and a gentle breeze blew through the tall trees surrounding the lake. She'd spent the whole of her life traveling from one space station or landing bay to another, and never once had she seen anything like the countryside around them. She could spend eternity just looking at it.

Devyn joined her at the window and snorted. "Yeah, it looks like a wonderful place to die," he said, retrieving the backpack that held the second blanket, food, and other supplies.

Alix frowned. How could he say such a thing? She punched him in the arm. "Just my luck. I always wanted to be gyved to a pessimist."

Tugging his blanket on as a makeshift poncho, he led her out of the craft, pulling and snatching her arm as he went.

Once they were safely outside, she scanned the woods surrounding the lake and listened to the beautiful bird songs and noises the strange animals made. She smiled, inhaling the fresh, incredible air. This was the type of place she wished she'd grown up in. She could definitely settle on a planet like this.

She looked at Devyn, who had his left hand up to block the glare of the sun as he, too, scanned the area around them.

"Is there civilization anywhere nearby?" she asked.

He nodded. "According to the computer, there should be a city just past these trees. Maybe a three- or four-hour hike."

"City, huh?" she asked, skeptical over the readout. "I don't see any buildings."

Devyn lowered his hand and tossed the backpack over his left shoulder. "The Energumen never build over two stories. They're afraid anything taller will offend God."

"Interesting," she mumbled, hoping the residents wouldn't take too much offense over her dress. Though her body was covered, the stitches on the side of her shirt left a lot to be desired. It did cover her, in most places anyway.

"Just watch your step," he warned, "and be very careful what you say when we meet the natives."

She stopped, jerking him to a halt as well. "I know you didn't have time to pull up detailed files on this planet, and you acted like you didn't learn much from Tiernan, so how do you know so much about the natives?"

He pulled his medallion out from under the poncho. "My father is Gelfarion and a Postulational, a separate branch of their religion. I grew up in his church, listening to the Postulational priests condemn the Placidian Energumen for heresy against the faith."

Alix nodded, partially understanding. "Are there still En-u-go—"

"Energumen."

"Energumen on Gelfara?"

He smiled at her and her heart pounded. He had to be the most handsome man she'd ever seen. "A few remain, but they're so persecuted only a moron would announce it publicly."

"Hmm," she said, thinking back to his treatment of her over the last few days. "Gelfarions aren't very tolerant as a race, are they?"

Devyn snorted. "Show me any time in history when the Gelfarions have been tolerant either religiously or politically."

"Or individually."

He glared at her and she could tell by his eyes that he had caught her meaning. "Can we start walking again?"

Alix bit her lip. Heat suffused her cheeks and she hated what she had to say next. "Actually, I could use a tiny stop before we go any further."

"For what?" he asked, his voice heavy with irritation.

She knew her face had to be as red as the sun. "I've got . . . well . . ." She glanced up at the sky and tried to think of a way to tell him. "I need . . ."

Oh, this wasn't working. How was she going to say this to him?

Staring off at a nearby bush, she heard his groan.

"I wish I could beat Sway for this."

At the moment so did she. "I really can't wait much longer."

He sighed. "All right. We'll figure something out."

Alix led him to the bush. Maybe if they stood on opposite sides, it wouldn't be so bad.

She quickly changed her mind when she realized where his hand fell as she unbuttoned her pants. Looking up, she caught the hungry look in his eyes a moment before he averted his gaze.

"Would you please hurry?" he said, staring off into the forest.

How could she even start when her left hand had to dangle above her head?

"Could you please stop up your ears or something?" she asked.

Lightly, he jerked the gyve. "I can't plug my right ear unless you stand up."

"Then hum!" she snapped, so embarrassed and frustrated she wanted to die. "Do something so I'll know you're not listening."

"I can't sing. I've never been—"

"Devyn!"

He groaned, then broke into one of the songs he and Sway used to sing while they launched.

Realizing now why they had turned the music up so loudly, Alix finished as fast as she could, her stomach knotting with humiliation.

After she straightened and stepped around the bush, Devyn gave her a small grin. "I just hope we get ungyved before I have to go."

"Me, too," she whispered, despite a wave of excitement tearing through her at the thought. After their recent experience, she knew exactly where her hand would dangle on his body.

The thought must have occurred to Devyn as well. A deep blush spread over his cheeks.

"We need to get going," he said, glancing away.

Alix held up their bound hands. "Wherever you lead, I shall follow."

"Very funny," he said, pulling her forward.

They walked in a tense silence that had Alix fidgeting with her right pants pocket. So much had happened since the first time she had reluctantly approached him.

She could still see him standing under his ship, his handsome, confused expression burning a place in her heart, a place where no other had been before.

And the day they'd made love. Even now, she could smell the rich leather scent and her heart pounded. If only Irn had waited a little longer, maybe she would have escaped and Sway would still be alive.

"I'm sorry for everything I've done," she said past the bitter lump that constricted her throat.

Devyn continued to stare into the forest in front of them. "I'm sorry for what I said about Sway. I was angry at myself and I shouldn't have blamed you for it. I'm the idiot who was flying through blockades without weapons. Sooner or later, either me or Sway was bound to die. I'm just sorry he's the one who paid the price."

Alix rubbed the chills from her left arm. "My mother used to say how death always turned the survivors against each other. She said it's easier if you can find someone to blame other than yourself."

"Your mother?" he asked, a strange note in his voice. "I've never heard you speak of her before."

Alix sighed, pain catching in her throat. "I was afraid to. You can't imagine the shame that goes with being a slave."

"Sure I can," he said, his voice soothing her. "You can't help what you are, but I chose my path, my shame." His lips curled. "I'm such a stupid bastard. Sway's life wasn't worth my stupid obsessions."

Alix stopped him. She stared into his eyes, into the torment they reflected, and she knew she had to ease his guilt. "You have a noble cause you believe in. There's nothing wrong with wanting to help defenseless people."

He fingered her cheek, then looked away and started walking again. "What I do has nothing to do with those people, not really."

She frowned in confusion. "What do you mean?"

"I joined the HAWC for glory. I wanted people to whisper my name with reverence like they do Rina's father's. You should see the way people look at him, listen to every word that falls from his lips. It's incredible. Even my own dad practically worships him."

He glanced at her as they continued down the small path they'd found, and she caught a first-hand glimpse of the anguish that resided inside him. "Uncle Alexei was furious when Adron and I joined the HAWC. At the time, I thought he was jealous that we might overshadow some of his glory, but I quickly learned what had him so upset. What he had tried so hard to tell us."

His eyes turned black, empty. "The HAWC eats at your identity, tears out your innards, and feasts on your soul. You have no thoughts except the ones they dictate. I woke up one morning and hated what I saw, what I had become."

"A piece-hacker?" she whispered.

"Yeah. I clinically executed convicted enemies of the HAWC."

Tears gathered in his eyes and she stared in wonderment at them. He blinked them away, his jaw so rigid it looked like steel. "One day, a young woman, no more than eighteen, was sent to my termination center. She was accused of being a rebel leader on the planet where I was stationed to treat the wounded."

He took a deep breath. "My High Commander brought her to me with her death authorization. Without any fear, she looked me straight in the eye, smiled, and said, 'I die for a cause in which I believe. No authority rules me save my conscience. Are you so lucky, HAWCer?'"

Alix hugged his arm to her in an effort to cheer him. "Did you kill her?"

He shook his head. "I couldn't."

"So what did they do?"

Anger and agony mixed in his eyes, stealing her breath. "They called Onone in to perform the order. I was demoted and fined. If I'd had any sense, I would have walked out that day, but I couldn't. I had made a commitment and my parents taught me to respect my oath. But from there it only got worse. I started noticing all the death we caused in the name of peace." His lips curled. "It made me sick."

"So you run missions to save lives."

He closed his eyes and sighed. "That's what I used to think, but it's not true."

He clenched his teeth and looked up at the sky above them. "I've been so damned blind. All I do is delay the inevitable. So I bring in a few supplies, who cares? What I carry can only feed a few hundred for a few days. In the end, they die or surrender. All I do is prolong their suffering. And I killed Sway for a stupid ideal that doesn't exist!"

She stopped walking. "Devyn, don't."

He faced her, and she wanted to know the right words to soothe him, to take away the regret and blame that gnawed at him.

"Don't what, Alix? Blame myself? It's too late for that. For the first time in years, I see clearly again. My life has been useless since the day I was born a pampered babe. I couldn't accept it and now I've killed my best friend because of it."

"That's not true!" she said, cupping his cheek.

245

"No? Then tell me what happens? Where does the happy ending come in? That girl died even though I didn't perform the execution." His breathing scorched her. "Even if we had made the trip to Paradise City, how long could the people have lasted?"

She just stared at him, not knowing what the answer was, or how to assuage him.

"Answer me!"

She jumped at his shout and dropped her hand. "Oh, God, Devyn, I don't know. All I know is what I feel, and inside I know you're decent, that you do care. Why is it so important to you that you make a difference? The majority of people pass through life making only minor contributions. It's enough for them, why not for you?"

"Because I'm different," he said, clenching his fists. "I come from money and influence and I haven't done anything to deserve it. I snap my fingers and I can have anything I want."

"Is that so bad?" she asked, wanting to know why that of all things would bother him.

"Yes!" he shouted. "My parents clawed their way out of the streets, starving, scraping. I couldn't even survive to do what they did. If I go more than three hours past my time to eat, I shake and sweat and pass out."

She opened her mouth in shock. Who would want to be able to starve? "Starving isn't fun."

"How would I know?"

Alix closed her eyes and searched her heart and mind for something she could say to him, something that would help him. "You have made a difference."

"Oh, yeah?" he asked in disbelief.

"Yes," she said, her voice strong and sure. "If not for you, Sway would have left Claria and never returned."

"At least he'd still be alive."

Her throat tightened. "Maybe, maybe not. But he wouldn't have had all the happy years he followed you."

She held up their hands to show him the gyve. "Remember what he said: 'I owe you for Claria.' He loved you, Devyn, and so do I."

# *Chapter Thirteen*

Devyn stumbled, almost jerking her hand off.

Alix bit her lip, unable to believe she'd said such a thing.

He straightened himself and stared at her with an awe-filled expression and she waited for his response, afraid, yet finally hopeful that maybe he might feel the same way about her.

But he said nothing. He just continued to stare at her as if he were dreaming.

She couldn't take back her slip, so she moved forward, unloading the rest of her secrets. "You've made such an impact on my life that I can't even begin to thank you. You and Sway are the only friends I've ever known, the only laughter I've ever had."

His gaze hardened and he looked away. "You can't love me. I'm nothing but pribber bait."

"At times," she said, offering him a smile when he whipped his head toward her. "But there are other times when you're more than that, and those times far outnumber the rest."

He scoffed. "This from a woman I chained in her closet?"

Fury burned through her. "I didn't say I wasn't angry at you. I am. I'd like to punch you in the belly until you scream for mercy. But I understand why you did it. I know you feel you can't trust me. I just wish I could fix this."

He looked so sad, she thought *she* might burst into tears. He took a deep breath and clasped her hand. His gaze probed hers, pleading, searching. "Will you lie to me the next time you're afraid?"

"No," she said emphatically.

Closing his eyes, he shook his head.

She sighed, knowing the very thoughts in his mind. "I know you can't even believe that. For all you know, I'm lying to you now, lying about my love."

Running his hand through his hair, he looked at the ground. "I can't accept empty words anymore. I did it three years ago and a lot of people lost their lives."

She frowned, wanting to understand why he couldn't accept her love. "What people?"

He sighed, looked away, and dropped her

hand. Silence hung between them until she was certain he had no intention of telling her anything more.

At last, he rubbed the back of his neck and said, "For the sake of love, I refused to report Onone when I found out she was running weapons, drugs, and information."

He clenched his teeth. "I allowed her to learn codes and sequences I never should have broken to begin with. Then when Jayce found out and told me she had been selling the weapons to HAWC enemies and selling poison-laced drugs to our troops, I called him a liar."

He met her gaze and she saw all the hate that ate at him. "Onone had sworn the weapons were for civilians to protect themselves and that the drugs were being used to treat their children."

His breath came in short, sharp gasps and she wanted to stop him, but she needed to hear the story.

"Of course, I didn't believe Jayce. I thought he was jealous that I'd found someone sophisticated and glamorous like Onone. But after a while I started getting suspicious. Bigger, heavier weapons were disappearing. One day a KP-X 480 vanished, and two weeks later Jayce was wounded with a four-eighty round."

He curled his lip, rage burning in his gaze. "There's no other way the soldiers we were fighting could have gotten their hands on one. There were only four prototypes and only one had been stolen."

"Devyn—"

"Listen to me," he said, and she gave up trying to shield him from his pain. "After I dug the grizzle out of Jayce's side, I confronted her. She laughed in my face and called me a fool." His gaze hardened.

"Probably the only truth she ever spoke in her miserable life," he said bitterly. "When I told her I intended to report her, she pulled her weapon out and shot me."

The last two bitter words branded themselves on her heart. So much pain, so much betrayal. "I'm not Onone," she said, needing him to believe that she could never do such a thing, especially to him.

Indecision filled his eyes. "I know," he whispered, taking her hand into his again. "But I can't help what I feel."

He held her hand in both of his and ran his fingers over her knuckles. Waves of chills spread up her arms and she ached for some way to make him believe in her again.

"I care for you so much," he breathed. "It's just that I can't offer more than I can give, and right now friendship is the best offer I have."

Pain gathered in her throat, choking her. "It's not your friendship I want."

"I know."

She looked up at him, a new fear burgeoning. "Is it because I'm a slave?"

"No," he said, his gaze sincere. "I couldn't care less about your birth stats. Those can be changed."

Alix nodded, her heart a bit lighter. She knew she'd probably have to leave him in the end, but she didn't want to leave him thinking of her like he did Onone.

She wanted to prove to him that not all women were users, that she wasn't a user. But how?

"What would it take to prove myself to you?" she asked.

His eyes widened. Emotions played across his face—agitation, confusion, disbelief, and finally anger, the source of which she couldn't understand. "I don't know what it would take. And I don't want you to walk around like some altruistic Bremen sister looking for a good deed to perform. I just want you to be you. I would never ask you to be anything or anyone else."

Alix gave him a sad smile. She wasn't even sure if she wanted to be herself. The Alix Garran she knew didn't belong with a handsome runner.

If only she could be someone else.

"Okay, I guess we'll just wait and see what happens," she said, using the same phrase she'd used countless times to see her through the never-ending cycle of days when she'd lived under her father's fist.

Devyn took a deep breath and started walking again. The trail led them out of the trees and into a small clearing.

As they neared the edge, Alix heard leaves rustling behind them.

"You, there!"

They turned around and saw three big, burly human men moving toward them. One of the men held a rifle cradled next to his chest like a beloved child.

"Is there a problem?" Devyn asked, stepping forward a bit to keep the men from seeing their gyve.

The man who must have been the leader raked his gaze over them. His eyes hardened as he noted her dress, but Alix didn't think he'd seen their gyve.

"Yeah," he said at last. "We saw the crash and were wondering if you're the ones who fell."

"Yes, sir," Devyn said.

The man's gaze became stone. "What race are you?"

"Kildarion," Devyn lied, and Alix stared at him in disbelief. "We were attacked by pirates and our ship destroyed. If you have a space port, we'll gladly be on our way."

The three men huddled together and whispered.

"Why did you say Kildarion?" Alix asked under her breath.

Devyn glanced up at the men, then leaned

down to her. "They hate Postulationals. If I told them I was Gelfarion, they'd never help us. Besides, my mom's Kildarion; it's half true in my case."

She shook her head, a smile curving her lips. Half true indeed.

Slowly, warily, the men came forward. Suspicion darkened their eyes and their reluctance was more than obvious. "We don't have a space port, but the Emir has a shuttle for emergencies. I'm sure he won't mind. . . ."

The man's gaze focused on Devyn's medal.

Alix sneezed and the gyve jingled. Without thinking, she reached up to rub her nose, only to realize she'd used the wrong hand.

"Uh-oh," she whispered.

Panic contorted the man's features, drawing his brows together. Widening his eyes, he looked at her, then at Devyn. "Dear Lord preserve us. He's the Chaldese!"

"Dear Lord, no!" the man with the gun said an instant before raising the gun with his trembling hands and aiming it at her head.

Devyn pulled her into his arms and threw her to the ground behind a clump of bushes. The gun fired, deafening her to everything except the frantic beat of her heart.

Devyn scrambled up, then quickly fell when she didn't follow.

"Damn it!" he yelled, pulling at the gyve.

He looked up, stopped, and listened.

Alix couldn't hear anything other than a sharp ringing. She pushed herself up beside Devyn, but was too frightened to look for the men. If she had to die, she didn't want to see the shot coming.

Rising slowly to his knees, he looked over the bushes and scanned the area. He drew a deep breath. "They ran, but I'm sure they'll be back."

Alix sat back on her heels and allowed her stomach to unknot. She shook all over. Her nerves would never be the same. "What happened?"

Bewilderment covered his features. "I honestly don't know. He looked at my chest, then you, then . . ." Devyn pulled up their joined hands. "Chaldese," he whispered.

His confusion melted under a grimace of rage. "Somewhere up there I know you're laughing, Sway. But this isn't funny!"

"What are you—"

"They think we're the Chaldese!"

Alix frowned, not understanding any of this. "The what?"

He clenched his teeth, his features furious and frustrated. "The Energumen have a prophecy that a destroyer will one day fall from the sky and claim their souls and those of their children."

It still didn't make any sense. Did they kill everyone who crashed on their planet in fear of one stupid prophesy? "Why would they think you're this Chaldese?"

Devyn sat for a moment, gazing into the forest as if searching his mind for something.

Finally, he looked back at her. "If I remember my lessons, the passage is something like, 'From the sky shall fall one of man and one of woman. Joined together to appear as one, the beast of light and darkness shall claim the souls of all true believers. Marked by the sign of our enemy, it will portend the end of time.' Or something like that. Hell, my aunt used to taunt me with it as a kid, telling me she'd call the Chaldese to take me if I didn't obey."

He shook his head. "If only I'd known then that *I* was the Chaldese, I could have stayed up long past my bedtime and eaten all the cookies I wanted."

Alix didn't find his jest amusing. "I still don't understand why they think we're this destroyer."

He looked at her as if she were a slow-wit. "Falling from the sky. Joined together, one of man—"

"I get that part," she said, her voice heavy with sarcasm.

Devyn smiled. "All right, light and darkness could be our hair color, and this"—he pulled at his medallion—"could be interpreted as the sign of their enemy, since the Postulationals persecute them."

The knot returned to her stomach. "Oh, no,"

she breathed, disbelief filling her.

Devyn shook his head and groaned. "Leave it to me. I lose my ship, my best friend, my future, only to crash on a planet chained to the point I can't even relieve myself." He raked his hands over his face and grunted. "But that's not enough. Oh, no. Now the planet's entire population thinks I'm the beast who'll eat their souls."

Despite the seriousness of the situation, Alix burst into laughter. She laughed so hard, she thought her sides would explode.

"This isn't funny!"

She sobered to small laughs. "Sure it is. Come on, it's not every day you get to be someone's dire prophecy."

He smiled and pushed himself up. "I guess not."

Looking back into the forest around them, he sobered. "Come on, we need to get out of here. I'm sure they'll return with a group of priests and locals. And all of them will want our heads as a trophy."

She rose.

Devyn tugged at the gyve, his jaw clenching. "We've got to find some way to separate. Maybe if we can get to the Emir, I can explain how this happened. Maybe."

Alix nodded and followed his lead.

Within a few hours, they found the walls of the city. As they stayed within the forest's shelter and out of the guards' view, Alix swallowed at the sight before them. Staring up at the twenty-foot wall, she couldn't believe her eyes. "Why do they wall themselves up?"

Devyn shook his head. "I don't know, but my guess is there's something on the outside they don't want in."

She studied the wall and the guard posts that were situated every few hundred yards. "Or maybe there's something inside they don't want out?"

He laughed. "All right, play the optimist. But with our luck, I'm sure there's some kind of monstrous beast roaming out here in the woods and no doubt we'll find it right about its dinnertime."

With her luck, he was probably right.

Alix considered their situation. "Maybe we ought to go on in. Surely there's someone in the city who doesn't believe we're the Chaldese."

Before Devyn could respond, a gate opened. Several hundred feet from them, a military fleet rolled out: three armored vehicles, followed by six hovercraft bearing soldiers, a craft full of priests, and a number of civilians all chanting, "Kill the Chaldese!"

Devyn looked at her and cocked his right brow. "You were saying?"

"Do you think we'll give the big beastie out here indigestion?" she asked flippantly, then allowed a wave of impotent frustration to roll over her. "What are we going to do?"

"Despite the irony, I suggest we pray for a miracle." A pained expression lined his brow.

"Is something wrong?"

"No," he whispered, leading her deeper into the woods. "We need to find someplace safe to sleep, and I'll have to have some food in about an hour. Unless you think you can carry me."

Hmm, a prone Devyn could lead to interesting developments. Then again, with her luck, he'd just pass out right about the same time the locals showed up to burn her. "I think we'd best keep you fed."

Devyn paused and scanned the area. The soft breeze blew through his hair, giving him an almost mystical appearance. His finely sculpted features didn't belong to the real world, but to that of dreams. White-hot desire set her heart pounding.

How could she have thoughts like these when they were being tracked by maniacs?

Then again, if she had to die, shouldn't she be enjoying her last few moments of life?

Unaware of her thoughts, Devyn started walking again. "Okay, since I don't know their military habits, I'm going to assume they follow HAWC tactics. Which means they'll probably take a little time to investigate the pod, then spread out and search the area from there to the city."

"With the vehicles and numbers they have, how are we going to escape them?" she asked.

"I have no idea."

"Wonderful," she said with a small laugh. "Why not just sit here and wait for them to find us?"

He stopped, then moved so close to her she could feel his breath fall against her cheek. "Do you know how they execute?"

She shook her head.

"It's not like the HAWC, where they knock you unconscious, then administer poison. Instead, they give you parphinerol, which renders you paralyzed, but keeps all your nerve endings functioning. Then they take lason knives and start methodically cutting off pieces of your body."

Alix's heart hammered. Who could think up such horrible things? And what kind of person could perform such an execution? "Maybe we should try the east."

"Maybe we should."

They traveled for the next hour, stopping every so often so Devyn could scan the area around them and listen for sounds of their pursuers.

At last, they stopped in a small clearing and Devyn opened up the survival backpack.

Sitting beside him, Alix wrinkled her nose at the wide selection of condensed food that had been pressed into dull, gray tubes. Her experience with such compressed food told her that each tube would be nothing more than a tasteless blob of vitamins and nutrients.

"If the natives don't kill us, this stuff will," Devyn muttered as he grabbed a tube and squeezed it into his mouth.

Alix repressed a shudder, then grabbed her own tube. "Who makes this stuff?"

"Someone without taste buds," he said, curling his lips.

She laughed. At least his old humor was coming back. She'd missed that most in the past few days when he'd avoided her.

He stared out into the forest and she took the opportunity to study him. Even with dirt smeared down his cheek and his hair tousled, she doubted she'd ever seen a man who could compete with him.

How would things have turned out if Irn hadn't interfered? The thought of Irn brought a lump to her stomach. Worried over the natives, she hadn't given a single thought to him in quite a few hours. "Do you think Irn will land here?"

A slow, evil smile curved Devyn's lips. "I should have thought of that and told those guys to watch for my minions. Damn," he said, snapping his fingers. "Missed that opportunity."

He met her gaze and she saw the resignation in his eyes. "I'm sure he's already here and probably helping them track us."

His eyes darkened as he watched her.

Alix shifted uncomfortably, certain that dirt and sweat only made her look repulsive. Her eyes widened at the thought. Twitching her nose, she tried to see if she stank.

Devyn pulled back from her, his own gaze searching around them. "Do I stink?" he asked.

"No," Alix assured him. "I was afraid I did."

He smiled. "You're fine."

Suddenly, a loud growl sounded nearby.

She snapped her head toward it. "What the—"

Devyn pulled her up.

The growling moved closer. Retrieving a stick from the ground, Devyn held it awkwardly in his left hand. "I just hope this thing has eaten."

"Me, too," Alix said, standing just behind him so she wouldn't block his swing. "Maybe we ought to feed it tube food. That should kill it."

Devyn gave her a look that told her how little he appreciated her humor.

Twigs snapped.

Alix held her breath, her blood pounding through her veins. With one loud scream, the creature broke into their clearing.

"Ah, jeez," Devyn said disgustedly as the small furry rodent caught a whiff of them, then dashed back into the forest. "It's nothing but a verrat."

Alix took a deep breath to steady her frayed nerves. "Do they always make that much noise?"

"I guess. I've never been this close to one before."

She wiped the sweat from her brow. "Well, I hope I never get this close to another one again."

Devyn shook his head and they resumed their seats. "We need to make a few plans," he said, tossing away his makeshift club.

"I'm listening."

He took a drink of water, then wiped his

mouth. "The way I see it, there are three things we have to do. The first is to avoid the locals; the second is to separate; and the last is to get into the city and steal the Emir's shuttle."

Her mouth dropped. "Steal the—"

"I didn't say any part of it would be easy."

Easy? Was he insane? How could they possibly break in and steal a shuttle? "The Emir will have bodyguards, alarm systems. All kinds of things."

"Yeah, I know," he said, taking another drink. "But my dad was the best hacker and clinch in the universe. He never taught me to hack, but I managed to get him to teach me how to clinch a few security systems." He smiled. "I even managed to clinch the one my father designed for our house. Believe me, if I can break curfew and sneak past his system, I can breach anything."

The way he talked, she almost believed they could do it. Almost.

Besides, what did they have to lose? Her life wasn't worth much anyway. Come to think of it, the last slave dealer only offered her father a hundred and fifty *cronas* for her. Devyn's boots were worth more than her body.

They certainly couldn't stay on the planet, not with the lunatics who lived here.

"All right," she said with a resigned sigh. "After we get the shuttle, what are we going to do? Where are you planning to go after we leave here?"

"To Paradise City, as we planned. I was supposed to meet Taryn there."

"What?" she asked in disbelief. "I thought you met him on Nera to get supplies for *you* to take to PC, and now you're telling me he was traveling there all along? Why did we have to exchange cargoes?"

Devyn shrugged. "He couldn't carry the cargo. His father has a treaty with the HAWC that Taryn doesn't dare break. If I get caught with illegal substances, it won't cause an intergalactic incident."

"Oh," she said, and picked up her bottled water. "So I guess from there Taryn will take you home."

He nodded.

Her heart stopped. His obvious omission slashed through her consciousness, bringing a searing pain to her chest. "And what about me?"

Devyn continued to dig through the backpack, apparently oblivious to how she felt, what he'd said. "I'll talk to my uncle once we reach PC and get the paperwork started on freeing you."

The pain eased under a surge of happiness. "You're really going to do it?"

He looked up at her, his eyes sincere. "I'm going to try."

She smiled. "Then let's get going. I have no intention of staying a slave any longer than I have to."

Laughing, Devyn packed the backpack up and

they started once more on their trip.

"Wait," Alix said, pulling him to a stop. "Why are we still heading away from the city?"

"They'll be searching for us there. If we keep heading east, then make a large circle north, we should come in on a side where they won't be looking for us."

She bit her lip, scanning the area around them. "I hope you're right."

"That makes two of us."

For the next few hours they walked until Alix feared her feet would melt. She'd never been so tired. They had finally reached a wide, rippling stream and were currently traveling along it.

Yawning, she stumbled.

"You okay?" Devyn asked, catching her against him.

She nodded, her blood warming from the close contact of his body against hers. "Tired."

He looked up at the darkening sky. "I guess we should stop for the night." He set the back-pack down on the ground and pulled the blanket out of it. "I don't know how safe we'll be from the animals, but I'm pretty sure the Energumen won't look in this direction for a while."

Alix rubbed her wrist under the gyve where some of the skin was chafed. "You know, I've been wondering why they haven't sent out probe eyes or flyers after us."

He shrugged. "Maybe they don't have any."

"It's strange that they wouldn't."

"There's a lot about them that's strange," he said, then noticed her rubbing. He dug into his backpack and pulled out a medical bag. "Let's just be grateful they don't have any high-tech junk to scope us with."

Alix didn't comment as he rubbed cold, pungent-smelling ointment on her sore wrist. It tingled a little, but not as much as the chills that spread over her from Devyn's touch. His fingers stroked her skin, sliding under the gyve, over her hand. She licked her dry lips and remembered only too well the taste of his flesh, the feel of his hands on other parts of her.

He pulled out a bandage roll and cut a small piece, then wrapped it around her wrist, padding it.

"Feel better?" he asked.

She nodded, too afraid her voice would betray the path of her thoughts.

He returned the bag to the backpack. She studied his profile, wanting desperately to run her fingers down his stubbly cheek, her hand under his poncho to explore the muscles that lay beneath.

*Stop it*, she ordered herself. They were out in the middle of nowhere with a bunch of angry locals looking for them, thinking they were some kind of demon out to kill their children. This was definitely not the time for romantic thoughts.

After they ate another tasteless meal, Devyn pulled out the large knife and started frantically cutting at the chain on the gyve.

"I don't think that's going to work," Alix said, tensing as the blade came a little too close to her hand.

Without comment, he continued to try for several more minutes, sawing at the chain like a man possessed.

Was being gyved to her so abhorrent he'd rather cut his own hand off to escape her?

Growling, he put the knife away. "I'd give anything for a palm torch."

So would she.

Once Devyn secured the backpack, he started scanning the foliage around them, his features pinched and worried.

Alix dropped her tube, her stomach cramping. "Do you hear something?"

He shook his head and, despite the darkening shadows, she could swear she saw a blush creep up his cheeks.

"What?" she asked.

"I've got to go," he whispered so low she barely heard him.

She tried to keep her laughter inside, but a small laugh escaped. He glared at her.

"Sorry," she offered. "You sure did hold it for a long time."

"Well, I kept hoping we'd find some way to break apart before I had to."

His glare intensified. "Stop laughing or I'll never be able to do it."

# Sherrilyn Kenyon

Biting her lip, she allowed him to pull her to her feet, but she could still feel the corners of her lips curving up.

Devyn said nothing as he led her to a nearby clump of bushes.

"Want me to help?" she asked mischievously.

"No," he snapped. "Turn around or something." He fumbled with his pants, and Alix couldn't resist a small caress of the bulge just under her fingers. "Stop that or I'll get a kidney infection."

Alix moved her hand away.

"Not so far," he growled when she jerked on the gyve. "Don't pull me over."

"Sorry," she said meekly.

"Yeah, right," he said, his voice hard. "I know you're enjoying every minute of this."

What could she say? She actually was. "Not so easy with someone standing nearby, is it?"

"It wouldn't be so bad if you'd stop talking to me," he snapped. "Can't you whistle or something?"

Alix started whistling an old tune her mother used to sing. By the time she hit the third stanza, he'd finished.

"Let's get some sleep," he said, leading her back to the blanket. "We'll wake at dawn and see about finding a farm or small house."

"Yes, boss."

They lay on the ground, side by side. Alix stared up at the stars, trying to forget how good Devyn

268

felt next to her. How much she would love for the nerve it would take to roll over and kiss his stubbly cheek, his soft lips.

"This isn't working," he said with a sigh, intruding on her thoughts.

"What?" she asked, her face flaming.

He sighed and sat up. "I can't sleep on my back. Let's roll over."

"Roll over? On our stomachs?"

"Yeah."

Alix sat up beside him. "I can't sleep on my stomach."

"You've got to be kidding."

"No," she said defensively. "I hate it. Why can't you sleep on your back?"

He ran his hand through his hair. "Well, I always sleep on my left side."

"All right then, roll." Alix quickly wished she hadn't said that. They pushed and pulled at each other, trying to find some way to lie and not have their arms trapped.

"I can't breathe," she choked out as his biceps crushed her throat.

"Sorry."

He twisted his arm under her head.

"Ouch!" he grunted. "Don't tear the muscles off the bone."

She sucked her breath between her teeth as he wrenched her arm.

"Sorry," he mumbled.

"Wait," Alix said, sitting up again. "I have an

269

idea." She placed her hands on his chest as he started to sit up. "You get situated."

He rolled over onto his side.

Crawling over him, she lay on her back and draped his arm across her chest. "How's that?"

"Perfect," he said, his voice deep and husky in her ear, his breath falling gently against her cheek.

Her face tingled as she realized his hand cradled her right breast and he brushed his thumb over her taut nipple.

# *Chapter Fourteen*

Like electricity dancing along dried wood, Devyn's body erupted into flames and he forced his hand away from the delectable curve beneath his fingertips.

He hadn't forgotten how good Alix felt in his arms, but his memory had definitely taken some of the edge off the sharpness of reality. Now that she lay so close beside him, and her chest rose and fell beneath his arm, he couldn't control the thoughts singeing his brain.

Sleepiness abandoned him and he knew if he slept at all tonight he'd be fortunate. He'd been such a bastard to her, he didn't have the right even to ask for what he wanted. Yet he wanted her more than he'd ever wanted anything.

His gut wrenched at the thought of a future with her. What could he really offer her? Death. She deserved a lot more than that, and he couldn't stand the thought of holding her in his arms while she died. As he'd done with Sway.

Tears choked him, but he forced them down. All his years of medical training and he hadn't even been able to save his best friend. He was useless.

Alix deserved so much more than him. She needed someone who could keep her safe, hold her on cold nights like this and protect her from her fears, her monsters. All he could offer were even more demons to stalk her sleep.

Just what was he going to do once they left here? Right now, he wasn't even sure he wanted to go back to being a runner. But what did that leave?

Why couldn't he just bury the past and forget Onone and the HAWC? Sighing, he shifted restlessly.

"What's wrong?" she asked, her voice like a caress to his battered soul.

"I was just thinking."

"About?"

He sighed, trying to sort through his jumbled thoughts. But he couldn't quite express any of them, so instead he reached out to her. "What do you want out of life?"

"What?" she asked, her voice unsteady.

He stroked the graceful fingers of her hand,

the knowledge that she lay with him somehow soothing the agony of his soul. "Do you still want a freighter?"

She turned and looked at him and his insides quivered. "Sometimes I still do. But I think I'd rather have a life."

He frowned at her word choice. "A life?"

"Yeah," she said, her eyes shining in the darkness. "I'd like to have a purpose. Like you with your missions. I've been thinking about what you said and it makes a lot of sense. Too many people just go about their daily lives without ever making any kind of mark. I'd like to leave behind something that says Alix Garran passed this way."

He smiled. "I guess we all crave immortality. My mom always wanted it by having a huge family. She used to say that the best immortality was to survive in the memory and genes of your children, to bring a smile to their lips years after you've departed their lives. And have them trade stories about how you held them close on cold, scary nights, or made them feel better after a bad day at school."

"That's beautiful," Alix whispered. "So why didn't she?"

"Didn't she what?" he asked, not following her question.

"Have a big family? You're her only child, right?"

Devyn nodded. "Yeah, I'm the only one." He

fell silent for a minute, impotent anger washing over him.

He didn't want to tell her the reason, yet he couldn't stop the words from leaving his lips. "My mother was raped as a teenager and the bastard who did it messed her up really badly. She didn't realize how much damage had been done until she was pregnant with me. There was so much scar tissue inside that she almost miscarried me four times, and she had one hell of a time delivering me."

Alix ran her hand over his arm, her touch reaching far deeper than just the skin she caressed. "Your poor mother. That must have been horrible for her."

His throat tightened and he wished once more he could have protected his mother. "I think that's why she spent so much time with Rina's family. She used to gather us all close and just hold on like she was afraid of losing one of us." He laughed. "I was almost three before I realized they weren't my real siblings."

Alix laughed with him. "You're kidding."

"No. Adron and Jayce still call her Mom." The laughter faded from him. "My mom wanted so desperately to have more kids."

"Did you resent it?"

Devyn brought her hand up to his cheek and rubbed the back of her fingers across his face. He closed his eyes, savoring the soft skin. "No, I didn't. In fact I used to pray every night that she would have ten kids. I kept hoping a real brother or sister would give me more freedom, or ease the pain in her eyes every time she looked at a baby."

Alix pulled her hand from him and brushed his hair from his eyes. "She really loves you."

"I know. I've spent the whole of my life coddled and kissed."

Alix frowned at him, wishing she knew some way to ease the pain in his eyes. "Don't sound so upset. I would have given anything just to have my mother hold me."

He raised himself up on one elbow and stared down at her. "Why didn't she?"

Alix traced the line of his cheek as memories tore through her. Memories she would give anything to bury. "She couldn't. My father would attack her every time she came near us."

"Why?"

She shook her head, her throat tight. "I don't know. He was just so mean. I don't think he ever had anyone growing up and I don't think he wanted us to have anyone either."

Even in the dark she could feel the hatred in his glare. "Your father and beasts like the one who attacked my mother are part of the reason I wanted to be an assassin. I get so sick of all the useless violence. Why can't I do something?"

Alix snorted. "Excuse me, but I believe part of the useless violence comes from the assassins themselves."

Devyn sighed, his anger wilting beneath a wave of frustration. "I guess you're right."

Her laughter caressed his ears, sending a warm chill down his spine. "I think your desire to help clean up the world must come from having a bounder as a mother."

A smile curved his lips. "I know you're right about that." He fell silent, thinking over the last few years of his life. In all that time, everything he'd tried had only ended up making him miserable.

He sighed, disgusted with himself, with what he'd become. "I never thought I'd be this old and not know what I wanted to do with my life. Everything seemed so clear when I was a kid— do my homework, join the HAWC, be an officer and gain immortal fame and glory. Why does it have to be so frustrating now?"

She brushed her hands over his face, sending chills up his spine. "Well, I once heard an old man say half the battle is knowing what you don't want to do. Then just keep trying new things until you find the one you enjoy."

"Is that what you do?"

She looked away from him. "No. Until I joined the *Mariah*, all I did was survive. I never once thought about options. There aren't very many for slaves."

Devyn thought about that. Did anyone really have options? Zarina felt trapped by her parents as had her brothers and he. "Maybe we're all slaves when it comes down to it."

She gave him a sad smile that tugged at the edges of his heart. "I guess, but I'd much rather be a slave to my conscience than a slave to a man."

"Freedom is more than a corporeal state; it is a state of mind. A man can be free in the abstract, but bound more securely by his responsibilities and conscience than the one who is restricted against his will. It is the man who thinks his own thoughts and travels his own route who is the freest. Be true to yourself and no greater friend will you ever make."

"What?"

Devyn smiled and smoothed out the frown on her face. "It's something my father used to say when I was a kid. I haven't thought about it in years."

She closed her eyes and leaned into his palm, her lips gently brushing his skin, sending a wave of torturous desire through him. "It's amazing how things like that come back when you least expect them."

Devyn watched her, the way the breeze laced itself through the soft golden brown strands of her hair and spread them over her cheeks. He wished for a fire so he could look in her eyes and watch the emotions play inside them.

"But you know what I'd really like at the moment?" she asked.

Devyn shook his head. "I can't imagine."

# Sherrilyn Kenyon

"I'd like a nice, unexciting life without people chasing me."

"Yeah, right," he said with a smile.

Her eyes dulled and he saw the need inside her to have her dream. To live free of harm and danger.

He wanted to offer her his protection, to keep her safe and chase away all her bad memories, but he couldn't. Besides, she wasn't really free to commit herself to him, not until she went through emancipation proceedings.

The law forbade marriage between a freeman and a slave. Not that he cared much for the law, but he wanted her to come to him on her own terms, not offer herself because he owned her, or because she was afraid of Irn. He wanted her love and he wanted to know that she hadn't been lying when she told him she loved him earlier.

She shivered.

"Are you cold?"

"A little."

Awkwardly, Devyn pulled the backpack to him and jerked the blanket out.

She touched his hand as he adjusted the blanket under her chin. "Do you know you're the first person I've ever really talked to?"

He smiled. "Do you know you're the first person I've ever wanted to possess?"

She stiffened. "How do you mean?"

"Not as a slave, but as a companion. When I

278

think of the future, it's your face I want to see when I come home."

Instead of relaxing, she actually tensed more. "I'm not free, Devyn."

"I know."

"And no matter how much I love you, I can't stay with you unless I do have my freedom."

"I know that, too," he said, his throat tightening. "I wouldn't ask you to stay with me unless you were free."

"Then what are you asking?" she asked, her voice full of a need he wasn't sure he could fulfill.

"I want you to consider staying with me once you have your freedom."

"As your mistress, your engineer?"

"As my wife."

She turned away and he sensed a sadness in her that burned him, pained him. "What about trust? You said you didn't trust me."

He turned her back to face him and he tried to see into her soul. "Would you ever hurt me?"

She stared into his eyes and there deep inside her crystal gaze he saw the truth. "No, I could never hurt you."

The weight in his chest lifted and he felt light enough to soar. "I don't want to lose you to my stupidity. Sway was right. You do mean more to me than my ship, than my life."

Suddenly, there was a strange look in her eyes.

## Sherrilyn Kenyon

"What is it?" he asked. Could his words have hurt her?

She shook her head. "Nothing."

"Tell me."

Instead of talking, she answered him with a hungry kiss. Desire blazed inside his veins, igniting his loins.

Alix opened her mouth to taste him. She needed to touch him tonight, to know he meant his words, at least for this moment in time. She could never marry Devyn, but she loved him for the offer.

Love was a virus that ate at a person's soul, and once it devoured that, it spread to the heart and in the end, it left its victim weak and bitter. Dried up and cold. Her mother had loved her father at one time, and look at what had happened between them.

Maybe Devyn's parents had managed to nurture their love, but she was of a different type. She didn't know or understand how to love someone else.

What he offered was more than she could take. She had too much of her father in her for that. No. Devyn needed a woman who had grown up with love, who knew how to give.

For now, she would take the physical side of love, the side she understood.

Pulling off his poncho, she ran her free hand over the wide expanse of his shoulders.

Devyn moaned, leaning his head back.

She nipped at his throat, her body afire with the heat of her desire. Tomorrow they might be found and terminated, and if this was her last night, she wanted to enjoy it to its fullest.

Devyn unbuttoned her shirt, then cursed when he realized it wouldn't come off.

"Want to cut it again?" she teased.

"Maybe I should bite it off."

She laughed until he lifted up her T-shirt, dipped his head, and nibbled on her breast. Fire radiated from his lips, dancing down her spine, tightening her stomach and bringing a longing throb. Moaning, she ran her fingers through his hair. Everywhere he touched, she burned.

She resented her bound hand. She wanted to run her hands down his spine and hug him close.

He peeled her pants off, then pulled back to stare at her. "You are beautiful in the moonlight," he said, bringing a sudden warmth to her breast.

"Love me," she whispered.

He removed his pants and returned to her, his body warming hers. His tongue danced over her neck, her jaw, sending wave after wave of throbbing heat in a hundred directions over her body.

He ran his hand down her side, caressing her skin and seeking out the aching throb that demanded his touch, him. She moaned from the

281

magic of his fingers and she wanted more.

Finally, he separated her legs. She opened her eyes and looked up at him. Never in her life had anyone made her burn as he did.

"Love me," she said, reaching up to partake of his warmth, his gentleness.

When he slid into her, she arched, her body quivering in ecstasy. She rose to meet each of his thrusts, delighting in the feel of raw strength that surrounded her.

Could she really leave him? The thought tore through her, scalding her soul.

Did she have any choice? She didn't want to live in his memory as Onone did, a bitter reminder of someone he shouldn't have involved himself with.

If she stayed, he would grow to hate her the same way her parents had hated her and each other.

Though she wanted to stay, she knew better. She could never cause him pain.

Holding him close, she resigned herself to this little bit of time with him and surrendered herself to the love blazing between them. She lifted her hips to draw him in deeper, needing to feel his fullness inside her.

Suddenly, her body tightened, then burst. Shaking, she gasped in wonderment. Wave after wave of ecstasy tore through her.

And with two more thrusts, Devyn joined her release.

He lay atop her, breathing heavily in her ear. "I need you," he whispered, nibbling the sensitive flesh of her neck.

She rubbed her cheek against his, adoring his rough whiskers. She closed her eyes and savored the feel of his strength surrounding her, lying atop her. If only they could stay like this forever. If only fate could be her friend.

Devyn pulled the blanket around them and returned to their comfortable position. She laid her head in the hollow of his shoulder and listened to his heartbeat slow. Caressing his steely muscles, she tried to envision living without him. Pain gripped her heart, squeezing it tight. Tears formed in her eyes and she begged herself to stop. Too late, a tear slid past her control.

"What's wrong?" Devyn asked, stroking her cheek.

"I was just wondering if you would regret knowing me," she whispered, hating herself for the trembling fear in her voice.

He kissed her forehead and chills spread through her. "I could never regret being with you."

She swallowed the lump in her throat. *I bet he'd have said the same thing to Onone when he made love to her.*

"Alix, please don't cry," he begged. "I didn't mean to hurt you."

"You haven't hurt me. I just feel sorry for myself."

He rested his cheek on her head and caressed her face. "What can I do?"

"Hold me."

His arms tightened around her and she lay for hours just listening to him breathe.

She stared at him while he slept.

Images drifted through her mind: images of them together in old age; of Devyn coming home to her and a house full of children; of festive dinners spent with his parents; of a lifetime of nights like this one, nights spent in his arms, listening to his soft, easy breathing.

And sometime long after the moon had reached high above her head, she, too, finally fell asleep.

Irn glared at the Emir, wanting to tear the man apart. "If you'll allow me—"

"I have already told you, we don't allow airborne crafts to search here. If you can't respect our customs and laws, you may return to your vessel and wait for us to find the Chaldese on our own."

Damned zealots. What could he do with them? He'd tried for hours to talk sense into them, but they wouldn't listen. He could have found both Kell and the whore long ago, but if he deviated from the Energumen traditions, the Emir had made it plain what he'd do.

"It can't hide from us for long," the Emir said, his voice full of confidence. "Tomorrow we'll bring out the verdogs and they'll track it down. Don't you worry. Our ways may not be in keeping with the advanced ways you're used to, but they've served us well for centuries and they don't offend God." He waved his ringed hand. "Now retire for the evening. We start early in the morning."

"Yes, Your Excellency," Irn said, making sure to keep his sneer to a minimum.

Leaving the Emir's tent, he made his way to the edge of the field where his men had erected canvas-covered dwellings for them to rest in overnight. He curled his lips. Not even a woman to ease his needs. How he hated religious people.

Well, it didn't matter. They would provide him with the grisly death he wanted for Kell. Too bad Alix had to suffer the same fate, but at least she, too, would be punished for her acts, and that was all that truly mattered to him anyway.

"Sleep well, Kell," he whispered. "Tomorrow I intend to feast on your roasted flesh."

# *Chapter Fifteen*

Devyn came awake with a start. He sat up so quickly, he almost jerked both his and Alix's arms out of joint.

"What's wrong?" she asked, her voice heavy from sleep.

"I thought I heard something." He stared into the forest, but couldn't see anything stirring, or hear any other noise. "Guess I'm getting paranoid."

She rose to her feet, taking care to keep the blanket wrapped around her. "Well, I need a bush break. That is unless you want to finish pulling my arm out of its socket."

Smiling at her surly tone, he stretched. "Be nice, or I'll get you back for your tug last night."

While she went about her business, Devyn glanced across the nearby river. The soft hiss of the water beckoned him like a lover. "You know, I could really use a bath."

"So could I," she said, standing up again. "Do you think the water's safe?"

"It should be. Of course, there could be huge water snakes or overgrown algae that like to feast on humans. Maybe even a water dragon."

He watched fear flicker across her face, then disappear under a wave of suspicion. "You're not funny."

"Yes I am, you're just not a morning person."

She rolled her eyes. "Lead me to the water before I decide to drown you."

"Ah, I know better. If you killed me, you'd have to drag my rotting corpse around."

She scanned his naked body, and a blush darkened her cheeks to the loveliest shade of pink he'd ever seen. "How can you walk around naked?"

"HAWC training. First thing they knock out of you is modesty. Why, does it bother you?"

A small smile curved her lips. "No, not really."

"Good," he said, pulling the blanket off her, scooping her up, and tossing her over his shoulder. "'Cause it would be difficult to bathe fully dressed."

"Wait!" she shouted. "I've still got my shirt on."

"It'll dry."

She laughed as he dipped them both into the water.

Her laughter died as soon as she touched the icy chill. "Oh, it's cold!" she said through chattering teeth.

"It's not so bad. Good wake-up water."

She stared at him as if he were mad. "I was awake enough. You didn't have to freeze me."

Devyn opened his mouth to retaliate, but caught a flash of silver from the bank. Turning his head, he saw a group of men and women step out of the forest and line the bank around them.

Alix gasped as she, too, caught sight of their scowling faces. Devyn stepped in front of her to shield her from the strangers and their curious stares.

"Is it the Chaldese?" a woman asked, stepping back, her hands clutching her throat as if to ward off a demon.

The man who must have been the leader looked at Devyn and Alix, his eyes widening as he saw their gyve. "Notify Gannon we've found them."

"Devyn?"

He looked at Alix, a hundred thoughts playing through his mind. Did he have time to scramble up the bank and disarm the man?

Maybe, but not with Alix gyved to him.

"We mean you no harm," the leader said, slinging his weapon up over his shoulder. "We've come to help."

Devyn cocked his brow and narrowed his gaze on the man. Should he trust them? "How can I be sure?"

The man smiled. "Do you have a choice?"

Looking at Alix, Devyn's sighed. "I guess if they wanted us dead, they'd have already shot us."

"I guess, but I still don't like this," she whispered.

Devyn nodded his agreement, then turned to face the leader. "We're not wearing any clothes. Could you get our things?"

A woman came forward with their clothes bundled in her arms and placed them on the bank. Almost in unison, the group turned their backs.

"You must hurry," the leader said. "The Emir's troops are moving closer. We must be back in our commune before they get to this area."

They left the water and dressed as quickly as they could.

Devyn straightened and admired the way Alix's wet shirt clung to her hardened nipples. His body stirred and he was grateful he'd already dressed. He didn't need any more embarrassing moments.

She finished buttoning her pants, then looked up at him, her eyes resigned.

He gave her an encouraging smile before moving toward the leader. "Why are you helping us?"

The leader turned around and faced them, his face blank. "We don't believe the same things as the Urbanites. We figured you must be crash survivors who only want to return home, not the Chaldese who wants to eat the souls of our children."

Devyn gave a half-smile. "Very perceptive."

The man laughed and extended his arm. "I'm Braw."

"Devyn Kell," Devyn said, taking his hand and shaking it. "This is Alix Garran."

Braw frowned. "Your wife doesn't share your name?"

Devyn started to correct him, then caught himself. Better not offend the man until he found out more about their beliefs.

"We're newlyweds," Alix said, planting a kiss on Devyn's cheek. "We both keep forgetting."

Braw smiled. "Welcome, then. We must move."

He led them toward the northeast and into a secluded valley. Mountains loomed up all around and each footstep echoed down the winding trail. Once the trail ended at the base of the largest mountain, Braw opened a concealed door that led to the interior of the mountain.

Wooden beams reinforced by steel formed an intricate rib structure to support the hollowed-out corridors. They passed a number of closed doors and several curious passersby who stopped and stared in awe.

"Ever get the feeling they're leading us to our doom?" Alix whispered to him, grabbing onto his biceps.

Devyn covered her tight grip with his hand in an effort to reassure her. "I think we'll be all right."

He offered her a smile, but she didn't return it.

Braw stopped outside a door and pressed an intercom. "I have them."

"Then enter."

The door slid upward to display a large glass desk and a man no older than Devyn. They stared at each other, measuring, assessing.

After a moment of scanning the maps and terminals in the room, Devyn realized what was going on. This had to be some sort of military base. The men and women around him were rebels not involved with the people after them.

The man rose slowly to his feet. "Are you a transplenum?"

"Yes," Devyn said, remembering the archaic word which meant "from another planet" as he led Alix into the room. He still wasn't sure if these people would help them or not, but at this point, he and Alix had little to lose.

"Then be welcomed." He moved around the desk and lifted their gyve by the chain that connected the cuffs. A frown lined his brow. "How is it you two are bound?"

Devyn smiled and looked at Alix. "It's a wedding custom. During the attack that destroyed our ship, I lost the key."

Sherrilyn Kenyon

Gannon laughed and clapped him on the back. "I understand." Looking past Devyn's shoulder, he focused his light stare on Braw. "Find a pair of wire cutters and have food—"

"Gannon, help me, please!" a woman shrieked, rushing into the room from a door located behind the desk.

Devyn watched panic play across her features. A small child of no more than four years lay cradled in her arms, coughing and sputtering for breath.

Gannon paled at the sight. "Dearest God, protect him."

Suddenly, Devyn realized it wasn't normal choking. Something had the child's airway blocked.

"What's wrong with him?" he asked, pulling Alix forward as he moved to the child.

The mother looked up, tears streaming down her cheeks. "It's a mysterious illness that has stricken our people these past months."

He had to do something; a few minutes more and the kid was as good as dead.

Devyn took the child from the mother's arms and laid him on the desk. Handing the backpack to Alix, he said, "There's a piece of clear tubing. Dig it out of the first-aid kit."

Gannon grabbed his hands. "What are you doing to my son!" he demanded.

"I'm a doctor," Devyn said, trying to clear the child's air passage with his fingers. "And if this

292

kid isn't helped quickly, he's going to die."

"Nay, Lord," the mother pleaded to Gannon, "he's the Chaldese. He'll claim our child's soul!"

Gannon shrugged her away and stared deeply into Devyn's eyes. "Can you help him?"

"I hope so."

Gannon released his hands. "Then do it."

Nodding, Devyn clenched his teeth and tried everything he could think of to open the child's throat, but some form of grayish mucus had it sealed tight.

The child continued to cough and wheeze until Devyn wanted to shout from frustration. He'd never before seen such a dense covering and he couldn't seem to pry it free from the child's throat.

"Hand me the scalpel," he said, holding his hand out to Alix.

Alix just stared at him.

Groaning, Devyn dug into the pack and found the laser scalpel. It had been a long time since he'd performed surgery, and his right hand twitched. He prayed his hands remained steady, his touch precise.

Alix sneezed, her body moving. His right hand jerked with her.

Devyn cursed. There was no way he could make the cut with her tied to him. One sneeze during the procedure and he'd kill the boy.

He looked up at her and by the fear in her eyes he knew she had already guessed what he wanted. "I need you," he said. "I can't make the incision with our hands joined. You're going to have to use your right hand to do it."

"Me?" she squeaked.

The child convulsed, his skin turning blue.

"He's going to die."

Alix bit her lip to steady herself and took the scalpel from his hands. She'd never in her life done anything like this and she prayed Devyn knew what he was doing.

"Cut here and here," he said, showing her an X cut over the child's throat. "I'll mop the blood."

*I won't pass out,* she told herself. Taking a deep breath to steady her nerves, she made the cut, cringing with each slide of her wrist. Blood rushed out, and Devyn quickly wiped it with a tissue and inserted the glass tube into the child's throat.

Her stomach twisted and heaved. She cringed as he began pumping blood and mucus up through the tub with a small hand pump. She'd never seen anything more disgusting. How could he do it? Shivering, she turned away and swallowed, hoping *she* would live through this.

Once the child began breathing through the tube, Devyn straightened up and padded around the tube with more tissue. He returned to the child's mouth and began scraping more mucus out.

She couldn't stand it anymore. Her knees buckled.

Devyn caught her, his heart pounding against her breast. "Be strong for me. I need you."

Those words worked a miracle.

She raised up, fighting nausea. If he could stand doing it, why couldn't she stand watching it? Gripping the edge of the desk, she promised herself she'd do whatever he needed.

He taped the tube to the child's neck, then moved to check the child's temperature and pulse.

Devyn looked up at her and smiled. "Good job, Alix. With hands like those, you ought to be a surgeon."

She warmed at his compliment, but judging by the way her stomach twisted and her legs shook, she knew she'd never survive training.

"I think he's going to make it. Now I just need to figure out what's wrong with him." Devyn looked at the mother, who cried in Gannon's arms. "What are his symptoms?"

She wiped at her eyes, her nose red and swollen. "It started with a sore throat, and his neck ached; then earlier today he started coughing and coughing, and finally this . . . this happened."

Checking the child's eyes, Devyn asked, "Don't you have a doctor?"

"In the city," Gannon said, his face drawn and pinched. "Our commune doctors are only medical technicians who have very basic medical

295

training. Our three surgeons never involve themselves with illnesses. We save them for battlefield emergencies."

Frustration burned deep in Devyn's eyes and Alix wished she could soothe it.

"Do you know what it is?" the mother moaned.

Devyn sighed. "Sore throat, fever, coughing, swollen lymphs. It could be about three thousand different things." He ran his hands over the child's body, poking and prodding, and dragged her hand right along with his.

The boy's body convulsed a moment before he opened his eyes and looked at Devyn, his face panicky.

Devyn smiled at him and stroked his cheek. "What's his name?"

The mother moved forward to touch her son's forehead. "Jory."

"Hi, Jory," Devyn said as the child continued to stare at him.

"No," he said gently, grabbing the child's hand to keep him from touching the glass tube. "I know it's not comfortable, but it needs to stay there for a little while."

Jory looked at his mother, tears welling in his big brown eyes, and Alix's throat tightened at the pain he must be in. She would give anything to relieve it.

"It's all right," his mother said, her own eyes brimming with tears. She looked up at Devyn, her gaze worshiping. "Thank you for saving him."

Devyn raked his hand through his hair and Alix could sense his anguish. "It's not over yet. I have no idea how to treat this." He looked over his shoulder. "I don't guess anyone here knows what it is?"

Gannon shook his head. "Not even the city doctors know. We've taken a few of our people to them, but they couldn't help them. They say it is the will of God because we are rebelling against the Order, and they have refused to treat it."

"I love new illnesses," Devyn said tersely.

Alix brushed his hair back from his cheek and offered him a smile. "Isn't there some kind of universal antibiotic that can treat this?"

Suddenly, Devyn smiled, and Alix could see the idea even as it formed. "Are there any survivors?"

"I've had it," the mother said.

His smile widened. He picked Alix up and twirled her around. His arms held her tight against him, his joy becoming her own as she watched the happiness play across his face.

"We've got it!"

"Got what?" she asked, her face flaming as she noticed the curious stares they collected.

He set her down, then returned to Jory. "Dig the centrifuge out of the kit," he said to her.

As if she knew what that was. "The what?"

He laughed and dug through the medical bag. He pulled out a strange, round contraption that looked like a multiarmed bug of some sort, a bottle of antibiotics, and a glass vial, and set them on the table.

Next he took out a syringe and moved toward the mother. "I need a sample of your blood."

The mother stared at him aghast and took a step back. "For what purpose?"

"For an antidote. Whatever this is, your body has already built up an immunity to it. I'm hoping I can transfer that to your son and help his cells fight off the illness."

Horror filled her face. "Gannon?"

Gannon came forward and picked up the centrifuge. "Will it work?"

Devyn took a deep breath. "I don't know. All I can do is try."

Nodding, Gannon returned his gaze to his wife. "Do it, Ila."

Alix could swear the woman paled as she rolled up her sleeve for Devyn. Not that her own face probably didn't look the same. Averting her eyes, she tried not to think about what he was doing, or how close her own arm was to the needle.

"Wait."

They turned simultaneously to see Braw move forward with a large pair of wire cutters. "For your gyve," he said with a triumphant smile.

"Thank you!" Alix said, wishing he'd shown up before she had performed surgery.

With a tiny snap, the gyve broke apart. Braw quickly snipped the thin metal from their wrists.

"You okay?" Devyn asked, a smile hovering at the corners of his lips.

"Much better," she said, moving to sit in a nearby chair.

He shook his head and turned back to his patient.

Alix watched him while he worked. There was a joy to him she'd never seen before and she knew that this was what he should be doing. This was his calling.

It amazed her the way he knew instinctively what to do, the way he soothed both Jory and his mother. And to her utmost shock, Jory let out a tiny, gurgling laugh in response to Devyn's teasing.

Happiness swelled inside her, bringing tears. She licked her lips, imagining what Devyn would be like as a father. He'd never abuse his child, never lock it in the closet, or kick it out of the way. No, he'd tickle and tease and be there to wipe away the tears, to cuddle and love. And she could see his face the first time he held his own child in his arms.

If only she could be the mother.

"Stupid dream," she whispered under her breath, knowing that for her such dreams never came true.

"Yuck," Devyn said, and wiped his hands on a cloth. "What did you eat, Jory, snail stew?"

Again the tiny giggle sounded.

"Now hold your breath a minute and let me try to get some of this yucky stuff out so you can breathe."

A tiny hand moved up to clutch Ila. Alix's stomach tightened. Would anyone ever love her so completely? Trust her so much?

After a short time, Devyn finished. "We need to leave the tube in a little longer until I'm sure his throat's not going to reclose."

He looked back at Jory and smiled. "Which means you can't try to blow icky stuff at any girls who might irritate you."

Ila grabbed Devyn's hand and pulled it to her cheek. "Thank you. Whatever you need, ask and it shall be given."

Devyn pulled his hand away and patted her on the shoulder. "Keep an eye on him and let me know if his condition changes at all. If that serum works, then I'll make more and try to treat the others who are sick."

Tears brimmed in Gannon's eyes. "You're no Chaldese. You're a godsend."

Devyn shifted uncomfortably. "Actually, I'll settle for something in between the two."

Smiling, Alix stared at him and the tired lines on his face, the relief in his eyes. She'd never even hoped to meet a man like Devyn, and now she cherished the time they'd had together.

Alix bit her lip to staunch her tears of happiness, grateful to whatever fate had delivered her into Devyn's hands.

Her wrist itched, reminding her of last night, and her body grew hot. In a way she regretted their separation. Now he could leave her behind.

Would he?

The door opened, giving her a start. "Lord Gannon, the Urbanites have entered the valley with scanning equipment! They say if we hand over the Chaldese, they'll spare our city."

# *Chapter Sixteen*

Devyn stared at the soldier, awaiting Gannon's decision.

"Tell them we haven't found the Chaldese and reinforce our shields."

A sour knot twisted Devyn's stomach. He couldn't be responsible for destroying a whole community. "Look, don't risk your lives for me. If you'll protect Alix, I'm willing—"

"Don't be ridiculous," Gannon said. "I owe you my son's life and I am not going to hand you over to imbeciles who can't see for their own stupidity."

Devyn started to argue, but the stubborn set of Gannon's chin told him the effort would be futile. "If you're sure . . ."

"Very certain." He grabbed Devyn into a hug and Devyn did his best not to stiffen. Having a man hug him was not something he enjoyed. "I owe you everything!"

"Thanks," Devyn said, pulling away. "But that's what a doctor does."

"But you didn't have to."

Devyn shrugged, embarrassed over Gannon's gratitude. "Well, anyone would have done the same."

Gannon shook his head. "Integrity. The City Elders used to claim transplenum had none."

"I always said Devyn was one in a trillion," Alix said, and Devyn could have kissed her for it.

Even exhausted she looked beautiful. Her eyes twinkled from an inner glow and he wished they were alone back in the forest. "If you two don't stop complimenting me, I'm going to swell three times my normal size."

He looked at Gannon. "If you don't mind, I need a place I can wash."

"Certainly." Gannon beckoned a servant. "Take them to their rooms and as soon as they're ready, escort them to my dining hall."

Devyn offered his hand to Alix. Her warm, slender fingers closed around his and a shiver sped up his spine and straight to a part of him he'd rather not have roused at the moment.

It shocked and amazed him that he could think of sex at a time like this. Who knew how many so-called Urbanites were waiting outside to tear their hearts out, and all he could think about was the way Alix felt in his arms. He must be going slanted.

Without a word, he followed Alix and the servant, who led them to a nice set of chambers.

When the servant showed them only one bed, he started to protest, then remembered their ruse. "I'll take the couch," he whispered to Alix.

She turned and smiled at him. How could something so innocent as a smile be so devastating?

"There are fresh clothes in the closets. Feel free to use whatever you wish." The servant paused at the door. "I shall wait outside. As soon as you're ready, I shall escort you to dinner."

"Thanks," Devyn said, forcing himself not to bury his head in the luscious curve of Alix's neck and taste the sweetness of her pale skin.

First he had to make sure he didn't give her any germs; then he might have time for a nip or two. Maybe three.

Once the door closed, he headed to the bathroom. "You need to wash your hands really well. I'm not sure how infectious that disease is, but I'm sure you don't want to catch it."

She came to stand beside him at the basin. Even without touching her, he could feel her presence as if she were a part of him, a part he needed as much as his lungs or heart.

Desire erupted and he closed his eyes against

the heated demand he couldn't yield to. Not yet.

She moved forward and he trembled from her nearness. Stunned, he watched as Alix picked up the soap, took his hands, and scrubbed between each of his fingers. Each stroke of her fingers sliding like silk in between his sent waves of heat pounding through him. Waves that instantly kindled his desire and set his entire body on fire. At the moment, he'd bet his body temperature would rival Jory's.

"Do you have any idea what a great doctor you are?" she said, her head tilted away as she studied his hands.

He cocked his brow, curious about her somber mood. "Am I?" he asked, his voice ragged to his ears.

She looked up into his eyes and his breath caught. His heart pounding, he wanted nothing more than to peel her clothes from her.

"You were magnificent."

He smiled. Somehow her praise meant more to him than anything else ever could. "I was just doing what I was trained to do."

"No," she said, her gaze boring into him. "You were making a difference."

He frowned. "I don't see—"

"You saved that boy's life," she whispered, her voice cracking. "He would have died today had you not been here. Now he will grow up and tell his children about the man who saved his life and made him laugh."

His throat tightened from the happiness running through him. No woman could ever compare to Alix. "I love the way you see things."

She swayed into his arms and he held her tightly, tasting the sweetness of her lips. He could never get enough of her touch, her laughter, her warm reassurances. He pressed against her, reveling in her delicate curves that molded against his body as he cupped her buttocks and brought her closer to his heat.

Her lips quivered beneath his and he ran his tongue over the soft sweetness of her mouth. No wine or candy could ever taste better, ever whet his appetite more.

"I couldn't have saved Jory without you," he whispered, nibbling the corner of her mouth.

"I didn't do anything."

He pulled back and smiled at her. "I don't know. For a seed, you did an excellent job."

She looked at him skeptically. "What's a seed?"

"It's a HAWC term for a recruit."

Her gaze turned mischievous. "Then what would that make a seedling?"

He loved her wit. Thinking about her words for a minute, he brushed his lips across the curve he'd ached to nibble earlier. "A very short recruit?"

She laughed, the sound cutting a place in his heart like lightning on a stone.

"I would give anything just to stay in this room

and make love to you for the rest of my life," he whispered, running his hand through the soft strands of her hair.

"But if you don't eat soon, you won't be able to do anything but shake," she said, pushing at him.

Despite her flippant tone, he sensed an inner restraint, a need to keep him locked outside. Her rejection shredded his soul, yet he still wanted her.

Why couldn't he gather his anger and push her away?

The answer stung him worse than a viper's bite. He loved her. She meant everything to him, and unless he returned them to their worlds and freed her, he would never have her by his side. She would never stay by his side.

"C'mon," he said, pulling away from her. "Let's get cleaned up."

An hour later, Alix stepped out of the bathroom and stole his breath. She wore a loose, flowing gown that added a femininity to her he'd never seen before. Her long hair was drawn up on top of her head, where it fell in soft curls he longed to free and bury his face in. She was perfection.

"Wow," he said, rising to his feet.

She smiled, showing him her little dimple, and a wave of electricity snapped through him.

He took her hand and kissed her soft palm. "You know, I sort of miss being gyved to you."

Her laughter caressed him. "Funny you should say that. I was thinking the same thing while I dressed."

Devyn started to smile, but it died instantly as his thoughts turned to Sway. Why did Sway have to die? It just wasn't fair.

"Devyn, what's wrong?"

He cleared his throat, but the pain remained inside, where it burned and ached more than any beating or wound. "I was just thinking of Sway."

She caressed his cheek, her fingers cold against his skin. For once, not even her touch could soothe him. "I'm sorry," she whispered.

"I know," he said, forcing himself to pay attention to what had to be done.

Alix needed him, and her life—her future—depended on him. He had to keep her safe. And even though he'd failed Sway miserably, he vowed he would see Alix freed no matter what.

Alix sat at the table, listening to Devyn and Gannon plot their escape. As each second passed and they discussed how they intended to break into the Emir's palace and steal his shuttle, her stomach shrank a little more until it was far too small to accommodate any of the delicious food before her.

She was getting tired of all the intrigue. A little quiet time would do her good.

"Do you not like the food?" Ila asked, a frown lining her brow.

"Oh, no," Alix assured her. "Everything's marvelous. I'm just not very hungry."

Ila wiped her mouth and nodded toward her husband. "Politics have a way of taking anyone's appetite."

Alix picked up another bite of klara soufflé, but decided she couldn't quite manage to eat it. Returning it to her plate, she looked back at Ila. "Why are all of you at war with the Urbanites?"

"They don't believe in free thought," Gannon answered from his end of the table. "The ruling council became convinced that if they allowed new ideas, then they'd lose power or be persecuted as we'd been on Gelfara. So they closed the space ports and limited our access to other cultures physically and mentally."

She bit her lip, thinking the matter over. "So all of you rebelled?"

"Not quite. My father, who sat at the council all those years ago, tried to make them see what they were doing. He warned that if we closed our minds, God would disfavor us and send a plague to our people."

Gannon sighed and looked down at the small map on the table where he and Devyn had been making notes. "Every day, both we and the Urbanites in all the cities on Placidity lose loved ones to this nameless plague."

He looked at Devyn. "The priests have been

warning all of us over the last six months that it was a sign the Chaldese would soon appear."

Devyn swallowed his food and wiped his mouth. "Then why didn't you believe them when you saw me?"

He retrieved his glass. "One of our scouting parties saw your pod. I might be wrong, but I don't think God will send a destroyer by conventional means. I think He'll move on a grander scale."

Devyn laughed. "I'm sure you're right."

He met Alix's gaze and her stomach unknotted. "I'm also sure there's a name for this plague. If you'll allow me to take a few samples from Jory, I'll have a colleague of mine run an analysis. Once we find out what you've got here, I can send you vaccines and cures."

"Do you think there are cures?" Ila asked desperately.

"I'm sure of it," Devyn said.

Alix saw the sadness behind his eyes lift. Devyn wasn't a runner or a soldier; he was a doctor. A slow smile curved her lips. Maybe now he could quit searching.

As soon as they finished dinner, Devyn went to check on Jory. Alix followed one step behind, carrying what she thought of as his magic bag. He might not be able to pull out a rabbit, but he'd found a solid future in it.

They entered the lavish blue nursery filled with toys. Jory's nurse rose from her chair and greeted them. "He's doing much better," she said, a huge smile on her face.

"Good," Devyn said, leaning over the sleeping child and taking a few quick readings. He handed a small recorder to Alix. "Real good. It looks like the serum's working."

Ila gasped happily and threw herself into Gannon's arms.

Alix cringed while Devyn pulled the tube out of Jory's throat and closed the wound with a laser seal.

Devyn looked up at Ila. "If you don't mind losing a little more blood, I can probably get a number of doses for the extreme cases."

Ila nodded. "You can have all my blood if it'll save the life of a child."

A strange light glowed in Devyn's eyes and Alix wanted desperately to know what thought hovered in his mind, what memory Ila had triggered.

"First thing in the morning, I'll send one of our doctors to assist you," Gannon offered.

"Good. I can also give them the anti-inflammatory drugs that I have. Maybe that'll curb some of this."

Gannon laughed. "Who would have thought the Chaldese would save our children?"

"Definitely not the farmer who took a shot at me," Devyn said wryly.

Alix laughed at the memory, grateful for Devyn's quick reflexes.

Clapping him on the back, Gannon pushed him toward her. "You two go on and rest. I'm sure you could use it after what you've been through."

Devyn gave her a mischievous smile and this time Alix knew the exact thought his mind entertained. She could definitely use a little of what Devyn had in mind.

To her surprise, Devyn took her hand and led her back to their rooms. His warm, strong palm chased away the coldness of her fingers and sent a chill up her arm.

As she followed, his words echoed in her mind. *As my wife.* Part of her wanted desperately to accept his offer of marriage. Every time she looked at him, she wanted nothing more than an eternity spent in his arms.

But dare she risk it? Could she rise above the depravity of her father?

A lump settled inside her chest. She wasn't even sure if Devyn could free her. What would she do if he couldn't? Stay with him as his slave?

No. She couldn't, not after what had happened to her mother. Closing her eyes, she could still hear her mother's pleading voice, still see her mother grabbing for her father, begging him not to sell her off. She'd promised him anything and he had coldly, callously unwrapped her fingers from his forearm and pushed her into the hands of the waiting slave dealer.

No one would ever do that to her. She must

refuse ownership, even if it meant leaving Devyn behind.

He closed the door behind her and pulled her into his arms. Touching her cheek, he stared deeply into her eyes. "Why are you so sad?"

Pain tore through Alix, searing her heart. "I'm not sad," she whispered. "I'm grateful for every moment I have with you."

He ran his knuckles along her cheekbone, sending chills across her face, down her back. "But you're still planning to leave me."

She drew a deep breath and forced the words from her throat. "I don't know, Devyn. Let's just wait and see what happens."

Sadness filled his eyes. "I'd rather have a firm promise. Something I can count on."

She looked up at him, and she wanted to give him that promise and more. She never wanted to leave him, even to think about leaving him, but she knew reality might dictate otherwise. "Now you're the one asking for more than I can give. I never expected you to marry me; I just wanted you to trust me, to . . ." She stopped.

What did she want?

Him. The answer seemed so clear, and yet she knew the impossibility of her desire. Slaves didn't marry the sons of wealthy parents. Like married like or they lived in complete misery.

"I know what you're thinking," he said with a sigh. "Let's wait and see what happens."

Alix pulled him into her arms and held him

tight, her desperation washing over her in resounding waves that pounded on the shore of her soul, rushing against her heart and threatening to tear it apart. She yearned to give him the reassurance he needed, to give it to herself, but she couldn't.

"I will get your freedom. I swear it."

She smiled, running her hands over his muscular back. "I know." But that wouldn't erase her past, nor her fears.

A knock sounded on the door, breaking them apart.

Devyn stepped away and opened the door to reveal Gannon.

"I'm sorry to disturb you, but there's been a confrontation with the Urbanites. They're bringing in wounded by the craftful, and we could use an extra pair of surgical hands."

Alix saw the pain flicker across Devyn's face. "I'll do what I can."

"Can I help?" she asked, stepping forward.

"We can use any volunteers."

The three of them rushed through the interior of the mountain, not stopping until they reached an enormous operating room. The odor of blood and seared flesh filled her head, invading her senses until she could taste the horrid bitterness of death. Moans echoed off the walls and for a moment she was too afraid to move.

Gannon directed Devyn toward an empty table, and as soon as the nurse had sterilized his hands, a body was deposited before him.

"Here," a nurse said, pulling Alix aside to cover her clothes with a surgical robe and scrub her hands clean.

She handed Alix a bundle of folded cloth. "Take these to the new doctor."

Alix headed toward Devyn, her heart pounding. All around her people lay suffering. They clutched at the nurses, begging, crying, praying.

Panic filled her head, making her senses light, her knees weak, and she wanted to scream.

"Don't take so long! Hurry or get out," an orderly snapped, grabbing the towels from her.

Biting her lip, Alix looked at Devyn, who leaned over his patient, oblivious to her. Blood covered his chest and his arms from the elbows down. A frown lined his handsome brow and she realized the screams and moans affected him every bit as much as they did her.

"Can't they ever shut up?" another doctor muttered. "I can't stand the way they moan like children."

"Let me open fire on you with a six-ninety round and see if you can hold in your pain," Devyn said, pulling shrapnel out of his patient's chest and dropping it into a tray with a loud ping.

The doctor looked up at him. "How do you know?"

"I've had one hit me in the shoulder," Devyn

said, meeting his gaze. "Blew my arm out of joint, splintered my scapula, and really pissed me off."

The doctor averted his gaze.

Alix gazed down at the man on the table and her stomach heaved. At one time that had been Devyn. She couldn't stand the thought of someone shooting him like that, nor of him lying on a table with strangers digging around in his body.

"Hey!" a nurse shouted, pointing at her. "You, there. I need help."

Alix blinked back her tears and forced herself to go, even though she feared she might collapse at any moment. These people needed her and she couldn't let them down.

Hours later, she again stood near Devyn. This time his patient was a young soldier, no more than nineteen or twenty. Immediately, she noted the strained frown on Devyn's face as he worked. She wanted to touch him and reassure him, but she knew he needed his concentration.

Suddenly, the boy convulsed.

"We're losing him," the nurse said, her voice devoid of emotion.

Devyn worked with frenzied haste. "Give him a shot of adrenaline with a cardiac needle."

The nurse injected it straight into the boy's heart.

Alix held her breath.

"We're still losing him."

Alix's own heart lurched at the pain in Devyn's eyes and she wanted to go to him, but she dared not.

"C'mon, buddy," he pleaded. "Don't give up."

The monitor blinked and emitted a shriek.

"He's gone."

"Like hell," Devyn snapped, moving to resuscitate him by massaging his heart.

Alix bit her lip, her stomach pitching. Each time Devyn squeezed the boy's heart, blood shot over him, but he didn't seem to notice. And every time he stopped, the boy's monitor flat-lined.

The nurse tried to help, but after a few minutes she pulled at Devyn's arm. "I'm sorry, Doctor, but he's gone."

Alix could feel the fury of Devyn's anger, and her own body trembled.

"Why don't you take a break?" the nurse suggested.

Without a word, Devyn left the operating room, his fists clenched at his sides.

Alix excused herself and ran after him.

"Devyn?" she called.

He stopped, but didn't turn around.

Alix closed her eyes and drew a deep breath. His pain reached out to her, bringing an ache to her chest that throbbed and burned with each breath she took. Closing the distance between them, she reached out and touched his arm. "I'm so sorry."

He shook his head. "Tell that to his family."

Tears constricted her throat. "You did everything you could."

"Big consolation," he snarled. "Sorry about your kid, folks, but I did all I could. I'm not responsible. Here's his body, hope you don't mind." He gave her such a look of hatred her heartbeat faltered. "Too bad I don't even have that much to offer Sway's family."

"Oh, Devyn, please don't do this to yourself."

He pulled his surgical cap off and moved away from her. "I'm tired of making jokes about death, and I'm through watching kids die for nothing."

"Where are you going?"

"To hell, no doubt."

# *Chapter Seventeen*

Devyn sat in the surgery lounge, listening to idle conversations around him. One nurse was talking about a party she wanted to attend later that night, and another man asked his companion if she wanted to have dinner with him. Everyone was going about their routine just like normal.

"I guess I flunked Disassociation and Callousness 101," he muttered.

He'd never been one of those doctors who could just walk away and feel nothing. No matter how many battlefields he'd worked on or how many soldiers died, he'd always felt somehow responsible.

God, how he hated being a doctor.

Sway's face drifted before his eyes. His stomach tightened in grief and guilt. Everyone he touched died. Maybe he ought to just throw himself under the nearest transport and end his uselessness as quickly and painlessly as possible.

"All right, a little self-pity never hurt anyone, but you look like you're wallowing in it."

He looked up at Alix. He had to admit just the sight of her made him feel better, but not enough to completely erase what bothered him. "I know. I'm tired and things always bother me a lot more when I haven't slept."

She fingered the empty cookie wrapper in front of him. "Should you be eating sweets on an empty stomach?"

He shook his head. "What the hell. All it can do is kill me."

"You're not funny."

Devyn pulled out the chair next to him and beckoned her to sit. "I was just thinking how much I miss Sway. If he were here, he'd kick my butt."

He picked up her hand from the table and toyed with her fingers. "He couldn't stand for me to do emergency surgery. I think the happiest I ever saw him was the day the HAWC held my court-martial and discharged me."

He captured her hand and sighed, enjoying the feel of her fist beneath his. "I'll never understand how my dad managed all the years he worked as a surgeon in an emergency room. I don't guess I was cut out to follow in his footsteps any more than Alexei's or Calix's."

She leaned forward and covered his hands with her free one, her gaze probing him. "Maybe you should quit trying to be like the men you admire and try to be yourself."

Devyn frowned. He'd spent the whole of his life just trying to find himself and now she acted like a sage who knew what course he should follow after a minute and a half of consultation. A twinge of anger went through him, but before he acted on it, he stopped himself.

Maybe she did know. He sure as hell didn't. "What do you mean?"

She smiled. "You're a great pilot, a fantastic surgeon, and I bet you were a fabulous soldier, but the thing I've seen you best at is when you were working on Jory."

He frowned.

"It's true," she said, caressing his fingers. "You were magnificent the way you had him laughing while he had a tube sticking out of his neck. Any other child would have been screaming his head off. *He* would have been screaming his head off had you not soothed him, distracted him."

He laughed at the thought of him treating children. "I don't think so. Kids make me nervous. I've never been around them much."

"You could have fooled me. I saw you, Devyn. You were great."

## Sherrilyn Kenyon

He took her hands and kissed her knuckles. He started to tell her how great she was, but Gannon picked that moment to approach them.

He gazed at Alix, then met Devyn's stare. "I just wanted to thank you for all you've done."

"No problem," Devyn said, stifling a yawn.

Gannon smiled. "Well, I know how much of a hurry you two are in to leave our planet. We've got a team working on a plan to infiltrate the capital and they think they can get you in there around midnight tonight."

"That's great!" Devyn said, relief filling him.

Gannon nodded, and his gaze wandered around the room as though he had bad news to relay. Devyn held his breath, afraid he and Alix would end up stuck here.

Finally, Gannon looked back at him. "There's just one last thing, and I hate to ask it."

"What?" Devyn asked, fearing his response.

"I know how hard you've worked in surgery, and I don't want you to think we don't appreciate it. . . ."

"But."

"But you mentioned helping out with our—"

"Oh, yeah," Devyn said, remembering his promise the day before to teach their doctors about the serum. "Are the doctors assembled?"

A smile lit Gannon's entire face. "You don't mind?"

"Not at all. Let me get cleaned up and I'll be right there."

"Thank you."

Alix spoke up to Gannon. "Could you please make sure someone brings him something to eat? He hasn't had anything since a small dinner yesterday and he could use a good breakfast."

"Of course." Gannon turned to him and winked. "You picked a good wife."

Devyn watched shock play across Alix's face. "I know," he said to Gannon. "And I appreciate your noticing it."

Her face turned so red Devyn half expected flames to ignite.

"Come, wife, and clean me up."

As soon as they were out of Gannon's hearing, Alix punched him in the belly. "You're awful!"

"I know, but I enjoy it so."

Morning passed quickly while he showed the doctors how to make the serum until he could get a real antidote and vaccine to them.

As he worked with the doctors and treated a number of children, he began to see what Alix had meant. A part of him adored working with them. The way they looked up at him with their trusting eyes and eagerly laughed and touched him.

He didn't know how to explain it, but a part of him responded to their needs like a flower unfolding before sunshine. Every time one of them laughed, he felt as if he'd accomplished something spectacular. And he hadn't felt like that in a long, long time.

A little after noon, he finally had to retire. Yawning, he made his way back to their chambers, his sight blurry, his eyes sore.

Alix greeted him at the door and pulled him into the bedroom.

He stared at her in surprise.

"You can't sleep on the couch," she said, a timid smile on her lips. "After the night you've had, you need your rest."

Devyn fumbled with his clothes, but accomplished little. Too tired to bother, he started for the bed only to find Alix blocking his way, a stern frown on her face.

"You can't sleep like that," she chided, reaching for the ties on his surgical jacket.

She helped him undress and tucked him into bed, her touch gentle. He wanted the energy to pull her into his arms and make love to her, but his body couldn't respond with anything more than hungry images that played across his mind and tortured him.

He caught her hand as she started to leave. "Stay with me."

Biting her lip, she scanned the room. "I don't know. . . ."

"Please," he whispered. "I just want to hold you for a little while."

Her smile warmed his heart. "All right."

She snuggled up beside him and a jolt of electricity tore through him. It felt so natural and so right that she should lie next to him. For the first time in his life, he had a sense of who he really was and what he really wanted.

"Alix?" He waited until she rolled over and looked at him.

Pulling the strands of golden brown hair from her cheek, he stared into her eyes and a part of him knew he'd never be happy with any other woman. "I've been thinking about what you said and I think I might go back to school and study pediatric medicine."

Her happy, loving gaze scorched him. "I think that's wonderful."

He smiled, stroking her cheek's softness. "I owe it to you. If you hadn't planted the seed, the tree wouldn't have fallen on me."

She lifted a confused brow. "Excuse me?"

"I would never have thought of it alone."

She laid her head on his chest and ran her hand down his ribs, bringing a wave of delight to his body. "You give yourself too little credit."

He took her hand in his and held it, wishing he could think of some way to keep her like this forever.

What would happen if he couldn't free her?

Everything he knew about her told him she wouldn't stick around. She wanted her freedom and if he couldn't give it to her, she'd run.

But would she let him follow?

No, she was too independent for that. She'd creep out one night while he slept and he'd never see her again. The thought suffocated him.

Pain tore through him and he knew he couldn't lose her.

No matter how much time and money it took, he'd get her freedom. He just prayed she would be willing to wait.

Gannon woke them up a little past nine that evening. Alix noticed the paleness of Devyn's face and the tiny shake in his hands that he fought hard to conceal.

As soon as he dressed, she took his hand and squeezed. "Is this what happens when you get hungry?"

"In a way. This is the beginning stage of low blood sugar. If I don't eat soon, it'll get worse, and finally I'll pass out."

Alix didn't like the thought of that. "Have you ever passed out before?"

"Not yet. I learned early to eat before I get too bad off."

Hand in hand they went to eat.

They entered the dining hall and Alix froze in shock at the number of people who had come to say farewell to them. Jory came running in a pair of spotted pajamas and threw himself into Devyn's arms. Devyn scooped him up. A wide smile lit Jory's face and he held out a large piece of paper with colored drawings on it.

"I made this for you, Dr. Kell. See, it's a doctor and he's helping people get better." He wiped his nose on his sleeve, then pointed back to the picture. "And this is me helping, 'cause I know what you got to do to make them okay 'cause you showed me, and over here is Mrs. Dr. Kell, and she's helping, too."

Devyn looked at her, his eyes shining, and heat sizzled through her. "Did you do this all by yourself?" he asked Jory.

"Uh-huh."

"Well, you did a great job. I'll have to frame this and hang it up when I get home."

Jory's mouth fell open, his eyes huge. "Really?"

Devyn smiled and held him close, tugging at Alix's heart as she watched him and yearned for a way to give him his own child.

"You bet," Devyn told the boy.

Jory leaned back. "Can I come see it sometime?"

"Now, Jory," Ila said, pulling her son from Devyn's arms. "You can't bother Dr. Kell on his planet. We have to stay here."

"But why?" he whined.

"It's the law."

Jory looked at Devyn and poked his lips out. "It's a stupid law."

Ila rolled her eyes and Alix stifled her laugh at the woman's aggravation. "Now say good night to Dr. Kell. It's past your bedtime."

"Okay." He wiggled out of Ila's arms, ran to Devyn, threw his arms around his leg, and squeezed tight. "Good night, Dr. Kell, and don't

327

let the bad people shoot you tonight."

"I won't," Devyn said, ruffling his hair.

Jory looked up at him, smiled, then ran to Alix. She started in shock at the contact of his tiny arms wrapped around her. She'd never had a child touch her before and she found the sensation incredible. Kneeling down, she pulled him to her and his little arms encircled her neck.

"Thank you for letting Dr. Kell help me."

Alix smoothed his hair where Devyn had messed it up, her heart pounding. "Anytime. Just promise me you'll try to stay well."

"Okay."

"Jory?"

"I'm coming."

Alix watched him tuck his hand in his mother's and walk away from her and she knew then that she wanted children. God help her, but the thought of growing old without that special devotion and love left a hollow place in her soul that threatened to tear her apart.

As she glanced at Devyn as he folded up his picture and conversed with another doctor, an ache seized her chest until she wanted to shout.

*Please,* she begged silently, *let me find a way to be free. Let me find a way to stay with Devyn.*

Dinner was a hurried affair. All throughout the meal, Gannon and his lead commander briefed them on how they intended to break into the Emir's palace and "appropriate" the shuttle. She stifled her laughter at their military euphemisms and wondered if they realized what they were doing. Even Devyn seemed caught up in the terminology.

After an eternity in which they discussed things she barely understood, Gannon led them to a small room, where they were given black battlesuits to don.

Devyn covered her hair with a black cap and smeared camouflage on her cheeks. His fingers glided over her skin, raising chills and bringing heat to her most sensitive parts. Even now, she'd much rather retire with him to their room than risk his life for anything, including her freedom.

"I feel so stupid," she said, smiling.

"You'd feel a lot worse if someone shot you."

"True."

He placed one last dab on the tip of her nose, then handed her the tube.

She took the camouflage tube from him and stared at the sick-smelling black goo.

"Now remember," Devyn warned. "There's a pattern to this. Put the tan color where my face is naturally dark, and the black goes on the light reflective zones."

She frowned. "The what?"

His amused smile thrilled her. "My ears, nose, cheekbones, and forehead."

"You're kidding." she said, laughing.

The humor fled his face. "This is serious, Alix. If my skin reflects light, a sentry could see me, and if you neglect to cover any part of my exposed

329

skin I could trip up the infrared scanners. Either way, I'm toast."

Her heart pounded at the thought. Images of him lying dead like Sway, or on a surgery table, haunted her. She couldn't stand even the thought that he might be hurt by their plans tonight. If anything happened to him . . .

*Stop it,* she ordered herself as hysteria poured through her. She had to keep control or she would mess up and get him wounded. No matter what, she would protect him.

Alix smeared the waxy substance between her thumb and forefinger. "Maybe you ought to do this after all. I'm afraid I'll make a mistake."

He kissed the tip of her nose, then brushed his finger there to reapply more camouflage. "Okay. Where's a mirror?"

Once they were dressed, Gannon handed them a pair of night glasses.

Alix started to put them on, but Devyn grabbed her arm. "Not inside. They amplify light and if you put them on in a bright spot, you'll be blinded."

She took a deep breath. "Did you learn all this in the HAWC?"

All emotion faded from his eyes. "This and more."

Before she could think about his words, Gannon handed them two small blasters. Alix hooked hers into the empty holster at her side.

Devyn shook his head. "I don't use those."

Gannon lifted a disbelieving brow. "Are you sure?"

"Positive," Devyn said. "But I'll take a herotosh if you have one."

Gannon motioned to a soldier to bring the small stun bombs to Devyn. He hooked several onto his belt and gave her a comforting smile.

"Are you two ready?" Gannon asked.

Devyn took a deep breath. Alix prayed her legs would quit shaking and nodded to him.

"Lead on," Devyn said, and her stomach knotted in fearful expectation.

Silently, they climbed aboard the hovercrafts and made their way to the dark, forbidding city.

They abandoned their vehicles outside the gates and moved in through the sewer system. Alix held her breath even though she knew the oxygen tubing that ran to her nose and mouth filtered out the smell. The filthy sewer just didn't *look* conducive to breathing.

They crawled out of the sewer just before the palace gates. Then they crept around back to a secluded place where they could breach the gate without being seen.

Gannon stopped the soldier who was working on the code and looked at Alix and Devyn. "Remember," he whispered, "we have thirty seconds to get inside the gate once we jam their scanners."

Devyn nodded and reached to take her hand. Alix appreciated his support. She needed it. Her heart thumped in her throat and her limbs shook.

This was it. One mistake and she could cost all of them their lives.

"Go!"

Devyn went first and pulled her through. Gannon and the other four members came in and disconnected the jam.

They took a moment to get their bearings, then headed off toward the east.

Devyn hung back just slightly.

Curious, Alix looked at him. Despite the heavy camouflage, she detected his worry lines. "What is it?"

"I don't know," he whispered. "I've got a bad feeling. It's like—"

A blaster charge sizzled just past her shoulder and into the back of the soldier in front of her. Screaming, she stumbled and fell to the ground, Devyn on top of her.

"Ambush!" Gannon shouted, running for cover.

Blaster recoil sounded and sparkled all around. Everything happened so quickly, she could barely follow who ran where and exactly what was happening.

Alix pulled out her blaster, but her fingers shook so badly she dropped it. She tried to pick it up, but Devyn's insistent pulling and another round of fire that barely missed her dissuaded her from getting it.

"What are we going to do?" she asked as he led her to a wall, then pushed her down and crouched beside her.

He reached out to her, holding her close, but didn't respond to her question.

"Gannon?" Devyn asked into his link. "Where's the ship located?"

Alix held on to him, watching the Urbanite soldiers fill the yard around them. Her entire body trembled from her fear and she prayed they'd make it out alive.

Lights came up and everything stood out in stark relief.

"Okay," Devyn said, in response to Gannon's words. "I want you and your men to get out of here. We can manage on our own."

He paused and she could just make out Gannon's excited chatter. "Trust me," Devyn said. "I can handle it from here."

With that, he threw down the link and grabbed her hand. "Alix," he said, forcing her to look up at him. "You've got to follow me, pay attention, and for God's sake don't trip."

Following the line of the wall, they made their way steadily to the east. The Urbanites continued to move to the south and she assumed that must be where Gannon was leading them.

She bit her lip, her palms sweaty. "Do you think Gannon and his soldiers will make it?"

"I hope so."

She took a deep breath and asked the question that weighed heaviest in her mind. "Do you think we'll make it?"

The silence that answered her wasn't comforting in the least.

Devyn grabbed her and shoved her down. He covered her with his body and leaned against the wall. She closed her eyes, inhaling the fresh scent of him, and somehow it soothed part of the terror consuming her.

"They're heading out the gate!" a soldier said, running past them.

Sweat dripped down her face, stinging her eyes, and she wiped it away, realizing as she did that some of her camouflage came off on her hand.

"C'mon," Devyn whispered, helping her to her feet.

They reached a long white wall. Devyn paused and opened a steel ventilation grate. "This should take us to the landing bay," he whispered. "Just follow behind me."

As soon as he was inside, Alix squeezed in. She'd never liked tight spaces; they reminded her too much of closets. The walls hugged her so tightly she could barely breathe.

How could Devyn move so effortlessly?

They seemed to travel endlessly through winding, tight metal corridors, and panic welled up inside her. Were they ever going to get to the end?

What would be waiting for them? Closing her eyes, she forced herself not to think about that.

After what seemed like an eternity, Devyn stopped and started scratching the grate in front of him.

"Are we there?" she whispered.

"Yes," he said. "I can see the shuttle."

Happiness swelled inside her. They were almost free.

Devyn crawled out of the duct, then turned around to help her through.

Dimly lit, the shuttle twinkled in the center of the bay like a star. No one loomed anywhere nearby and for once it looked like fate had befriended her.

She smiled at Devyn.

"So, Kell, we meet again."

They turned simultaneously to see Irn step out from behind the shuttle with a group of Urbanite soldiers. All of their vile group held rifles aimed straight at her and Devyn.

# *Chapter Eighteen*

"This is not a good day for a reunion," Devyn said under his breath, and Alix had a strange urge to kick him.

Irn walked forward. "This time, Kell, we're going to settle it."

Faster than she could blink, Devyn jerked a herotosh from his belt, tossed it, and pulled her against the wall. A piercing white light exploded and the sound of blaster recoil filled her ears.

Devyn ran, pulling her after him.

Alix reminded herself not to stumble. They ran toward the shuttle, but a group of soldiers cut them off.

"Don't panic," Devyn said, leading her off to the side of the bay. But it was too late. Urbanites seemed to materialize out of the very walls.

Her vision dimmed. Her body trembled violently. She thought she would pass out.

"Wait!" Irn screamed. "You can't see what you're shooting at. Wait until you see them."

Devyn slid to a stop so fast she collided into his back.

"There is a God and he's definitely on our side."

Had he lost his mind? She stared at him in disbelief, then saw over his shoulder what had made him so happy. The *Prixie* and her companion ship stood docked just outside the bay.

But would it do them any good? "They'll have people on board."

"Let me worry about that. C'mon."

Let him worry about it? How could he be so careless with both their lives?

Another blaster shot sizzled past.

Okay, she was willing to trust him.

Rushing inside, Devyn sprinted up the ramp of the companion ship and she followed. He pulled another herotosh off and held it over his head. Three men looked up from their controls, their faces horrified.

"Get back, get off, or die," Devyn snarled. "You have two seconds to choose."

Two of them ran for the door.

The third man laughed. "That won't kill anyone." He shook his head and flipped the switch to seal the door. "But you've got guts and I admire that in a captain. So what coordinates do I punch in?"

Disbelief cut through Devyn. Why would this guy help them? A loud thud sounded on the door. He turned, half expecting the door to open.

The man cursed. "They're attacking. You two had better get strapped in."

As the ship started to tilt away from the bay, Devyn pushed Alix into the nearest chair.

"Don't worry," the stranger said. "I'd much rather kill that sonovabitch than either of you. Since I can't get to him, I think stealing the three things he wants most is vengeance enough."

Devyn had no idea what the man was talking about, but he was taking them off the planet, and until he determined exactly what was going on, he wasn't about to start complaining.

Once they'd cleared orbit, the man turned around and faced them. "Now where do you two want to go?"

"Paradise City," Devyn said.

He nodded, turned around, programmed the coordinates, then said, "You don't remember me, do you?"

Devyn exchanged a shocked glance with Alix. "Who are you talking to?"

"You, Devyn. Or should I say 'little toggle'?"

Heat suffused his cheeks at the old nickname. "I'm afraid I don't remember you, but you have to know my uncle to know that stupid nickname."

He held his hand out to him. "Werren Nemus. I used to run watch for Calix. Last time I saw you, you were about six years old."

Devyn smiled. "Oh, yeah. I do remember you. You're the one who gave me that huge piece of gleryl that I laid on my mom's new sofa."

Werren laughed. "I bet you hate me. Malena Laing's wrath is not something I welcome."

Devyn scratched his chin and watched Werren run over his gauges. "Is that why you're helping us?"

"Well, let's see," he said with a smile, lifting up his fingers to count off his reasons. "I fear your mother's abilities, I owe your uncle my life, and I hate Irn with a particular ardor. So given all that, helping you seemed like the right thing to do."

Alix leaned her head in her hands and drew a pain-filled breath that cut through Devyn. "Why does Irn want me so badly?" she asked, her voice cracking.

Devyn took her hand, trying to reassure her.

She looked up at him and he wanted to soothe the agony that burned in her eyes, tell her that he would never allow Irn to harm her. And he wouldn't. Irn would have to kill him first.

"Honey, you're just the sweetmeat. It's Devyn he wants as main course."

"What?" they asked simultaneously.

Werren turned around and looked back and

forth between them. "You mean you didn't know?"

Devyn clenched his armrest. "Know what?"

Werren shook his head and sighed. "He really is a slanted scab," he said under his breath. He stared at Devyn. "He wants to tear you apart and mail your body parts home to your mother."

Incredulity washed over him. "I don't even know the guy. Why would—"

"Your mom sent him to prison."

Devyn scoffed. "My mom sent a lot of people to prison, including my father."

"Yeah, but Irn's brother was torn apart during a riot. He blames your mother for it and he wants to do to you what was done to his brother."

Devyn just stared into space, thoughts whirling. "And all this time I blamed Alix for his pursuit."

Fury ripped through him and he wanted to beat Irn. "You mean that sonovabitch killed my best friend trying to get to me?"

Werren nodded.

A tic started in Devyn's jaw. "I'm going to rip his heart out and feed it to him."

"Looks like you're going to get the chance," Werren said, flipping switches. "Irn's headed in at three o'clock."

Devyn snapped to his feet. "Where's the gunner's chair?"

"End of the corridor."

"Devyn," Alix said, rising, "be careful."

He kissed her, then ran to his station.

Alix moved to the nav center and helped keep track of Irn. "It's just one ship," she said, unable to believe no other ships were flying after them.

"I guess the Placidians didn't want to get involved with transplenum business." Werren laughed. "Although I bet you two had a time. Chaldese . . ."

His laughter continued until Alix wanted to shoot him herself.

He sobered and punched in coordinates. "I think Devyn must have inherited his family's bad luck. Only a Laing could have that kind of fiasco."

A shot hit the ship and rocked it sideways.

"I'm getting sick of this," Alix muttered, straightening herself.

She heard Devyn fire several rounds.

"Hey, I think he got them. They're listing off and slowing down." Werren opened the link. "Toggle, stay in your seat. I'm about to enter a wormhole."

Alix strapped herself in.

After the initial entry, the ride smoothed out. She closed her eyes, grateful they'd all made it in one piece.

Devyn returned to the control room and touched her cheek. "How are you holding up?"

She shook her head and tried to ignore the heat that suffused her body. "All right, I guess. How about you?"

"Honestly, I think I should have blasted Irn out of the sky. I can't believe I only nicked him."

Werren snorted. "Well, you got him off our tail. That's the most important thing."

"For now." Devyn sighed. "He'll be back."

"Yep," Werren said. "You can count on it."

"What are we going to do?" Alix asked.

Devyn shook his head, wishing he knew. "Let's hope Taryn hasn't left Paradise City. If—"

"Taryn Kyrelle?"

"Yeah, you know him?"

Werren turned several shades paler. "Know of him. He's a real mean sonovabitch."

Devyn smiled. "He can be."

"Well, if you don't mind, I'll drop you two off and head out immediately."

Alix swallowed the lump of fear in her throat. "What about Irn?"

Werren smiled. "If you've got Taryn Kyrelle and Devyn on your side, I figure you can tear Irn apart. No point in my sticking around. Besides, all I wanted was my ship back, which you've now given me. No offense, but I'm not sticking my neck any further out."

Devyn pulled Alix into his embrace and rubbed the chill bumps on her arms in an effort to calm her. "We appreciate your help."

"No problem. Just make sure if you don't kill Irn, you let me know so I can prepare myself for his attack."

"Deal."

Werren sighed and turned back to his console. "We should be in Paradise City in about twelve hours. You two make yourselves comfortable and take whatever you want."

Devyn rubbed his chin against Alix's hair and inhaled the fresh floral scent. "Do you have a rec area?"

"Yeah, it's four doors down on the left," Werren answered without looking up.

Alix went after Devyn, who led her by the hand.

The rec room wasn't very big or impressive, but at least it was clean. A large game table was set up with some type of card game.

She took a seat in the chair next to a relaxation terminal.

Devyn stood next to her, looking down with a frown. "What's wrong?"

She stared at Devyn in shock. How he could tell something troubled her? "I was just wondering how all this would end. Here we've thought all this time Irn was after me, and now we find out you're more important to him. Me he wants to torture; you he wants dead."

She closed her eyes, a knot forming in her stomach. "What are we going to do?"

Devyn sighed and raked his hands through his hair. "I think you had the best advice on Placidity. Let's wait and see what happens. For now we're safe enough and Irn doesn't frighten me. When he shows up in PC, I'll take care of him."

Fear closed her throat. She couldn't stand the thought of Devyn facing Irn and what Irn might do to him. "How? You won't even use a blaster."

He smiled, but not even that could alleviate the anxiety gnawing at her. "Don't let that worry you. I *will* take care of him."

But she did worry. She had a bad feeling about this. Something deep inside her warned her that all this would explode in their faces.

She knew first-hand how Irn was. Devyn didn't understand how slanted the man was. "Devyn, Irn's not normal."

He laughed. "I think I've figured that out on my own."

He knelt on the floor by her side and took her hand, his gaze warm, reassuring. "I'm not going to let him hurt you."

Tears welled in her eyes. "It's you I'm afraid for."

One corner of his mouth twitched up into a precious smile that eased some of her pain, and he ran a finger down her cheek. "He's not going to hurt me either. I know you think I'm a pacifist, but I've lost Sway, and I'm not going to let anything happen to you. The only way I can make sure you stay safe is if I stay alive."

She smiled, taking his hand from her cheek and kissing his palm. "You've got to look after yourself."

"I swear it," he whispered, his voice hoarse.

He brought her hand to his lips and nibbled her fingertips.

Ecstasy broke through her melancholy and stole her breath. Nothing would happen to Devyn; she'd make sure of it. Somehow, she would keep him safe.

"Here," he said, breaking into her thoughts as he pulled a wipe out of his pack. He glided the tissue over her face and removed the camouflage.

She smiled. Even covered with silly makeup, he was gorgeous. Indeed, it only served to make him look like a wild, untameable beast, and she knew if she held out her hand, he would feast from her palm. She closed her eyes against the joy that knowledge brought.

But what of tomorrow? Would he grow to hate her as her father had her mother?

Her mother used to tell her stories about how gallant her father had been when he'd saved her mother from her former abusive owner. The first years he'd owned her mother had been like a dream, or so her mother had said. It wasn't until after her mother had children and her looks began to fade that her father began cursing her.

Well at least she knew Devyn wasn't playing the gallant because of *her* looks.

"Why do you want me?" she whispered, needing desperately to hear his answer.

He paused over her cheek and stared, aghast. "Don't you know?"

She shook her head.

A smile curved his lips, one that lifted her spirits. He was so handsome, so strong.

He returned to wiping her face. "I love the way you laugh, the way you look at things, the way you always know how to make me feel better, or even like a heel."

He pulled back and stared deeply into her eyes. "Mostly, I just love the way you make me feel when you walk into a room."

Tears fell down her cheeks. "Now look what you've done," she snapped, wiping at them as a wave of anger tore through her. "You've made me a ninny!"

He laughed and wiped them away. "And you've made me a hero. You've made me strong again."

She took the tissue from him and wiped at his camouflage, uncovering with each stroke a little more of the man she loved. "But what of tomorrow? What if my presence in a room starts to annoy you?"

He frowned at her, his eyes troubled. "Why would you think that?"

She wiped the tissue over his nose and steeled herself against the pain and fear inside her. "My mother used to say love comes quickly to men's hormones, but seldom to their hearts. As long as you give a man your body, you have a piece of his heart, but once he tires of you and starts looking for another body, you become useless and forgotten."

He cupped her face in his hands. "I could never forget you," he whispered.

But could she believe that? Could love really work?

"Love me, Devyn," she breathed, needing physical reassurance more than empty words.

His lips covered hers.

Alix pulled him into her arms and ran her hands down his spine.

*Please don't forget me,* her soul cried, and she ached to say the words aloud, but no amount of forcing could bring them to her lips.

Devyn laid her down on the floor, wishing he had a more comfortable place for her. She looked so vulnerable, so afraid, and he wished he knew what it would take to make her believe in him.

Her hands clutched at him, her desperation cutting to the core of his soul. She'd been alone so long that now even when he offered her all he could, she still couldn't accept it, or him. His heart pounded in agony.

He touched her cheek, delighting in the way she closed her eyes and sighed like a contented verrago. "Don't leave me," he whispered.

She held his hand against her cheek. "I won't."

Devyn smiled and dipped his head to taste the luscious silk of her throat.

He unbuttoned her shirt and slid the thick material slowly off. When he bent to remove her pants, she rolled to her side and he saw her mark. His heart lurched at the sight of the three intertwining circles and he ran his fingertips over the smooth area. He would give anything to wipe the mark away as easily as he had done her camouflage.

"Don't," she said, her voice trembling as she grabbed his hands. "It's repulsive."

He leaned down and kissed the mark, then looked up into her troubled eyes. "Nothing about you could ever repulse me," he said, and once more tears shone in her eyes.

She pulled him to her lips and he gladly went, holding her close against him, afraid to let go. Afraid that if he did, she would leave him.

Without her, he would have nothing. He would be nothing.

No one had ever made him feel as she did.

She unbuttoned his clothes and he laid his head back, reveling in the sensation of her warm hands running over his body, bringing chills and fire everywhere they touched. He allowed her to explore him until he thought her touch would drive him slanted.

Unable to take any more, he rolled over and pinned her beneath him, her body molding to his. He tasted her skin, running his tongue over her throat, her breasts. Her hands danced along his spine and he sucked his breath in, fire burning through him.

He would never be happy until she bound herself to him as his wife, until she stood by his side

as an equal and proclaimed to the universe that
she had chosen him and that she would remain
by his side for all eternity.

She lifted her hips to him and he took her
hint. Separating her legs, he slid into her, gasping at the warm feel of her body welcoming
him.

He made love to her slowly and savored each
beat of her heart against his chest.

"Don't ever leave me, Alix," he whispered in
her ear as she convulsed with her release.

The hours went by far too quickly and with
each one, Alix's worries tripled.

A buzz rent the air. "I just wanted to let you
two know that we're coming up on Jarun. I
did a preliminary news scan and it sounds as
though they've surrendered to HAWC troops.
Good thing we're not smuggling anything. The
HAWC's under orders to blast any supply ship
out of the sky. Anyway, it's about dinnertime in
Paradise City and I've gone ahead and checked
the two of you into the Murid Hotel, if that's
okay."

"Sure," Devyn said, pulling away from her.
"Just buzz when we land and we'll be out of
your way."

Pulling on her clothes, Alix watched Devyn as
if this were the last time she'd ever see him. Why
did she have such an awful feeling?

Why couldn't she banish it?

Too soon they were leaving Werren and his ship behind. She and Devyn said their good-byes and headed toward the hotel.

A number of buildings stood in fragments from bombs and blasts, reminding Alix of giant, rotting corpses that attested to the brutality they had silently witnessed. HAWC Keepers patrolled the streets in such a huge number that she saw one every few hundred yards, each poised as if ready to kill anyone who looked threatening. Children ran about, filthy and half dressed. She and Devyn passed a number of street people who begged them for food or money. Devyn gave them all he had on him in cash, and by his face she knew how deeply he felt for each of them.

"You'd think the HAWC could feed them," he muttered, his voice heavy with hatred.

Alix rubbed her hand down his arm to soothe him, and his tensed muscles relaxed a bit.

Every few feet, they passed more HAWC soldiers.

"Don't look at them," Devyn warned. "They'll take that as an open invitation to harass us."

She kept her gaze on the ground in front of them and followed him to the hotel.

Without any problems, they checked in and got their rooms. A smile curved Alix's lips as she realized Werren had ordered them adjoining suites.

They propped open the door that separated

their rooms and Alix joined Devyn in his suite while he ordered dinner.

Hanging up the link with the kitchen, he sighed. "I'm going to call Calix first; then I'll see about finding Taryn."

Alix nodded. "Do you want me to leave while you talk to your uncle?"

He shook his head. "It involves you. You might as well stay and listen."

The speed with which the emperor came to the link to talk with Devyn amazed her. She guessed Uncle Calix to be in his late forties, though he could easily have passed for thirty-five. An air of power and charm clung to him.

"Hey, little toggle!" he said with a smile. "Your mother has been crazy with worry over you. She's about made me slanted."

Devyn laughed, the sound warming Alix's heart. "I'm sorry. I'll call her as soon as I hang up."

"So what's happened? Why haven't you been answering her calls?"

Pain flickered across Devyn's face and she saw Calix react to it. "Are you in trouble? If you need me—"

"No trouble," Devyn assured him. "My ship was attacked and destroyed."

"Are you all right?" the emperor asked, his face even more concerned.

"Yeah," Devyn said, his voice ragged. "But Sway was killed."

Calix looked as though Devyn had slapped him.

He closed his eyes and winced. "Have you told Crill and Claria?"

"Not yet."

Calix shook his head. "I'll do it. You've been through enough. How are you dealing with it?"

"I guess I'm all right."

"If you need me—"

"I know. That's why I'm calling. I've got something that I need you to handle."

Calix lifted his brow expectantly.

Alix stiffened, knowing this was it. She held her breath, praying the emperor could help.

Devyn glanced at her and she caught his smile of reassurance. "What are the procedures for freeing slaves?"

"Why?" Calix asked, his gaze suspicious.

"I've got a friend who needs emancipation."

The emperor stroked his chin, his features pensive. "Well, there's paperwork that has to be filed on the home planet. You need a team of investigators to talk to present and previous owners."

Hope burgeoned inside Alix. Only her father had ever owned her. Maybe she would be free after all.

Calix continued, "Once the investigators get release from all the owners, then they run a posting with slave dealers to see if anyone else has an additional claim. If anyone comes forward with a legitimate claim, you can buy your friend from them, provided they're willing to sell."

A lump closed her throat.

"And if they're not?" Devyn asked.

"Then there's nothing you can do."

Alix's heart slid into her stomach and she feared she might be sick.

Devyn nodded. "How long will all this take?"

"A while. Maybe as long as a year or two."

Pain consumed her. A year or two. The words echoed in her mind. Dear God, she would never be free.

"Can you get started on it?" Devyn asked, his voice sounding like a stranger's to her hollowed-out soul.

"Sure," the emperor said, picking up a pen and a scrap piece of paper. "What's your friend's name?"

"Alix, A-L-I-X, Garran, G-A-R-R-A-N."

"And where's he registered?"

"*She's* registered on Praenomia."

"Okay," Calix said with a smile. "I'll get on it. You take care and please call Malena."

"All right. Thanks a lot, Uncle Cay, I owe you much."

"My pleasure."

Devyn turned to face her, expecting to see joy. Instead, terror darkened her features. "What's wrong?"

Tears welled in her eyes as she looked up at him, her face as pale as a ghost. "Irn will never let me go."

"Does he own you?"

"No, but what if he comes forward like he did—"

"He won't," Devyn assured her.

One tear ran down her cheek. "How do you know that?"

"Alix," he said, moving toward her, "trust me."

"How can I?" she asked, and put more distance between them, her voice becoming hysterical. "I'd rather be dead than have him . . . have him . . ."

She broke into tears and ran into her room, slamming the connecting door.

"Alix!" he called, trying to open it, but she had it locked. "Please let me in."

"Just leave me alone."

Devyn clenched his fists, his fury blinding him. Why wouldn't she listen to reason? Irn had no claim to her. So why was she frightened? Why wouldn't she believe him when he said he would get her free?

Women, what could you do with them?

Sighing, he turned around and went to call his mother.


Alix lay on her bed, staring at the ceiling. Devyn had invited her to eat two hours ago, but she hadn't answered him. Instead, she lay here trying to think of some way to free herself.

*As long as two years.* The words kept echoing in her head. Two more years of fear, of worrying that someone could come forward and claim her.

Over and over she could feel the sting of the scanner burning her slave code into her back, hear her mother's last pleas, see her brother's face when the dealer sold him, feel the groping hands, the humiliation.

Dear God, she couldn't stand the thought of being placed on an auction block, or one of her children suffering that horror.

She loved Devyn, but she couldn't stay with him and hope for something she knew she could never have. No, her freedom must come first.

"Alix?"

She started to open the door, but stopped herself. If she saw Devyn one more time she'd never find the courage to leave.

"I know you're upset," he said, his voice tired. "I've left a plate on a warmer in here for when you get hungry. Taryn's staying at the Lira Hotel down near the south landing bay and I'm going to see him for a while. If you need me, you can call the desk and they'll transfer you to his room. I also got you a new debit card. I'll leave it on the bureau, in case you want something."

She listened to the rich, refined tone of his voice. Pain wrapped around her heart. This was the last time she would ever hear him.

She held her pillow to her face and sobbed.

*Stay with him, you fool.*

But how could she? Even if Devyn didn't treat

her as a slave, it wouldn't change her legal status. If something happened to him, where would she be? Sold to the highest bidder. Their children right at her side. Fear and pain tore through her. If she did stay with Devyn, she could never have a child.

Yet how could she stay with Devyn and not have children?

Suddenly, a new horror occurred to her. What if she were pregnant now? Her sight dimmed and her heart sped up. Why hadn't she thought about that sooner?

"Because you are a fool," she snapped at herself, angered over her stupidity.

No, she must get out of here before it was too late. Before Devyn could stop her, and before she found out something she didn't want to consider.

"I'm sorry, Devyn," she whispered, knowing it would tear him apart for her to leave. "I just don't have a choice."

Forcing herself up off the bed, she waited until she was certain he'd left. She entered his room and took her debit card, ignoring the pain in her stomach, then quickly crossed back into her own room.

With a deep breath for courage, she tossed the key card for her room on her bed and left the hotel.

# *Chapter Nineteen*

Devyn entered his hotel, his mind churning over Taryn's words. Take Alix and run. He smiled. Leave it to Taryn; he always came up with a radical solution.

And yet it didn't seem so radical; in a weird way it almost made sense. Why not take her and live on Twrdr? At least stay there until Calix could get her freedom. That way if anything happened, no one would be able to claim her.

Come to think of it, they had a pretty good pediatric school in the capital city. His smile widened. It'd be perfect.

He wanted to fly upstairs and tell her; instead he had to wait for the lift, which seemed to take an eternity. He tapped his foot against the floor, anxious to get to his room and tell Alix the good news.

At last the doors opened on their floor. He took four steps into the hallway before he saw the HAWC troops leaving his room.

"There he is!" one of the Keepers said, pointing at him.

Devyn frowned, not quite afraid, but definitely cautious.

"Captain Devyn Kell?"

He looked at the sergeant who approached him with a frown. "Yeah?"

"We've got a warrant here for your arrest."

Anger scorched him. He hadn't done anything wrong. "For what?"

"Murder and smuggling."

Not this again. Was this a horrible replay of his brief trip to Nera? Only this time, he didn't have Zarina here to pull him out of the fire.

"Look," Devyn said, trying to maintain his calm. "There's some kind of mistake."

"No mistake," the Keeper said, handing him a computer ledger with the posted charges.

Devyn scanned it until his eyes fell to the name of the informant—Alix Garran.

Disbelief poured through him, only to be quickly replaced by cold fury.

"Alix!" he shouted, dropping the ledger and running past the Keepers and into his room.

They came after him, blasters drawn, but he

didn't care. He had to find Alix and see what the hell was going on.

He pushed open the adjoining door and immediately his gaze hit on her key card. All the fight drained out of him with sickening slowness.

She'd not only left, but turned him in for crimes he hadn't committed.

How typical of the female sex.

The Keepers slammed him against the wall and gyved his hands behind him. Devyn grunted, but the physical pain couldn't compare to the agony that shredded his heart. The Keepers could beat him, for all he cared.

Alix had betrayed him. After all they'd gone through together, she'd left him behind and fried his gizzard worse than even Onone.

He was a fool. He almost deserved to die for a crime he hadn't committed. Life no longer seemed worth the effort anyway.

Alix stopped to eat at a small, homey restaurant.

Taking a back corner seat, she scanned the occupants, who appeared the typical motley assortment of city clientele. She typed her order into the table ledger and waited, her stomach rumbling.

Maybe she'd been rash to leave Devyn behind. She buried her head in her hands and stared at the glass-topped table. If only she knew what to do.

Why couldn't she see into the future for just an instant? Long enough to divine a course of action. Or see what she should do.

Devyn or freedom. What a choice.

And now that she had it, what would she do with her freedom? Sign on board a new ship? Keep running from Irn, always looking over her shoulder?

How long would it take to earn enough money for a down payment on her own vessel?

A waitress brought her food out. Alix tipped her, then sat and stared at her food, her appetite suddenly gone. Devyn had given her so much more than a job. He'd given her hope. For the first time in her life, she'd had a reason to look forward to getting up in the morning—seeing him.

Even now, her skin tingled from the memory of his touch, his warmth. Could she stand even one day without seeing his bashful smile, hearing his laughter?

But slavery . . .

Her stomach twisted. Possibly two years before she could be free.

"Oh, Devyn," she whispered. If only she had someone to talk this over with. But the only friend she'd ever had was Devyn. The only person who had ever held her when she was hurt or lonely was Devyn.

Could she really give that up?

Sliding her debit card into the slot to pay for

her food, she left without tasting it. She would probably regret this. But there was still the tiny part of her that hoped. The tiny part of her that Devyn had created.

And there was one thing she knew for certain—without Devyn she would definitely be miserable.

"Okay, flyboy. Two years, or I'm gone." She pushed open the door of the cafe and laughed at herself. "Okay, maybe two and a half."

Alix wanted to run the distance back to the hotel, but she forced herself to continue her walk.

As she approached the hotel, she saw a group of Keepers milling around.

Frowning, she edged her way around them, trying to look inconspicuous.

Why would they hover around her hotel? Coincidence? No, not the way her luck ran.

Links hissed and popped.

"We've got him," a voice said from one link. "We're headed out. Open the shuttle."

Alix took two steps, then froze on the corner. The hotel doors opened and out stepped Devyn, surrounded by Keepers.

What the . . . ?

They forced him into the shuttle and took off before she could even blink.

"Move along," one Keeper said, pushing her.

Alix stumbled forward, her mind numb. What was happening? "Why was that man arrested?"

# Sherrilyn Kenyon

she asked the Keeper who had spoken to her.

"He's a wanted felon," he said, his voice dispassionate. "Now go about your business."

Her eyes widened as fear gripped her. The charges on Nera! But Devyn had said they were phony. And she believed him. Devyn wouldn't murder anyone.

Panic tore through her. She had to get him out of jail. But how? What was she going to do?

She closed her eyes and let the frustration consume her. If only she were Zarina, she could think of a brilliant plan, but she lacked military abilities or connections.

Connections . . .

Taryn. Maybe he could help.

Alix licked her dry lips and whispered a small prayer that Taryn hadn't left the planet. He had to be here or else she didn't know what she'd do.

No longer caring if she caused a scene, she ran in the direction of the south landing bay.

It didn't take long to find Taryn's ship. The sleek, black Trebuchet freighter stood out among the smaller, older ships.

Running up the ramp, she met a large, burly Deucalion, his hands crossed over his chest, his frown fierce.

"What do you want here?" he asked in a strange, melodic accent.

"I need to see Taryn."

The guard scanned her body, a sneer on his face. "I do not know you, human."

"Please," she begged, realizing this must be one of Taryn's bodyguards. "I'm here on Devyn's behalf. He's in trouble."

The Deucalion's features changed immediately to concern. "Come with me."

He paused at the ship's entrance and faced her. "If you lie, human, I'll tear out your heart and eat it."

"I'm not lying."

He nodded, then continued down the narrow corridor.

Alix followed him into the ship, but almost stumbled at the rich luxury surrounding her. And she had thought the *Mariah* exceptional!

"In here," the Deucalion said, opening a door for her.

Alix walked in and stopped. Taryn sat at a card game with another Deucalion male.

He looked up and frowned. "Hi, Alix, where's—"

"Devyn's been taken by Keepers!" she said, too excited for niceties.

His mouth fell. "He's been what?"

"I saw them put him in a shuttle." Tears rolled down her cheeks, but she didn't care. She had to help Devyn. "When we were on Nera, they said he was wanted for smuggling and murder."

Taryn shook his head and rubbed his neck. His frown deepened. "HAWC charges?"

"That's what Claria said."

Taryn looked at his Deucalion guards. "This is weird. Then again, Devyn always stumbles into weird situations."

He rose to his feet and held out a chair for her. "Sit down and relax. We'll get this mess straightened out." He handed her a handkerchief and she quickly wiped her eyes.

Moving to his link, he punched in a series of numbers.

"Code?" a strange voice asked.

"Six million, six hundred and twenty-four thousand, five hundred and eight, Blue Rising."

"One moment for transfer."

Taryn turned around and smiled. "Don't worry. If Rina had done this on Nera, we wouldn't have this trouble now."

Before she could ask him what he meant, a man's voice boomed, "Yo, Terry, how's my runamok kid brother?"

"I'm fine, but brother Devyn has landed himself in the proverbial verrago's hole."

"What happened?"

"HAWC trouble. I need you to run a scan and see what his charges are."

"Hold on."

Seconds ticked by, each one punctuated by the sharp beating of her heart.

Finally, the voice returned. "He's not wanted by us."

Taryn looked at her with a lifted brow.

Alix shook her head, puzzled by the denial. "That's what they said on Nera, and the HAWC Keeper I spoke with here said Devyn was a wanted felon."

"Did you hear that, Jayce?"

"I heard it, but I'm staring at the main data base and it shows a blank file. Besides, if a felonious charge had been leveled against Devyn, I would have been notified."

"All right," Taryn said. "Hold on a minute and let me run my stats on their local system and see what shines."

Alix clutched her hands together, trying to sort everything out. Suddenly, she knew. Irn. It was the only answer.

Damn him and his interference!

Taryn straightened and returned to the link. "I've got three murder charges, espionage, and smuggling here."

"It's a plant," the voice said.

"Looks *real* authentic."

Alix clenched her teeth. "Irn did it."

Taryn looked at her. "Who's Irn?"

She sighed, suddenly so tired she just wanted to crawl under the table and sleep.

Or better, find Irn and beat him senseless. "Devyn's mother sent him to prison, and after he was released, he worked for my father." Her throat tightened and she forced herself to say the last. "I led him to Devyn and he's been after us ever since."

365

"Irn what?" the voice asked.

"Penisky."

"Okay. Terry, I've got one of my operatives there. I'm going to stat her Devyn's real readout and have her straighten this mess out. Meet her at the Keepers' station and make sure the Keepers haven't ruffled his fur any. If they have, get their names and numbers and let me handle it. No stupid bravado tricks," he snapped. "After the stunt Rina pulled on Nera, the High Command is blistering my neck. I'll also send out a stat on this Irn Penisky and bring him up on forgery charges and interfering with HAWC affairs. I'll bury him so deep, he'll never move against another one of us."

"Thanks, big brother. I knew I could count on you."

"Anytime."

Taryn switched off the link. "All that worry. See how easily things work out?"

A shiver ran down her spine. Nothing ever went easily for her. "If it's that easy, why didn't Rina do it on Nera?"

Taryn rolled his eyes. "My parents should have locked her up in a cage from the time she turned two. If there's an easy way to do something, she makes a point of avoiding it. And if she can run away from her nosy brothers at any time, she leaves so fast you can see the vapor trail for miles."

Alix smiled.

"C'mon," he said, "let's go find Devyn."

Devyn sat in his cell staring at the odd group around him. The man to his left had killed three members of his family and was now involved in a boasting contest with another occupant who claimed he'd killed four HAWC Keepers.

At least all six other occupants kept away from him. He just wasn't in the mood to deal with anyone. Although he did keep imagining himself strangling Alix.

He couldn't believe she'd turned him in. Why? If she didn't want to wait, she could have told him.

Women. Who would ever figure them out?

A guard walked to the door. "C'mon, Kell. We made a mistake."

"You made a mistake with me, too!" one of the other guys shouted.

Devyn sighed and pushed himself off the floor. Leave it to Taryn. He had known all along it would only be a matter of time before Taryn came looking for him.

As he walked out of the cell, the guard caught his arm. "Make sure you tell them we didn't do nothing to you."

"Other than slam me against the wall?" Devyn couldn't resist asking.

The man's face blanched.

A twinge of guilt tweaked his conscience.

"Relax. I needed someone to slam some sense into my skull. You guys probably did me a favor."

Devyn made his way down the corridor and stopped at the window to collect his belongings. After signing the forms, he entered the waiting area and stopped.

Alix and Taryn stood by the door. Catching sight of him, Alix smiled.

Amazing how people changed. Did she think him so stupid he didn't even know?

"What?" he asked as she approached him. "Did you start feeling guilty about shoving me into the grinder?"

She frowned. "What are you talking about?"

"You turned me in," he sneered. "I saw the form with your name on it."

She pursed her lips and said sarcastically, "I didn't turn you in."

"Yeah, right. I guess the Keepers just happened to choose a name to assign blame and out of all the names in the universe, Alix Garran was the one name they chose." He looked at Taryn. "Gee, what are the odds of that?"

Anger darkened her eyes. "I should have just kept on walking. I don't know why I even came back."

"Neither do I."

She clenched her fist at her side and he half expected her to hit him. Instead, her eyes narrowed. "Go rot, for all I care."

Turning around, she headed out the door and into the street.

"That was a nasty thing to do."

He turned to glare at Taryn. "What do you know about it?"

"What I know is that I was going to leave in about fifteen minutes and if Alix hadn't shown up in tears and told me you'd been taken, you would still be locked up, if not executed."

Fury burned through him. How dare Taryn stand up for her after what she'd done. "She turned me in!"

"How do you know?"

"Someone had to give them the info. If not her, then who used her name?"

Taryn frowned, then went to the processor's desk. "Excuse me, could I see the warrant on Devyn Kell?"

"Yes, Your Highness," the secretary said. "For you, anything." He shuffled through the papers on his desk until he found the warrant and gave it to Taryn.

Taryn scanned the papers, then handed them to him. "Look at the description of the inform-ant. Male, dark hair, five foot ten inches. Gee, but I could have sworn Alix—"

"Irn," Devyn snarled, his vision clouding. And if Irn had done this, he was here.

And if he was here . . .

"Oh, my God," he breathed.

He had to get to Alix before Irn did, before Irn hurt her. Panic riding him like a demon, he ran from the building and out into the street. People

Sherrilyn Kenyon

surrounded him, but nowhere did he see Alix.

Which way would she go?

Devyn turned around, his blood pounding. If she were hurt because of him, he'd—

Color sizzled past him, narrowly missing his arm. The crowd screamed and ducked, running all through the street.

"Kell!" a voice shouted.

He turned to see Irn holding Alix in the center of the street, a blaster aimed at her head. The smile on the man's face bordered on insane.

Devyn took a step toward them, but Irn's grip tightened on the blaster.

Keepers spilled out of the building and froze as they caught sight of them.

"I'll be in touch," Irn said.

A Keeper fired his blaster at them. Irn and Alix dissolved into wavy lines a second before they disappeared.

"Hologram," Devyn snarled.

The *Prixie* zoomed overhead. He knew without a doubt that it had been the hologram's source.

"Who is this guy?" Taryn asked, moving to stand beside him.

Devyn whirled around and pulled the blaster from Taryn's holster. "A walking corpse."

# *Chapter Twenty*

"Devyn, wait!" Taryn shouted, rushing after him. "What are you planning?"

"I don't know. With any luck something will occur to me when I need it."

Taryn's face blanched. "Don't do this."

He tried to take the blaster away, but Devyn shoved him aside. "Don't try to stop me, Taryn. I don't want to hurt you."

Taryn shook his head. "I lost one brother this way. Do you want to end up like Adron?"

Devyn paused, his anger only building. For the first time, he understood why Adron had had to pursue his wife's murderer. He knew if he failed to get Alix back, he'd end up as Adron's bunkmate in the slanted zone.

"Go on and get your shipment to Terria. This is between me and Irn."

He started to move away, but Taryn caught him by the arm. "Devyn, look at yourself. You've become one of those guys you hate. You swore you'd never touch a gun when you left the HAWC. Now you're ready to kill this guy?"

"No, now I'm protecting Alix, and if that means killing him, so be it. She's lived her life in fear and terror. No one deserves her past, and I intend to guarantee her future will not be a repeat journey to hell."

"You sound like you've gone slanted."

Devyn met his gaze. "I love her, Terry, and I'm not going to let her get hurt."

Taryn shook his head and sighed. "Women aren't worth it, but if you're determined to do this, I'm not going to let *you* get hurt."

Alix sat in the large rec room of a house on some forgotten planet in a forgotten corner of the universe, her hands gyved in her lap. Irn sat at a table across from her and eyed her with triumph burning in his eyes, his body encased from head to foot in a HAWC battle uniform.

"Cap'n, our spy says Kell is holed up with Taryn Kyrelle."

A glimmer of fear flashed in Irn's eyes. "It doesn't matter."

Alix bit her lip, her entire body trembling. "He's not going to come after me," she said, trying to keep the fear out of her voice. "He hates me."

"You know, boss, she might be right. What with you using her name and all—"

Irn grabbed him by the throat. "You don't think, *kruna*. I do. He'll come after her. Just send the message like I told you. Make sure he has all the coordinates for my brother's place."

"Yes, Cap'n."

Irn moved to pace around her chair. "Kell's smart enough to realize you didn't turn him in. I only used your name to get under his skin."

He grabbed her face, his fingers biting into her cheeks, and forced her to look at him. "I would have had him by now if you hadn't interfered. I had everything planned so carefully, but you couldn't just sit and wait."

He backhanded her. "That's for making me take you first."

Her cheek throbbing, she stared at him. "Why do you hate me so much?"

His lips curled. "Why?" he asked, his voice high and whiny. "Are you truly that stupid?" He raked her with a glare. "Then again, I guess you are."

He returned to pacing around her. "I spent thirty years in prison taking orders—when to get up, when to go to the bathroom, when and how much to eat."

He faced her, his eyes glowing from inner madness. "There was a time when I was the one who gave orders. My brother and me were the best drug- and gun-runners in the universe. We had over two hundred people working for us, and then that bitch came and infiltrated our ring."

His lips curled and he raised his fist as if addressing the Lord himself. "She handed me and my brother over to the HAWC in chains. I always knew I'd get back at her for that and then when Janoff died, I knew I could never rest until she had received her true reward."

His gaze returned to her, and Alix wanted to shrink from it. "After they finally let me out, I had to earn money. Have you ever tried to find work with a prison record?"

Alix swallowed, her panic rising. She grasped at the one last chance she had to reach him. "That's right. My father and I were good enough to give you a job even with your prison record and this is how you repay us?"

He slapped her again. "You didn't hire me."

Blood ran from the corner of her mouth and her head swam from the pain throbbing along her cheek and lips. Alix closed her eyes and drew a deep, fortifying breath.

She must stay conscious and alert, or she and Devyn would die. "I told my father to hire you. I knew you had forged your credentials, and I hacked into the HAWC's computer banks. I found your prison file and hid it from my father. I was stupid enough to think you had done your time and could use a job."

"Liar!" He drew back to hit her again and she tensed, but for some reason he refrained.

Slowly, he lowered his hand, his eyes blazing. "It was you who told him about my record. You who sent him to fire me!"

She frowned in confusion. Her father had never wanted to fire Irn. "What are you talking about?"

"I'm talking about the night he went into the Gilded Cage to fire me," he said, gripping the arms of her chair and leaning so close she nearly gagged on his putrid breath.

"He told me that he refused to have me on board his ship making passes at his daughter. He said he'd found out about my rape charges and other crimes and that you might be nothing but a slave, but you were his flesh and blood and as such he had no intention of having you harmed."

Her mouth dropped. Her father had defended her?

No, it had to be a lie. Her father had never defended her, would never have defended her.

"So I gutted the ignorant bastard."

Her stomach lurched at his cold, callous words. "You were the one who killed him?"

"Of course, you fool. Who did you think ended his miserable existence?"

Pain burned through her. Her father had died protecting her? She still couldn't believe it.

But why would Irn lie? He had nothing to

375

gain. Dear Lord, it had to be true. Her father had cared for her, at least for one moment.

Not once had he ever said a kind word to her and now to find out too late . . .

"You sorry—"

He lifted his hand again. "Don't tempt me, woman. The only thing keeping you alive is your lover. Though why he'd want to come after something as ugly as you, I can't imagine."

Each word tore through her, made worse by the fact that she knew he was right. She'd never understood why Devyn had wanted her, what he could possibly see in her.

Then suddenly she knew.

"This is what he sees in me," she said, and kneed Irn in the groin.

Irn doubled over next to her. Jerking the keys off his belt, she quickly ungyved her hands and sprang from the chair. "Thanks, *skagen*," she said, and ran for the door.

She went out into the yard and pulled up short when she saw two guards headed toward the house.

Dashing right, she hid herself behind a clump of shrubbery until after they'd passed.

An alarm rent the air. Alix clenched her teeth. She had to get out of here and find some way to warn Devyn, to make sure that he, too, didn't die trying to protect her.

Taryn stared at Devyn in disbelief while Devyn strapped on the flexible black body armor.

Over the years, he'd seen his friend drink until he couldn't walk, seen Devyn cry by his side when they brought Adron into the hospital one heartbeat shy of death, seen him furious to the point of murder, but only years ago had Taryn seen him like this.

What Taryn faced now was the old Devyn Kell. The Devyn who had emerged from HAWC training with a purpose, who had sworn to uphold the Code. The Devyn Kell who made *him* look like a nice little kid.

Not since Devyn had left the HAWC had Taryn seen him like this—cold, unreadable, deadly.

Devyn straightened and caught his scrutiny. "What?" he asked, strapping the blaster to his hip.

"I was thinking how much you remind me of your parents."

He lifted his brow. "What do you mean?"

"You've got your mom's stubbornness and your dad's icy demeanor. How long did you have to practice to get that menacing glare down?"

Taryn hadn't thought it possible, but Devyn's gaze turned even chillier. "If you ever lose the most precious thing you treasure, you'll have the same look. I guarantee it."

Taryn snorted. "I already lost it. Except mine left me by her own free choice. I just hope after you go through all this, Alix doesn't do you the same way."

*Me, too,* Devyn thought, remembering the way she had left the hotel room without so much as a note.

But that didn't matter, not at the moment. "I don't care if she does leave me. I can't leave her in danger, especially since that bastard wants me more."

The link buzzed. "Your Highness, we're approaching Cranora."

Taryn met his gaze. "You ready for this?"

"Let's dance."

They lowered the ramp and moved cautiously from Taryn's ship. The location Irn had given them was through the dense forest, half a mile to the south.

If they could take him unawares, maybe they would stand half a chance.

As they reached the edge of the woods, a large estate came into view. Thick, fortified walls surrounded it, and even without the guards posted every few feet, there was little doubt who owned such a place.

"You can really pick them," Taryn muttered. "Druggers."

Devyn smiled at the irony. "I won't think badly of you if you decide to wait in your ship."

"What?" Taryn asked, his eyes wide in feigned shock, "and miss the chance to see a Kell infiltrate the uninfiltratable? I want to see if you remember any of the stuff your dad taught you."

Devyn pulled out his decoder and began

punching in data. "The electronics don't scare me. But I think I hear girbeasts."

"Yeah," Taryn said, his voice cracking. "Let's hope they're on a leash."

Devyn was almost ready to breach the code when a guard walked past.

Ducking down into the shadows of the wall, they heard the guard's link. "She's down in the refinery. We've found two of our guys shot, so she's armed. Remember, shoot to wound."

Devyn's heart stopped. Alix was in trouble. He had to find her.

Where was the refinery?

As soon as the guard moved past, he breached the alarm. Steeling his nerves, he crept through the yard with Taryn one step behind.

Devyn crouched as another guard approached. He drew his knife. Then when the guard reached their hiding place, he lunged and grabbed him from behind, laying his dagger against the man's throat. "Where's the refinery?"

"I don't—"

Devyn tightened his grip, cutting the man's words off. "One more lie and I'll slit this nice juicy artery."

"To the east. The gray building."

"Better," Devyn said.

Taryn zapped him with a sonic disrupter and the man crumpled to the ground.

"Hope he has some potent painkillers," Taryn muttered.

"I hope we have some potent luck."

Stealthily, they continued until they reached the refinery. Shouts filled their ears and a number of armed men ran inside.

"Boy, Dev, you sure can pick them," he repeated in the same fatalistic tone. "Looks like your girlfriend has ticked off the entire staff."

Recoil fire filled the air.

"Alix," Devyn breathed, rushing forward.

Taryn caught him by the arm. "Wait a minute. Are you trying to get both you and her killed? We need a plan."

Devyn clenched his teeth. "Fine, you sit here and plan. I'm going to help."

He removed Taryn's hand from his arm and sprinted into the refinery.

Smoke surrounded him, blinding his sight. He choked on the thick, pungent fumes and moved through the huge warehouse as quickly as he could. He heard the guards running and cursing, but he could barely make out anything other than passing shapes and swirling fog.

Something moved behind him. Whirling, he took aim.

"It's me!" Taryn snapped.

Devyn removed his finger from the trigger. "Finished planning so soon?"

"No," he muttered, stopping next to him. "But if I get shot, I'm holding you responsible."

Self-recrimination tore through Devyn. He'd already killed one friend. He didn't want to lose another. "You go back. I can fight my own battles."

"No, thanks. We're in this till the end."

"But—"

A blast sizzled between them.

Taryn spun and shot the guard. "C'mon."

Devyn followed him through the haze. Voices came at them from all directions. Several guards rushed past them, not even seeing them in the smoke.

"She's up on the catwalk," one of them said. "But she's got a nerve deflector."

"Ouch," Taryn whispered. "I hope she doesn't hit one of us."

Devyn didn't think about that. All he cared about was finding Alix safe and alive, and he had a feeling that if they didn't get to her soon, there wouldn't be enough left of her to identify.

Stifling heat hovered in the air, making it thick, almost unbreathable. They ascended the ladder and had to walk single-file on the thin metal planking that ran over huge vats of chemicals. Devyn looked down and took a deep breath as his heart slid into his stomach. He hated heights, but the worst part was that if they fell, they'd no doubt land in something very hot or very acidic.

Suddenly, a scream rent the air, sending a chill down his spine. Fear nearly buckled his knees.

Devyn ran toward the sound, no longer caring

how high above the ground he was. Rounding the corner, he froze. Alix dangled off the walk and two guards stood above her.

"Maybe we ought to tell Irn she fell," one of them said, picking up his rifle and aiming it at her.

*No!* Rage descended on him.

Before he could think, he rushed forward, snatched the rifle from the man's hands, and backhanded him. The guard fell from the walk, screaming until he landed on the ground with a solid, sickening thud.

The other guard started to fight, then caught sight of Taryn and decided against it. Turning on his heel, the guard ran in the opposite direction.

Taryn moved to go after him.

Devyn grabbed him by the arm and holstered his blaster. "Leave him," he said, and knelt on the planking.

"Alix!" he called, grabbing her hands.

She looked up at him, her eyes large and fear-filled. "Devyn," she breathed, her grip tightening beneath his.

"It's okay," he said, relief pouring through him. "Let go and I'll pull you up."

"I can't," she cried, the horror in her voice slicing through him. "Please, don't let me fall!"

"I'm not going to let you fall," he said, curbing his irritation. "You have to let go."

Her hands trembled in his. She looked up at

him and he knew how close she was to breaking. "It's all right," he said. "Trust me."

Her eyes widened a second before she let go. Her unexpected surrender almost pulled him over.

Devyn braced himself and pulled. His sweaty palms slipped. She screamed.

Taryn grabbed him by the waist and helped pull.

With a strong tug, she came over the edge and into his arms. Devyn held her tightly, his heart pounding in relief.

"Thank you, God," he whispered against her hair, holding her close.

She wept in his arms and clutched at him, her entire body trembling.

"How precious," a voice sneered.

Devyn looked up and saw Irn standing just before them with a blaster angled at him and Alix.

"Now be good children and hand me your weapons."

It had been a long time since Devyn had intentionally killed anyone, and now that he stood facing Irn, the familiar bile rose in his throat.

For the ideals and power games of the HAWC he had killed so many, watched even more die. He couldn't stand the thought of killing anyone else, not even the vile creature before him. Could he do it?

Taryn and Alix slid Irn their weapons.

Irn's gaze hardened as he waited for him to do the same. "Kell?"

Steadying his nerves, Devyn took a deep breath and moved away from Alix. "Will you let Alix and Taryn go?"

"I'll say yes if it'll ease your mind."

Devyn pulled his blaster out of its holster. "Wrong answer," he said, then aimed and fired.

The blast caught Irn in the shoulder. He screamed and dropped his weapon. Hatred glared in his eyes and he ran toward Devyn, fists raised.

Devyn caught him and the two fell backward over the edge of the walkway.

Alix's heart stilled as panic wrenched her soul. Irn's scream echoed in her head, followed by the thud of bodies hitting the floor.

"Devyn!" Alix shrieked. She blinked, praying her eyes had lied and that she hadn't seen Devyn go over.

Her heart pounded in her chest and tears sprang to her eyes. She crumpled to the floor, wanting to die, unable to believe she'd lost her Devyn.

Gazing up, she met Taryn's horrified face and saw the tears that gathered in his own eyes.

She couldn't bring herself to look over the edge and see Devyn's body on the floor below.

"Dammit, Terry, give me a hand!"

Tears coursed down her cheeks at the familiar

frustrated voice. Relief filled her, stealing her breath.

Taryn sprang to his feet and leaned over the edge.

Smiling, Alix joined him and grabbed Devyn's right hand.

"God bless HAWC training," Taryn said with a laugh and latched onto Devyn's hands.

Alix stood back, unable to believe he'd survived. "How?" she asked, pulling him into her arms.

"The armor plating caught on a hook or something when I fell." Devyn held up his left arm and she saw the twisted body armor and blood pouring out of it.

"You're wounded!"

He smiled. "Yeah, but it's a hell of a lot better than the alternative."

Holding her close, he looked at Taryn. "Let's get out of here before more guards show up."

Taryn retrieved their weapons. "Right behind you, *shidan*."

# *Epilogue*

Alix stood inside the rectory, staring out the window, her stomach knotted. She clutched at the small white rose Zarina had given her and her mind whirled.

What was keeping Devyn? Had he changed his mind?

Fear gripped her and she tried to press it back. He wouldn't do that to her. Would he?

After a year and a half of waiting, she found it hard to believe he hadn't changed his mind about marrying her. Or had he?

She checked her watch and bit her lip. He should have been here an hour ago.

"You okay?" Zarina asked, touching her arm.

With a sigh, Alix turned away from the window and walked back to where the priest sat. His old eyes offered her comfort. She gave him a timid smile but would rather have cursed her luck.

Even now her back throbbed from where her brand had been removed three days earlier. And she had wanted to marry Devyn the second the brand had been stripped.

But Devyn had insisted they wait an extra few days and have a real wedding. She'd wanted to elope and have the whole thing behind her.

What was the point of a wedding when she had no family and her only friend was Zarina?

But Devyn had been adamant, and now she didn't even have a bridegroom.

Well, enough waiting. He wasn't going to show and she had no desire to stand here all day looking like a fool. Handing the rose to Zarina, she turned to leave.

The doors opened.

Valerian and Malena came through, a wide smile on their faces, and right behind them was Devyn.

Alix closed her eyes in relief, her heart pounding. Maybe dreams really did come true.

"I'm sorry I'm late," Devyn said, picking her hands up and kissing her palms. "I had a few people to pick up."

She smiled, all irritation gone. "I'm glad you brought your parents."

"Yeah, but they weren't the ones who were

late," he said, a gleam of mischief in his eyes.

She frowned, wondering what he'd been up to. "I thought we agreed to keep this small."

"Well, I had to make two exceptions."

"Who?" she asked, expecting Taryn and Claria.

Devyn stood aside and Alix's gaze drifted to the door. She blinked in disbelief, her body flashing from hot to cold.

Tears welled in her eyes.

It couldn't be.

"Mama?" she asked, her throat tight. "Piran?"

Tears streamed down her face as Alix dashed across the room and pulled her mother and brother close. She'd never even dared hope to see them again.

Now they stood before her.

"You've grown so tall!" her mother said, touching her hair, her face.

"Yeah, you don't look anything like a ship rat anymore."

She clutched Piran to her. "But you're still as handsome as ever," she said with a laugh.

Alix turned around.

Devyn stood just behind her, his eyes filled with love and warmth.

"Thank you!" she said.

He smiled. "I got all the thanks I needed when I saw your face the minute they stepped in."

Laughing, she held him close, her heart nearly bursting from the fullness of her love. "How did you do it?"

"While Calix worked out your release, I had him do a background check on your mother and brother. It took a little creative bartering, but it wasn't hard."

"Don't listen to him," her mother said. "He's a saint."

Alix smiled. "I know, Mama."

Devyn's cheeks flamed. "Well, I thought I came here to get married, not stand around while people tell fabrications about me."

Zarina came forward and returned the rose to Alix.

Alix kissed her mother's cheek and watched while Piran helped her to her seat.

She took Devyn's hand and they approached the altar. The priest came forward and started the ceremony.

Alix listened to the prayer, her heart pounding. It was really happening. The day she had barely allowed herself to think about had finally come and it wasn't a dream. It was better.

She took the ring from Zarina, her hands icy. "I, Alix Garran, in the presence of God and His representative, swear to uphold the vows of marriage, to protect and cherish my husband, Devyn Kell, against all enemies who would do him harm. To stand by his side for the whole of my life and offer him comfort, companionship, and all the love in my heart."

The priest blessed the ring. Her hand trembled as she slid it onto Devyn's finger.

# Sherrilyn Kenyon

Smiling, he stared into her eyes, and the love that shone there stole her breath. "I, Devyn Kell, in the presence of God and His representative, swear to uphold the vows of marriage, to protect and cherish my wife, Alix Garran, against all enemies who would do her harm. To stand by her side for the whole of my life and offer her comfort, companionship, and all the love in my heart."

The warmth of his hand on hers sent a chill down her spine. He slid the ring into place and she stared at the sparkling tarias.

Lifting her hand to his lips, Devyn kissed her knuckle just above the ring. His gaze burned into hers. "I love you, Alix, and so long as breath remains in my body, I swear you will never again have to fear the past or the future."

Alix smiled, knowing for the first time in her life she had the one thing she had wanted most— love. And the one thing she had barely dared hope for—an unexciting future with Devyn.

Yeah, right. Unexciting indeed.

# TIMESWEPT ROMANCE
## *TIME REMEMBERED*
### Elizabeth Crane
### Bestselling Author of *Reflections in Time*

A voodoo doll and an ancient spell whisk thoroughly modern Jody Farnell from a decaying antebellum mansion to the Old South and a true Southern gentleman who shows her the magic of love.

\_0-505-51904-6                    $4.99 US/$5.99 CAN

# FUTURISTIC ROMANCE
## *A DISTANT STAR*
### Anne Avery

Jerrel is enchanted by the courageous messenger who saves his life. But he cannot permit anyone to turn him from the mission that has brought him to the distant world—not even the proud and passionate woman who offers him a love capable of bridging the stars.

\_0-505-51905-4                    $4.99 US/$5.99 CAN

# Futuristic Romance

### Love in another time, another place

# Topaz Dreams

## Marilyn Campbell

"A story that grabs you from the beginning and won't let go!"

—*Johanna Lindsey*

Fierce and cunning, Falcon runs into an unexpected setback while searching for the ring that can destroy his futuristic world—a beauty who rouses his untested desire. Tough and independent, Stephanie Barbanell doesn't need any man to help her track down a missing scientist. But tempted by Falcon's powerful magnetism, she longs to give in to her burning ardor—until she discovers that her love for Falcon can never be unless one of them sacrifices everything for the other.

__3390-9                                          $4.50 US/$5.50 CAN

# *Futuristic Romance*

# *The New Frontier*

## JACKIE CASTO

*Love in another time, another place.*

Raised to despise all men, Ashley has no choice but to marry when she is sent to the New Frontier, man's last hope for survival. Surrounded by women-hungry brutes, Ashley chooses the one man she is sure will refuse her. But before long, she begins to wonder if Garrick will set her free from his tender grasp...or if she'll lose herself in the paradise of his arms.

_3201-5                                          $4.50 US/$5.50 CAN

## TIMESWEPT ROMANCE
### *TEARS OF FIRE*
#### By Nelle McFather

Swept into the tumultuous life and times of her ancestor Deirdre O'Shea, Fable relives a night of sweet ecstasy with Andre Devereux, never guessing that their delicious passion will have the power to cross the ages. Caught between swirling visions of a distant desire and a troubled reality filled with betrayal, Fable seeks the answers that will set her free— answers that can only be found in the tender embrace of two men who live a century apart.

_51932-1                                        $4.99 US/$5.99 CAN

## FUTURISTIC ROMANCE
### *ASCENT TO THE STARS*
#### By Christine Michels

For Trace, the assignment should be simple. Any Thadonian warrior can take a helpless female to safety in exchange for valuable information against his diabolical enemies. But as fiery as a supernova, as radiant as a sun, Coventry Pearce is no mere woman. Even as he races across the galaxy to save his doomed world, Trace battles to deny a burning desire that will take him to the heavens and beyond.

_51933-X                                        $4.99 US/$5.99 CAN

# Futuristic Romance

*Journey to the distant future where love rules and passion is the lifeblood of every man and woman.*

**Heart's Lair** by Kathleen Morgan. Although Karic is the finest male specimen Liane has ever seen, her job is not to admire his nude body, but to discover the lair where his rebellious followers hide. Never does Liane imagine that when the Cat Man escapes he will take her as his hostage— or that she will fulfill her wildest desires in his arms.
\_3549-9                                         $4.50 US/$5.50 CAN

**The Knowing Crystal** by Kathleen Morgan. On a seemingly hopeless search for the Knowing Crystal, sheltered Alia has desperate need of help. Teran, with his warrior skills and raw strength, seems to be the answer to her prayers, but his rugged masculinity threatens Alia. Even though Teran is only a slave, Alia will learn in his powerful arms that love can break all bonds.
\_3548-0                                         $4.50 US/$5.50 CAN

**LEISURE BOOKS**
**ATTN: Order Department**
**276 5th Avenue, New York, NY 10001**

Please add $1.50 for shipping and handling for the first book and $.35 for each book thereafter. PA., N.Y.S. and N.Y.C. residents, please add appropriate sales tax. No cash, stamps, or C.O.D.s. All orders shipped within 6 weeks via postal service book rate. Canadian orders require $2.00 extra postage and must be paid in U.S. dollars through a U.S. banking facility.

Name _____
Address _____
City _____ State _____ Zip _____
I have enclosed $_____in payment for the checked book(s).
Payment <u>must</u> accompany all orders.☐ Please send a free catalog.